THE JUNKYARD

RON FISHER

Fisher, Ron. The Junkyard (J.D. Bragg Series Book 3). Published by MysteryRow.

ISBN-13: 978-1-949073-10-02 (paperback)
ISBN-13: 978-1-949073-08-9 (Kindle)
ISBN-13: 978-1-949073-09-6 (epub)
ISBN-13: 978-1-949073-11-9 (hard cover)

"There are no secrets that time does not reveal"
Jean Racine

This book is dedicated to the memory of
Ruby Anderson Fisher.
7/18/1919 – 7/9/2018

ACKNOWLEDGMENTS

I want to thank all those who helped me so much with THE JUNKYARD, the third book in my J.D. Bragg mystery series. First, my Beta Readers, Jeff Upshaw, Patrick Scullin, Tom Monroe, and Ross Puskar. THE FISHER GROUP as always—Hal, Mary Ann, Travis, and Wil Fisher—for all their insight, design and production wizardry. Thanks for Dylan Fisher too, for being there as an inspiration for all of us. Thanks to my Tasmanian friends Jason and Marina Anderson at Polgarus Studios for their excellent work and advice, and to my new Australian friend Graeme Hague whose copy editing makes this a much better book. Finally, thanks to my incredibly smart and talented family—Michael and Staci, Chip and Beth, and Mackenzie and Jamie. You guys remain the greatest.

PROLOGUE

Pickens County, South Carolina.

Kelly Mayfield sat in her living room in her favorite chair, re-reading William Least Heat-Moon's *Blue Highways* for the third time since she'd discovered the book in her teenage years. The author's unforgettable journeys along America's backroads always made her spirits soar, creating a wanderlust that made Kelly want to pack a bag, gas up the car, and go on a road trip. The destination wouldn't matter, as long as an untraveled road lay ahead, and an unexplored adventure waited around a bend somewhere.

Maybe she could talk J.D. into a drive into the mountains this weekend and stay at some cute little bed and breakfast somewhere. He was on his way up from Atlanta, but with the ridiculous traffic there on Friday evenings, there was no way to know what time he would arrive.

John David Bragg, my long-distance lover, she thought. She closed the book and shut her eyes, thinking about him. She loved him, there was no doubt about that, but theirs was a relationship difficult to maintain. He lived in Atlanta where he was happy with his work as an investigative journalist, while she was a hundred and forty miles away and the editor of a small-town newspaper. Running the *Clarion* was her dream job.

And the *Clarion* had its own complications where she and J.D. were concerned. It was how they met. John David had inherited the paper when his grandfather died, but J.D. had no desire to operate it. Kelly had worked for his grandfather and with family money bought a twenty-five percent interest in the paper. J.D., with his seventy-five percent, became absentee publisher, leaving her and his older sister Eloise to run it.

J.D. stayed entirely out of the business. It left them with a relationship dilemma that they would eventually have to face; she didn't want to give the paper up and move to Atlanta, and J.D. hated the thought of running a small-town newspaper, especially when it was in the same small town where he grew up.

This was the elephant in the room which kept them from ever discussing the subject of a permanent future together.

Kelly heard a rattle in the kitchen. It sounded like ice cubes falling into the ice bin in the refrigerator and triggered a thirst for something cold to drink while she waited for J.D. to arrive. Something with a little scotch in it, perhaps. After all, it was the beginning of a weekend with the man she loved, and not the time to dwell on that elephant in the room.

She went into the kitchen, took a cocktail glass out of a cabinet, placed it in the refrigerator door, and punched the button for ice cubes. She heard the rattle again, but it wasn't the icemaker. It was coming from the back door that led off the kitchen to the patio. If it was J.D., she thought, why would he come to the back door?

As she stared at the door, the molding beside the lock splintered and the door crashed open. Two men wearing ski-masks rushed in. One of them overwhelmed Kelly quickly, driving her into the kitchen table and bending her backward.

He was on top of her, eye to eye, their faces so close she could smell garlic and onions on his breath. Kelly couldn't see enough through the small openings in the mask for any chance to recognize who he might be.

She pounded her fists frantically against the side of his head.

With the weight of his body pressing her flat against the table, he released his grip from her shoulders and tried to grab her flailing fists.

"Get off me!" She yelled, raging inside, determined to fight. She gritted her teeth and tried to head-butt him hard, hoping to get him in the nose. He sensed it coming and turned away, taking the blow on his ear and the side of his head. He grunted, and Kelly knew she had hurt him. He swore at her with a guttural, almost animal-like growl that she barely understood. He grabbed her by the hair and yanked her off the table, her head bouncing on the tile. A kick to the ribs shot pain through her like a stab from a knife. Another to her head sent the room spinning. A final kick made Kelly's whole world go dark.

The doorbell chimed.

The two men stood frozen, listening intently. The doorbell rang again, accompanied by a rap on the door. A phone somewhere in the house rang several times, then stopped. There was another bang on the door. Louder, and more aggressive. Kelly's assailant looked down at her body for a moment, then both men fled out the back door and into the night.

On the front porch, a pizza delivery guy turned and walked back to his car, angrily pitching the pizza box he carried onto the front seat beside him. He stared at it, then lifted the lid, pulled out a slice, and took a big bite. He drove away, cursing under his breath and eating the undelivered pizza. It was the second time Kelly Mayfield had been called a bitch that night. This one she didn't hear.

CHAPTER ONE

I walked up onto Kelly Mayfield's front porch, a headache from the hundred-and forty-mile drive from Atlanta beating a tympani solo in my head. The first twenty miles had taken almost as long as the rest. If Atlanta rush-hour traffic wasn't usually dreadful enough, a recent fire underneath an Interstate had collapsed a bridge and shut down a main artery, turning all of Atlanta into a parking lot.

A cardboard hanger like the "Do Not Disturb" signs that come with your hotel room was attached to Kelly's doorknob. It had the logo of a chain of pizza restaurants on it—*most likely our dinner for tonight*, I thought. I rang the doorbell, and when Kelly didn't show up right away, I used my key and let myself in.

I sat my suitcase down, called her name and she didn't answer. *In the bathroom, probably.* I went into the kitchen and found her. Prostrate on the floor. I shouted her name and rushed over, but she didn't move. Someone had savagely beaten her, bloody wounds on the side of her face and in her hairline, her right eye almost swollen shut. I checked for a pulse and found a heartbeat, thank God.

A call to 911 got the police and an ambulance coming. Kelly didn't stir once while I was waiting for them. At least, she was still breathing—if only haltingly.

First responders were there in minutes. They took one look at Kelly and ordered a Medivac helicopter to rush her to the Greenville Memorial Hospital, saying something about it being the nearest Level One trauma center. They worked on her until the chopper set down on the golf course fairway across the street. Kelly had leased a home in the Pickens Country Club neighborhood only for the view; the verdant golf course out her front windows, and the Blue Ridge Mountains on the northern horizon behind.

They let me ride in the chopper with her, and if her condition changed, I didn't see it. She was still breathing, and I took that as a good sign.

When we arrived at the hospital, they rushed Kelly in and pushed me away from the gurney, pointing to a waiting room, saying they would inform me when they knew something.

This was the first moment I had the opportunity to call anyone, but I didn't know who to call, other than my sister Eloise. She was not only Kelly's partner at the Clarion but loved Kelly almost as much as I did. I couldn't call Kelly's parents, they were elderly with advanced Alzheimer's, and both in a memory unit of a nursing home in North Carolina. They probably wouldn't understand what I would tell them. And Kelly was an only child with no brothers or sisters. She had other relatives somewhere, but I didn't have their names or phone numbers. I decided not to worry about that now and hoped her condition wouldn't reach a point that would make me have to find them.

I called Eloise. She answered on the third ring and sounded sleepy. She must have gone to bed early, which she often did.

"It's me," I said.

"Oh, hey, little brother, are you up here? Kelly said you were coming for the weekend."

"I'm at Greenville General Hospital. I've got some bad news."

"Are you hurt? Did you have an accident?" she asked anxiously.

"It's Kelly, not me."

"What? What's happened to Kelly? We left the *Clarion* together today. She seemed fine. She said she was going home, order a pizza, and wait for you."

"Someone broke in on her. She's been assaulted and severely beaten. I found her lying on her kitchen floor, unconscious. They brought her here by Medivac air transport, and I made them let me ride in the helicopter with her. She was breathing when they brought her in, but still unresponsive. I'm waiting to hear something from the doctors now."

"Do they know who did it?"

"Nobody has any idea. Do you?"

"No. I can't even imagine who would do something like this. I'm on my way, John David, and I'm bringing Mackenzie. She'll want to come too."

That didn't surprise me. Mackenzie was my teenage niece, and now a cub reporter at the *Clarion*, working part-time and juggling it with her senior year in high school. Kelly was teaching her the newspaper ropes, and the two had become very close.

"Can I bring you anything?" Eloise was saying. "I'll bet you haven't eaten a bite."

One of my sister's firm beliefs was that any crisis is better handled on a full stomach.

Another of her tenets as a true Southerner was that home cooking was the only real food.

"Don't eat that hospital food," she added. "I made fried chicken and biscuits for dinner. I'll bring you some."

CHAPTER TWO

Pickens County Sheriff Arlen Bagwell came into the waiting room along with who turned out to be two plain-clothes detectives. I knew Sheriff Bagwell. We'd first met way back when I was a teenager, and he was just a deputy. Then we became better acquainted two years ago when he investigated my grandfather's death. Our other connection was on a personal level. Sheriff Bagwell, a divorcee, held an unreciprocated crush on my sister, Eloise. I wondered if he'd decided to come along with his detectives for that reason—hoping to see Eloise here. He would get his wish. Eloise would soon be here.

I stood up and met them. Bagwell was a tall, lean man with a brush-cut and the deportment of a marine drill sergeant. Soft-spoken, he had a zero-tolerance for those on the other side of his ideas of law and order. He was an honest man whom I'd grown to respect and even *like* despite his lack of a gregarious nature and the fact that we didn't always see eye-to-eye.

After Bagwell introduced the men as Detectives Jud Chapin and Clyde Bates, he offered his commiserations for what happened to Kelly. He knew all about our relationship.

I told him I was waiting for the doctor to come out and tell me how she was, and I asked him what he knew so far about Kelly's assault.

"We haven't been able to learn much yet," he said. "Other than her attacker was most likely a male and he broke in through the back door. The CSI people are at the scene. Do *you* have any idea who could have done this, Mr. Bragg?"

"I can't imagine *anyone* who would do this to her," I said. "Was she sexually assaulted?" I was afraid to hear the answer; fearful she would suffer emotional injuries as well as the physical ones that this animal had inflicted.

Bagwell hesitated a moment. "I don't know. I haven't spoken to the doctors, but I doubt if they've done a rape kit yet. The doctors are probably attending to more critical matters right now."

"Oh Kelly . . ." I said before I realized I'd even said it.

"Do you know if she had seen any strange or suspicious men hanging around, or following her lately?" Bagwell asked.

"If so, she didn't tell me. My sister may know."

"Do you know if Ms. Mayfield had any enemies?"

I thought about that. "Every reporter makes their share of enemies if they're good at their job," I said finally. "They write things about people that can make them mad. Or they come down on the side of some issue that angers its opponents. But I don't know, or can't imagine, a specific incident that would cause anyone to do this. Eloise would know more about that than I would. I'm pretty hands-off when it comes to the *Clarion*."

"If there was a theft of anything, we can't determine it," Bagwell said. "She still had her watch on, and her wallet and cell phone were in her purse, found in the living room along with a laptop computer. Nothing in her bedroom seems to have been disturbed, and it appears that her jewelry wasn't touched. So, this doesn't look like a burglary. The beating was such an act of utter savagery that it seems like there was something personal to it. I guess it could have been some violent sexual pervert, but hopefully, the rape kit will help us determine that.

Did Kelly have enemies? Last spring a man on horseback tried to take my head off with a polo mallet because I was sticking my nose into his business. Why not Kelly? I needed to find out what she was working on.

I thought of the pizza delivery hanger on the front doorknob and told Bagwell about it.

"My guys saw that," he said. "We're tracking down the delivery guy right now to see if he saw or heard anything."

Bagwell was giving me an uneasy look. "Mr. Bragg, Detective Chapin here will need to take a sample of anything that might be under your fingernails, and we're going to need your shirt. We'll round up a hospital gown for you to wear."

"You think *I* did this?" I asked, surprised.

"Honestly, no, I don't. I know you, and I don't believe you would do something like this. But you're covered in her blood, and as a matter of procedure we need to eliminate you as a suspect. Detective Chapin here has a fingerprinting kit, and we'll need to get those too."

"You know my fingerprints will be all over her place," I said. "I've only been there a thousand times. And I'm the one who found her lying there, for God's sakes. *Of course*, I've got her blood on me."

"I know, I know," Bagwell said, appearing genuinely sorry. "But it's standard procedure, and I know it's hard, but let us do it. By eliminating you, we can put all of our efforts toward catching and convicting the real perpetrator. And we *will* catch and convict him."

He was right, I guess, but I didn't have to feel good about it. I tried to calm down and react logically. But it was hard not to get emotional over being tested for beating senseless the woman I loved.

"But I'm not wearing any hospital gown," I said. I'd seen them, and they were covered in pink and purple flowers. I had to maintain some dignity. "Before you get the shirt off my back, someone will have to bring me my suitcase from Kelly's house. It's sitting in the foyer."

"We can do that," Bagwell said and nodded at Bates, who pulled out his phone and stepped aside to make a call. Chapin was taking a fingerprint kit out of a briefcase.

I sat in the waiting room while Bagwell's men took scrapes from under my fingernails, hair follicles, swabs from my cheeks for DNA, and my fingerprints. A voice in my head kept saying that I was stupid not to get a lawyer. But one, I was innocent. Two, I didn't know any defense lawyers. And three, I just couldn't believe Sheriff Arlen Bagwell thought I was guilty.

Right now, I couldn't think about that. The only worry I could focus on was whether Kelly's injuries were fatal.

CHAPTER THREE

An hour later, Eloise burst into the waiting room with Mackenzie right behind her. They were both wearing concerned looks and made a beeline for me. After they hugged me and expressed their shock and horror at what had happened, Eloise stood back and looked at me.

"Have you talked to the doctor about her condition yet?" she asked.

"No, I'm still waiting to see him."

"Oh my God," she said, staring at my shirt. "Is that . . .?"

"Kelly's blood, yes."

"Oh, John David, it must have been horrible finding her like that."

"I should have been there earlier. Maybe I could have prevented it."

"Don't you dare blame yourself," she said. "This isn't your fault."

I glanced over at Sheriff Bagwell, thinking he might not agree with that.

Eloise followed my look and only then did she acknowledge his, and his men's presence. I was sure I saw Eloise blush when their eyes met.

He spoke to her, and I swear Bagwell blushed too. Eloise needed to give the guy a break and go out with him, I thought. Then I had another thought. Maybe she already had.

Eloise opened a large bag and took out a covered plate along with a thermos. She took off the aluminum foil covering the plate and showed it to me. It was the fried chicken and biscuits she'd promised.

"The coffee should still be hot," she said. "And I'm sure there's a microwave in the cafeteria you can use to heat the food."

"Thank you, sis," I said. "Wrap it back up, and I'll eat it later. I don't feel very hungry right now."

As she put the food away, a uniformed sheriff's deputy walked in, delivering my suitcase.

I took the bag from him, set it on the floor, and removed a fresh shirt. When I took my bloody shirt off, Eloise reached for it.

"Here," she said, "I'll take that home and wash it."

"I need to give it to Sheriff Bagwell," I said.

"Why does he want it?" Eloise asked with a frown, looking first at me then at Bagwell.

"Because he and his people want to do some tests."

"What kind of tests?" The crease between her eyebrows deepened.

"Blood tests, DNA, fingerprints, things like that."

The realization of what I was saying came ominously across her face like an approaching storm cloud. She turned to Bagwell and gave him such a look of anger and disappointment that he flinched.

"*Arlen Bagw*ell," she said. "You can't think John David did this terrible thing to Kelly. That's preposterous."

He said, "Of course I don't, Eloise. As I explained to Mr. Bragg, this is simply the standard procedure—not to accuse him, but to eliminate him from any evidence we may find at the scene."

"He's right Eloise," I said. "As much as I don't like it, he's just doing his job."

She held her disapproving gaze on Bagwell. He wore an expression like he was seeing any chance of ever capturing Eloise's heart disappear. I actually felt sorry for him.

Eloise was usually a mild, easygoing person, but if you attacked one of hers, she could exhibit the fury of an avenging angel. And I was the younger brother she helped raise.

We all went quiet for a moment, and I watched as the anger in her eyes slowly subside. After a moment, she smiled at Bagwell. I got the feeling that she liked him more than she let on. He seemed very relieved and smiled back at her.

During all this, Mackenzie said very little. My niece was no longer a child, becoming a beautiful young woman right before our eyes with long dark hair and a full figure like her mother. She was a senior in high school now, and according to Eloise, was leaving a trail of broken-hearted, lovesick boys in her wake. A straight-A student, and with the experience she was getting at the *Clarion*, she was talking college and a major in journalism. With her looks and brains, I could easily see her anchoring the TV news one day.

I placed my hand over hers on the arm of the chair and said, "Are you okay, sweetie?"

"Is *Kelly* going to be okay?" she asked, concern flooding her face.

"It's out of our hands, but I hope to God, she will be."

"Is that whose hands it's in?"

"God and the doctor's, I guess,"

"I love her like she's another mother, J.D.," she said, and placed her other hand over mine, her eyes welling with tears. "She *has* to get well. She just *has* to."

"I love her too," I said and looked over at Eloise. She was weeping, listening to us.

With the drama over, Bagwell introduced Eloise to Chapin and Bates and began asking her the same questions he asked me. Did she know who could have done this? Had Kelly mentioned anyone strange hanging around her? Had she made any recent enemies, and so on.

Eloise didn't know any more than I did and didn't even know if Kelly was pursuing a story that might place her in danger. Eloise offered that there might be something on Kelly's computer.

"Maybe she has notes on there that will show if she's working on some story we don't know about," I said.

"We have the laptop from her house," Bagwell said. "Does she also have a computer at work?"

"No, she doesn't," Eloise said. "She uses the laptop as her office computer and takes it home every day."

Bagwell said, "We will look at it and her cell phone, for any emails or texts of a suspicious nature. Do you know if there's a password for either of these devices?"

"There's a password for the laptop," I said. "*CherokeeGirl.* I've used it a couple of times. I don't think there's one for her cellphone."

"We also need to get her cell phone records," Bagwell said, turning to the Detectives.

"What's the number?" Detective Chapin asked.

I told him, and he entered it into his own cell phone.

Bagwell gave Eloise a tentative look. "Would you give me permission to look around Ms. Mayfield's office tomorrow? Check any notes, appointment calendars? Maybe there's something there that would help."

"Of course," Eloise said. "If John David agrees."

"I want to be there too," I said, and half expected Bagwell to say *no suspects allowed*. But let him try to do it *without* me. I owned the damn place—at least the majority of it. If the *Clarion* were a major newspaper like the *Atlanta Journal and Constitution*, the cops would never get a free hand to look at its records. The AJC would demand the right to protect the confidentiality of its sources. I just hoped my journalistic peers would never hear that I was allowing it.

Bagwell didn't mention my suspect status, and said, "I'll bring the laptop and cell phone. I doubt if the phone company will have given us Ms. Mayfield's phone records by tomorrow. It usually takes a little while. But when we do get them, you two can help me look at those, too".

Eloise and I agreed to meet Bagwell at the *Clarion* at 11:00 a.m. on Saturday. He and his detectives finally ran out of questions to ask and left, perhaps to go back to the scene at Kelly's house.

I turned to my sister. "So, you really don't know what Kelly was working on? How could you not?"

"I got the feeling she was chasing *something*," Eloise said. "But

I don't know what. She's got this thing about keeping her stories completely to herself until she has enough to start writing. Believe me, she hasn't said a word about it to me. I would have told Arlen if I'd known."

The three of us sat quietly for a moment, alone in the waiting room, worrying about Kelly. I tried to hold on to positive thoughts that she would be okay, but the fear that she wouldn't, kept getting in the way.

CHAPTER FOUR

We saw a doctor coming down the hall and stood up to meet him. I couldn't read his expression well enough to guess what kind of news he was bringing.

"I'm Doctor Mathis," he said. "Are you Kelly Mayfield's family?"

I nodded. I didn't think he needed more introduction or explanation than that. All three of us stayed silent and focused on his next words.

"She's breathing normally and appears to be stable now," he said.

Eloise said, "Thank God." Mackenzie burst out crying.

Somehow, I knew there was a "but" coming. There was.

He said, "However, she's suffered severe injuries to her head, and sustained some neurological damage. She came to us in a state of unconsciousness, and we've put her in a medically induced coma to keep her that way. That will support the healing process by allowing the brain to rest and decrease swelling. If we can relieve the pressure on the brain, hopefully, it will prevent further brain damage from occurring. She will remain in ICU while we do that."

I could see the wind go out of Eloise and Mackenzie. I guess it was up to me to ask the questions. "How long will she be in a coma?"

"When the swelling comes down, and she's ready, we gradually reduce the anesthetic drugs until she regains consciousness."

"And how long before you do that?"

"We do it as soon as we can. In most cases, a coma is induced for a few days, perhaps for up to two weeks. Induced comas longer than a month are extremely rare."

I asked the tough question. "What are the chances she *never* wakes up?"

He looked at me for a moment. "That's always a possibility of course, but in her case, I believe it's improbable unless her condition were to change for the worse."

It wasn't as definite as I wanted to hear, but at least there was hope.

He glanced at Mackenzie and Eloise as if he wasn't sure he wanted to continue in front of them. "There are no indications that she was sexually assaulted," he said. "We've done a rape kit, and no bodily fluids or any signs of penetration were found."

Despite what I'd told Eloise about this being the least of my concerns, I was hugely relieved. Can we see her?"

"You can, but she can't respond to you. So, prepare yourself for that. And if you will, please make your visits short for the time being. Rest is a big part of the healing process in something like this."

He paused. "Are you the one who found her?" he asked me.

"Yes," I said.

"Then you saved her life by finding her so early and calling it in so quickly. Another few minutes and she wouldn't have made it." He let that sink in as if it would be some consolation. "I'll keep you informed on her progress."

"Thank you, Doctor," I said.

He gave us an encouraging look, managing to smile. "Stay positive," he said, and left.

A nurse showed us to Kelly's bed in the ICU, and we all stood around it, looking at her. Kelly lay unresponsive, tubes and lines running in and out of her. I held her limp hand, wincing at the damage done to her lovely face, which was swollen and bruised, the eye, completely swollen shut. The nurse said she also had a broken rib.

I willed her to open her eyes and speak to me, but of course she didn't. I wondered if I could ever be truly alive again if I lost her. This monster, whoever he was and whatever his reasons, had tried to beat her to death, and still might succeed. I imagined the brutality of the act she'd suffered. What kind of sick bastard would do this to her? I would find him and see him punished, if it were the last thing I ever did.

We were sent back to the waiting room. Eloise and Mackenzie both eventually fell asleep in their chairs, sprawled in contorted positions. I was still too wired to sleep, even if I could have bent my six-foot-three frame into a position in the chair that would have allowed it.

I woke them up and told them to go home. There was nothing they could do here, and I promised to keep them posted to any changes. They begged me to come with them, but I was determined to stay, although I knew there was nothing that *I* could do, either. I just wanted to be close, in case somehow, Kelly could sense it. The girls left, and I took my seat, staring down the hallway toward the ICU, hoping for someone to appear with good news.

I went back and looked in on Kelly, my mind turning to the beginning of our relationship—to when we met. The first time I even knew there was a person named Kelly Mayfield was when I read her name on an editorial in the *Clarion*. What amazed me was that it was the first time I'd ever seen someone other than my grandfather handle an editorial in the newspaper he'd ruled with an iron and non-sharing hand. The article was written a week before he died, so he had to have approved it. The second shock was when I looked at the *Clarion's* employee list and saw that Kelly Mayfield was named as editor—a title my grandfather had selfishly held along with "publisher" since the day he bought the paper. What the hell was going on here, I'd wondered?

The editorial was well-written and thoughtful, and I remember thinking whoever this woman was, she was good. The first time I laid eyes on her was at Grandfather's funeral a couple of days later. She was nothing like I expected—which was some egg-headed woman with glasses on a chain, on the road to being a spinster and with a fundamentalist view of a heroic press that some believe still exists in small-town newspapers.

Boy, was I wrong. She was beautiful. Long black hair, big dark eyes, and high cheekbones suggesting Cherokee blood in her from way back. She was taking my grandfather's death as badly as Eloise. Certainly, worse than I was—or at least worse than I was showing.

I think I fell in love with her on the spot. But there was a problem. She despised me. I learned later, on a visit to the newspaper, that she believed I'd treated my grandfather meanly, and the estrangement between us was entirely my fault. Kelly Mayfield accused me of breaking the heart of a man whom she obviously adored and didn't deserve having someone like me as a grandson. Not true from my point of view, but that didn't get me anywhere with her. She thought me a heartless, mean-spirited bastard who only cared about selling the *Clarion*, firing everyone, and lining my pockets with the proceeds.

I should have left Kelly to her beliefs. Some unavoidable and inexplicable inner force drove me to want her to like me. My actions and behavior from that point on, along with my sister's good character references, eventually softened her opinion of me somewhat. And like the quarterback I once was, I saw an opening and went for it. Now here we were, both claiming our love for one another, but neither knowing what the future held. As I studied her lying there, I only knew one thing for sure. I didn't want to lose her.

CHAPTER FIVE

Morning came and sunshine began to peek through the ECU waiting room blinds. Nurses came and went in the hallway all night. As far as I knew, Kelly hadn't awakened or even moved. At least no one said so when I peeked in on her on my periodic visits. I hadn't moved much either beyond my visits to her bedside. I sat drinking Eloise's thermos of coffee, eating a little of her chicken and biscuits, and going to the bathroom. I could feel the effect of the waiting room chair in my shoulders and back. I'd managed very little sleep with people coming and going all night, and it seemed like most of the bones in my body ached.

I went back to see Kelly again.

Doctor Mathis came in and took a quick look at Kelly and checked her vital signs. I wondered if he had slept any.

"No change," he said to me. "Which is a good sign. She isn't any better, but she isn't any worse either."

The doctor was obviously more of a "glass half full" person than I was, I thought.

He said, "I learned that none of you are actually immediate family. Is there someone we can help you contact?"

"The only family she has are both in nursing homes for Alzheimer patients in North Carolina. They wouldn't recognize her any more than she would recognize them. We're her family now."

"And you're the significant other?"

"You could call me that," I said.

"Well, you don't need to stay here around the clock. We'll call you the minute there is any change in Ms. Mayfield's condition."

I thought about that for a moment. "If she remains stable, I'll probably stay tonight with my sister over in Pickens County." I fished out one of my *SportsWord* cards and handed it to him. "You can reach me on my cell."

He glanced at my card. "Leave one for the nurse at the station in the hall, too, Mr. Bragg. And go get some rest." He nodded at Kelly. "You'll wear yourself out staying here, and she wouldn't want that, would she?"

I got the message. It was his way of saying my being there was getting in everyone's way and wasn't helping Kelly. So, from today on, I decided, I would visit her daily, and sleep in a comfortable bed at Eloise's at night. I did have other things I could do to help. Even when Kelly awoke, she wouldn't be going back to work anytime soon. I could help Eloise get the paper out until Kelly could come back. The *Clarion* was Eloise's and Mackenzie's only source of income. I would need to become more than just the absentee publisher for a while.

I sat with Kelly until mid-morning, and then went to meet Eloise and Bagwell at the *Clarion* offices in Pickens.

#

Sheriff Arlen Bagwell's cruiser was sitting in one of the parking spaces by the *Clarion's* front door when I arrived. Eloise's Honda Accord was parked next to it. I found Bagwell inside, standing by the reception desk with Eloise and Mackenzie.

After a couple of unenthusiastic "good mornings," I asked Bagwell if there was any progress in identifying Kelly's attacker.

"Not from what we've found at the house," he said. "But we did catch a break. A couple of teenagers came forward and said they may have seen the assailants—and notice I said, *assailants*. Looks like there were two of them. These kids, both from the neighborhood—a girl and her boyfriend—were out on the golf course last night at about the time it happened. They saw a dark SUV come up the street and pull in behind a maintenance shed, like whoever it was didn't want to be seen by any passers-by. The kids found that suspicious, so they hid to keep from being seen. My guess is, they were already there, lying on the grass, involved in a little teenage hanky-panky.

"We're lucky they contacted us," he added. "Seems the girl's dad ain't too happy about them being out there together, but when the kids heard what had happened to Ms. Mayfield, they did the right thing and called us, despite the dad finding out about it.

"They say they saw two men get out of the SUV and go across the street and into the trees behind the houses that line the fairway there—Ms. Mayfield's house is one of them. They said the men were walking fast like they knew where they were going. They described one of them as a big guy with long hair pulled back in a ponytail. Too dark to tell the color. He was wearing a T-shirt under a vest of some kind, either denim or leather. His arms were covered in tattoos, but it was too dark to make them out. All they could say about the other man was that he was a little shorter, stocky, and dressed in dark colors that sort of blended in with the shadows. They couldn't offer anything on the ages of either one other than they weren't really young or really old. That's the best I could get out of them.

"They say the men were gone probably twenty to thirty minutes, then returned and left the way they came. They didn't get the make or model of the SUV, or the plate number. My guys are canvassing the area to see if any of the neighbors saw or heard anything."

"This doesn't sound random to me," I said, "As if these guys knew where they were going."

"I agree," Bagwell said. "Which says Ms. Mayfield was targeted. By the way, we found the pizza delivery guy. When he learned that Ms. Mayfield was probably inside and being attacked when he showed up at her door, the only thing he seemed to care about was her stiffing him for a pizza, and him skinning his knuckles banging on her door. The guy was a real self-centered little shit—pardon the French, ladies—but he didn't see or hear anything going on inside. He had nothing else to offer."

I said, "Could his banging on the door have scared these guys off?"

Bagwell considered it. "Well, it does look like her attacker was trying to kill her, but didn't finish the job for some reason. So, maybe the kid might have helped in spite of his self-serving manner."

"Maybe the Dixie Demons did it?" Mackenzie said.

We all stopped and looked at her. She didn't seem to be joking.

"Ponytail, T-shirt and vest, tattoos?" she said. "The one guy was dressed like a biker."

"Dixie Demons?" I said and gave her a puzzled look.

"It's a biker gang, J.D.."

"I know who they are, but what do they have to do with Kelly?"

"Kelly saw some of them. She went to a biker bar on Tiger Boulevard in Clemson, and there was a bunch of them there. She said they were rough-looking characters, and warned me to stay out of Clemson when they have their big gathering. As if I'd hang with outlaw bikers," Mackenzie added, and rolled her eyes.

"Gathering?" I said.

Eloise explained. "The Dixie Demons are having their annual get-together, or reunion, or whatever they call it, in Clemson later this summer. There's a few of them in town this week making plans and arranging things. We covered this months ago when the city agreed to let them come. There could be five or six hundred of them in Clemson for several days. It's the biggest thing to happen there since the parade for Coach Swinney and the boys when they won this last national championship."

Another example of how little attention I paid to the newspaper that listed me as the publisher. Grandfather would be rolling over in his grave.

"Was Kelly doing another story on these bikers?" I asked. "She wouldn't just stop by a biker bar for a happy-hour cocktail—unless she's leading a double life that I don't know about."

"She didn't say anything about it to me," Eloise said. "But as I said, she never tells anyone what she's working on until she's ready to go to press with it."

"Where is this biker outfit based?" I asked.

"Some little town in North Carolina close to the Virginia line," Bagwell said. "Mt. Airy,

Yadkinville, someplace like that. But they have chapters in other Southern states."

"Mt. Airy," I said. "Wasn't the fictional town of Mayberry from the Andy Griffith show based on Mt. Airy, or shot there, or something? It's hard to imagine an outlaw biker gang coming out of there. Reminds me of a story a guy I know named Tom Monroe told me. He grew up in Iowa and said biker gangs in the Midwest weren't all that tough. Instead of 'Born to raise hell,' the tattoos on their arms read, 'Born to raise corn.' Are these Dixie Demons really dangerous?"

"Around the South, they might even be worse than the Hells Angels," Bagwell said. "They add hate crimes to their list of criminal activities."

"And the people who live in Clemson are okay with hundreds of them coming to town all at once?"

"They had a public vote on it," Bagwell said. "A majority voted to let them come, which surprised me. I was against it. I think they're just asking for trouble. But Larry Watson, the Clemson Chief of police, checked with other towns that have hosted this thing in past years and there's never been any trouble to speak of. The tourism director for the Clemson Area Chamber of Commerce said it's almost like a family reunion for them— and they don't come looking for trouble."

"When was Kelly at that bar?" I asked Mackenzie. "Maybe one them of followed her when she left there or found out where she lived."

"Thursday night," Mackenzie said. "She told me about it yesterday when I got to work."

Bagwell said, "I'll get with Larry Watson and see if he can talk to these bikers, or stop by this bar to see if anyone there remembers Ms. Mayfield and if she was seen talking to any Dixie Demons."

I gave him a look.

"Hey, I would do it myself," Bagwell added. "But I don't want to step on Larry's toes. Clemson is his jurisdiction, and he's probably sensitive about hearing that these bikers may not be behaving. He came out strongly in favor of hosting their gathering. But my thinking is, just because they show up with their women and kids somewhere for four days every year and play family reunion, it don't change the fact that for the other three-hundred and sixty-one days of the year they're into things like drug dealing and trafficking in stolen goods. The Department of Justice classifies the Dixie Demons as an outlaw motorcycle gang, and I happen to agree with them. We don't need these kinds of people in Pickens County. A leopard ain't gonna' change its spots just because he's bringing his family with him."

"So, why *did* the town throw out the welcome mat?" I asked.

Bagwell sighed. "I hate to say it, but *money*. Plain and simple. Students are not in town, and business can be slow in the summer. The town fathers and local merchants estimated that this reunion will have an economic impact of over a million dollars on the Clemson community. They put pressure on Chief Watson. I doubt he had a choice if he wanted to keep his job."

"Wow," I said. I wouldn't have thought a bunch like this

would spend *that* much money. *A million dollars.* That's a lot of fried chicken and beer."

Eloise said, "We interviewed one manager of a Clemson restaurant and bar and she said their business will be welcoming the riders with open arms. She said with the experiences she's had bartending for fans on football game-days, she can put up with anything the Dixie Demons can dish out."

"Okay," I said. "Changing the subject, let's see if we can find anything here that might help." I motioned for Eloise to open the loose-leaf notebook on the reception desk.

"This is our sign-in-sign-out book," Eloise said to Bagwell. "If we leave during the workday, we must sign out with the time of our departure, and our destination. That's so we can be reached if necessary. Then we sign back in on our return. Mrs. Mozingo, our receptionist, jack of all trades, and mother hen, makes sure she always knows where everyone is, and you know her," Eloise said to me. "She enforces this company policy like a guard on a gate."

We went through the pages one by one, starting with the latest. The first that caught my eye was an entry by Kelly. It was a sign-out at two-fifteen the previous Monday afternoon, the destination, a Doctor Stefans. No address was given.

Eloise saw it too. "This isn't Kelly's regular doctor, Doctor Jamison is. I've never even heard of this doctor."

Neither had I, nor had I knowledge that she'd seen *any* doctor lately.

"Has Kelly been sick?" I asked Eloise.

"I don't think so. If she was, she didn't tell me."

She didn't tell me either, I thought, and suddenly the word

"pregnant" popped into my mind, followed by a scattered mix of emotions. But wouldn't that appointment still be with her regular doctor? And wouldn't Doctor Mathis at the hospital have found that out and said something about it last night?

"Maybe he's a specialist of some kind that Doctor Jamison referred her to," Eloise said. "But I can't believe Kelly wouldn't have told me."

"There's a Doctor Stefans in Clemson that I know of," Bagwell offered. "If this is him, he's a general practitioner. A family doctor, not a specialist."

"Why would Kelly see a doctor in Clemson?" Eloise asked.

I wondered the same thing. The college town of Clemson was on the southwest corner of the county and a long way to go to see a doctor for someone who lived here. I took out my cell phone and Googled, "Doctor Stefans in Pickens County." Bagwell was right. I found a Doctor Michael Stefans on Highway 123, in Clemson.

Bagwell looked like he didn't think the doctor held any pertinence to the case and was ready to ignore him. My thoughts lingered on. I wanted to find out if this Doctor Stefans was treating Kelly for something I didn't know about. I saved his information on my phone.

Eloise could explain most of the remaining entries in the book: routine business, people, and places that were well known, easy to figure out, and beyond suspicion.

We finished looking at the sign-out book and went into Kelly's office, searching for any story notes, telephone scratch pads, or anything of interest, but found nothing suspicious or unexplainable. If Kelly had notes on some story, they would probably be on her missing laptop, as would her emails.

Bagwell had brought Kelly's laptop and cell phone and said they'd found nothing suspicious or enlightening on them. Eloise and I sat down and looked for ourselves. We didn't find anything either. No revealing emails or texts, and no files or documents that looked like story notes. If Kelly were working on something, she wasn't keeping notes on her computer about it.

We searched Kelly's office and desk, and found nothing there either. We still didn't know what Kelly was working on—if anything—or who her attacker might have been, or why she had been attacked in the first place. As unlikely as it was, Mackenzie's news that Kelly had visited a biker's bar was the only thing we had to go on.

Bagwell told us he would be in touch with Kelly's phone records when he got them, probably not until Monday. The phone company's priorities didn't always coincide with his.

I thought about the idea of Kelly attracting the attention of someone dangerous. From what I was just told about the Dixie Demons, they were definitely dangerous. So, whether or not there was merit to it, and regardless of how much Sheriff Bagwell and the Clemson Police Chief would look into Kelly's visit to the Tiger's Tail, I would pay the place a visit too. To Chief Watson and Sheriff Bagwell, it might be just a job.

But to me, it was personal.

CHAPTER SIX

We were right behind Bagwell leaving the *Clarion* offices, and as I passed through the lobby on the way out, I spotted a stack of back issues of the *Clarion* on a coffee table and picked up a few to read later. I threw them in the back seat of my time-worn Jeep Wrangler, and from there, Eloise, Mackenzie, and I went to the Gatehouse Restaurant in Pickens for lunch.

We ordered soup and sandwiches, and spent our time rehashing the subject of the Dixie Demons, why Kelly would go to a biker bar, or why she visited this Doctor Stefans. I didn't mention my thought about pregnancy. I planned to ask the doctor at the hospital.

Afterward, we went our separate ways. Mackenzie and Eloise went to the hospital to look in on Kelly, and I went to Still Hollow to crash for a couple of hours. After spending the night in a chair at the hospital, I was exhausted. I'd found myself almost drooping my chin into my tomato soup a couple of times during lunch and realized that the best thing I could do for my efforts to help track down Kelly's assailant was to get some sleep.

\#

In my old boyhood bedroom at Still Hollow, which Eloise always kept available for me, I set a bedside alarm clock for three hours, stripped down to my underwear, and climbed into bed.

But while my body was tired, my brain was restless. I lay there for the longest time, eyes wide open, thinking about everything that had happened since arriving at Kelly's, and looking back on it like watching a nightmarish slide-show.

I was up and about to leave for the hospital when Eloise and Mackenzie returned from their visit there. I'd slept only an hour or so out of the three that I lay in my old bed. Just being comfortable and quiet for a while had charged my batteries some. I seemed to have a bit of a second wind.

Eloise said that some of the *Clarion* staff had come by to see Kelly and brought flowers. They didn't stay long, and neither did Eloise and Mackenzie. We were all starting to get the picture that there was nothing any of us could do for Kelly, although I guess we all felt the need to be there by her side. As I left, I told Eloise not to wait up for me. I would probably stay out quite late. I didn't tell them that the real reason was that I planned to pay a visit to the Tigers Tail bikers bar.

#

At the hospital, Kelly was still hooked up to wires, tubes, and monitors. They had her lying on her side with one arm moved aside and supported to allow for lung expansion, and her legs crossed. According to a nurse, this afforded the unconscious, breathing patient the best protection from airway occlusion or aspiration of fluids into the lungs. My emotions continued to swing like a pendulum between worry and rage as I looked at her.

There was a colorful bouquet of flowers by her bed, and the card revealed they were from the *Clarion* staff. They were beautiful, but they gave the room a heavy floral smell and reminded me of a funeral. I thought about removing them and decided against it. Maybe the cloying odor would bring Kelly back to life just to get rid of them herself.

I stood and held her hand for a long time, looking at her. The bruises on her face were already going from reddish-brown to yellow and green. Her eye was still swollen shut but somehow seemed a little better. That she had begun to heal externally was clear, It was the inside of her head I was worried about. Was that healing too?

I sat by her bedside until darkness began to settle on the landscape outside the hospital windows. Then I left for the Tiger's Tail Bar and Grill in Clemson.

CHAPTER SEVEN

The Tiger's Tail sat along Highway 123, or Tiger Boulevard, just north of the small college downtown and the sprawling campus of Clemson University.

The bar was a cinder block building painted blue and with few windows and a flat-topped roof. A large neon sign hung over the front door with a bright orange cartoon image of a tiger riding a motorcycle and trailing a large curled tail. What windows there were, all displayed brightly lit beer signs.

The place sat back off the highway, fronted by a large cracked asphalt parking lot scattered with Harley hogs and tricked-out pickup trucks. I could hear an old Lynyrd Skynyrd rocker coming from inside when I got out of the Jeep.

I parked and went inside. The place was smoky and noisy. I didn't think the customers were ignorant of the smoking laws, they just didn't give a shit. There were a lot of steel-toed boots and jeans and leathers, along with shaved heads or long hair, and a majority of shaggy beards. This was no place for the mild-mannered and meek. I couldn't picture Kelly ever coming here without an excellent reason.

A long bar ran down the right side, with a couple of bartenders behind it. To the left stood a dozen tables and beyond them, a small stage and dance floor on against the wall. A homemade sign sat on an easel next to the bandstand that announced that "The Roadrunners," were performing Friday and Saturday nights from 9:00 p.m. to midnight. It was still a little early for them, the only music coming from a jukebox. It was playing another Skynyrd number.

In the back were more tables and booths and a couple of pool tables. A half-dozen Dixie Demons surrounded the pool tables, easily recognized even from where I stood by their "colors," the club emblems on their backs.

I walked down the bar and found an empty stool, sat down and ordered a tap beer from a bald-headed bartender with a drooping Pancho Villa mustache. A man on the stool next to me turned and gave me the once-over. I returned the favor. He was probably in his fifties and had thinning short hair, going gray, He wore blue coveralls with a label on the pocket that read, "Dave's Tire and Wheel." He had ground-in grease on his knuckles. Not a Dixie Demon, I assumed.

"How ya' doing," I said.

"Fair to middling," he said. "How 'bout you?"

"Doing better now," I said, lifting my mug at him.

"Ain't that the truth," he answered, nodding.

"You come in here much?" I asked, already knowing that he probably did. I'd caught a bit of his conversation with Pancho Villa when I sat down, and they sounded like old friends.

He raised an eyebrow and gave me a quizzical look.

"If that's a pickup line, my friend, you're in the wrong bar," he said. "There's one of them kind of places down the street."

He had chuckled, so I guess he was pulling my leg. Maybe.

I chuckled too. "I'm just looking for anybody who hangs out in here a lot."

"I guess I fit that bill, I'm Dave," he said and stuck out his hand.

"J.D.," I said as I shook it, and I pulled out my wallet photo of Kelly and showed it to him, "Have you seen this woman in here recently?"

He studied the picture for a moment. "You a cop?"

"No, I'm just trying to find her."

"You got woman trouble, that's your business, friend. I ain't getting in the middle of nothing like that."

"There's no trouble, I met her once but lost her number. I'm trying to find her again. Can you blame me? Look at her."

He looked at the picture again. "Naw, I don't blame you," he said and studied my face. "Yeah, I seen her. A couple of nights ago. Hard to miss somebody in here looks like her. She was talking to the bartender."

I glanced over at Pancho Villa, standing a few feet away, talking to another customer.

"Not *him*, "her," Dave said, pointing down the bar at another bartender.

I turned and saw an attractive redhead with freckles and a cute little turned-up nose, probably in her twenties somewhere. I watched her for a moment, then turned back to Dave and nodded toward the pool tables in the rear of the bar.

"What about those boys in the back? You see her talking to any of them?"

"So far, they been pretty much keeping to themselves," he

said. "They ain't really been socializing with the local folks much. They tend to bring their party with them. A close-knit bunch. Some of the local riders ain't taking that too well, but nobody's screwed up enough courage to front them about it. Everybody knows there's only about six or eight of them here now, but, come August they say there'll be over five hundred of them.

"Them that's here now seem to be on their best behavior," he added. "What with making arrangements and stuff, nailing down campgrounds, and lining up box lunches for a big ride I hear they're gonna' take into the mountains, they're playing nice with everybody. God knows what they'll do when the whole bunch of them get here.

We both discreetly watched the bikers for a moment.

Dave added, "But I did see one of them belly up to the bar next to your lady in the picture. He said a few words to her, but she must have cooled his tater pretty quick, because he didn't stick around her but about a minute, and he was in the back again with his buddies."

"You remember which one of them this was?"

"Yeah, it was the one with the curly black hair and the beard that ain't so wild and woolly like the rest of them. The big guy, standing by the pool table on the right. I think he fancies himself God's gift to women. He sort of swaggers when he walks, and I've seen him hit on several young ladies who come in here. He's the only one of em' who seems like he wants to fraternize. As long as it's with somebody with tits."

I saw who he was talking about and the guy did cut a striking figure, well-built and looking a little bit like the Jason Momoa, the actor.

"She talk to anybody else in here?" I asked Dave.

"I don't know, I went home. She was still up front at the bar when I left."

I thanked Dave and dropped a five-spot on the bar for Pancho Villa. I took my beer and went to see if the cute bartender would talk to me. There was an empty stool in front of her, and I took it.

"Something I can getcha'?" she said, coming over. She didn't have that I've-heard-everything-and-nothing-you-can-say-would-shock-me look that many bartenders have, especially in places like this. She had a sweet girl next door innocence about her.

"I'm fine," I said, setting my beer on the bar and placing the photograph of Kelly next to it. "But I would like to talk to you about this girl."

She leaned over and studied the photograph. When she straightened up, her whole demeanor had changed. The photo had disturbed her somehow, and she was trying hard to hide it.

"Pretty girl, but I'm sorry, I don't know her."

"I was led to believe you were talking to her right here at the bar a couple of days ago."

"Who told you that?" she asked and glanced up the bar at Pancho Villa watching us. "If I did talk to her, I don't remember her. A lot of people come in here."

"You sure about that?" I said.

"Positive." There was something in her eyes that said she wasn't telling me everything. "Let me know when you're ready for another beer," she added, and turned to begin washing glasses in a sink behind her. I watched for a moment, her shoulders bent and scrubbing away. Whatever else she was, I thought—the girl next door or toughened bartender in a biker bar—there was one thing she wasn't. A good actress. She was scared of something and the picture of Kelly had caused it.

Pancho Villa was still staring at me.

CHAPTER EIGHT

I grabbed my beer and headed to the pool tables. I didn't see any reason not to get acquainted with some of the Dixie Demons while I was here. If they knew anything at all about Kelly's beating, I'm sure they wouldn't tell me, but I could at least try to read between the lines of what they *would* say—and get a feel for the Jason Momoa look-alike. Besides, what could they do to me if I pissed them off? Dumb question. They could take me out back and beat me senseless, for one thing. But what the heck. No risk, no reward, they say. But I wondered if anyone ever tried that old saw out on a murderous outlaw biker gang.

These particular Dixie Demons would be gone soon, and I wouldn't get another chance to take a look at them until they returned in August. As for the red-headed bartender, who I could see out of the corner of my eye watching me, I had plenty of time to talk to her again. I would just need to find a different approach, or a different place to do it.

I walked up to several of the bikers standing in a group. They were either between games or just using the table rails as a place set their beers. Look-alike Jason Momoa was one of them. All of them were wearing what you'd expect outlaw bikers to wear, mostly denim and leather, and looked their parts as if cast in Hollywood. They were laughing loudly at something as I walked up.

"Pardon me, fellas," I said, interrupting them.

They all went suddenly quiet and turned to stare at me as if I were an alien from another world—which to them, I probably was. I was definitely an unwelcome guest at their party and could only hope they weren't trying to decide whether to throw me out, or beat the crap out of me first and *then* throw me out.

"Can I ask if any of you have seen this woman in here?" I said, holding out

Kelly's photograph. "She's missing."

"No," one of them said, not even looking at the picture.

"No, you haven't seen her, or no, I can't ask?" I said.

"What do we look like, Ace?" he said. "The lost and found department?"

Another one of them leaned in closer and looked. "Hot. I ain't seen her, but I'll sure-as-shit keep an eye out."

A hairy guy with a large gap between his front teeth took a look. "Hey, Hound-dog? Ain't that the chick who shot your ass down?"

Look-alike Jason Momoa stepped over and took the photo out of my hand, studied it a moment, and handed it back. "That your woman?" he said to me.

"I'm just looking for her."

"Why?"

"She won the Publisher's Clearing House Sweepstakes. I need to notify her."

"Fuck you, you a cop?"

"No, why do they call you Hound-dog?"

"Because he hound-dogs every chick he sees, man," Gap-tooth said, and sniggered.

A couple of the others chuckled. Hound-dog didn't. He gave Gap-tooth the evil eye, then turned it on me. "If she's your woman, he said, "why don't you know where she is? She take off on you?"

"*Did* you hound-dog her?" I asked.

"Maybe I did. Maybe she's back in my motel room right now, waiting for this." He grabbed at his crotch.

"Your buddy there said she shot you down. I can see why. You're not her type."

"What, she don't like grade-A meat? Looking at you, she's probably ready for some."

"She don't like guys with an IQ smaller than her bra size," I said.

A couple of them laughed again. Hound-dog still didn't.

"This son-of-a-bitch is craving hospital food," he said, his eyes never leaving me. He took a step toward me and I wondered if my smart- mouth had just attracted a big fist.

An older guy stepped forward and placed a hand on Hound-dog's arm.

"Let's all just calm down here," he said and looked at me. "And you need to be leaving, friend. I don't know who you are or what kind of suicide wish you've got, but we ain't having any of it today."

His short brush-cut was greying, and he was smaller than the others, but by the steely look in his eyes and the way Hound-dog quickly backed off, I gathered that this guy out-ranked him—both in club hierarchy and in mettle. Something told me this was the most dangerous guy of them all.

"We're in town with peaceful intentions," he went on, still holding his gaze on me. "We're here to make plans for a family get-together we'll be having here later in the summer. So, why don't you just go on about your business, and leave us to ours? None of us know anything about this missing woman. And while Hound-dog here might have put the moves on her at the bar, he's a horny bastard, and that's just what he does. But if she's missing, he ain't the reason. None of us are."

Without any real evidence against this Hound-dog character, I did the only thing I could. I took my leave. The good news was that after a testy face-to-face encounter with a bunch of in-the-flesh Dixie Demons, I walked away under my own steam and with no broken bones, bloody nose, or missing teeth.

My inquiries were at a dead-end with the Dixie Demons. I would have to leave their investigation up to Sheriff Bagwell, the Clemson police, and crime scene investigators.

The barmaid was different. She hadn't seen the last of me.

CHAPTER NINE

Sunday morning, I woke up late, finally getting a good night's sleep. I felt much better, at least physically. I still had a brush fire going on in my head over Kelly's health, but at least I had the energy now to deal with it.

I smelled bacon frying from the kitchen, got up, dressed, and went down to join my sister and my niece.

"Good morning," Eloise said, as she and Mackenzie were getting breakfast on the table. It was a huge country meal of bacon, eggs, grits, and cathead biscuits with sawmill gravy. It was as if we were expecting a group of field hands to join us before they went to tend the crops for a hard day's labor. Some things in the south never changed.

"Are you guys going to church?" I asked Eloise. Sunday services were a ritual for my sister.

"God can hear my prayers for Kelly from here just as well as at church," she said. Besides, Sheriff Bagwell called this morning to say he has Kelly's telephone records and volunteered to bring them out for us to look at. I want to see them. Maybe I can help."

"When's he coming?"

"He's on his way. According to him, he pulled some strings and got more cooperation out of the phone company than he'd expected. They sent them to him sometime during the night."

I was about to tell Eloise about my trip to the Tiger's Tail last night and meeting the Dixie Demons, then quickly changed my mind. I'd wait for Bagwell to arrive. They would both be angry with me, albeit for different reasons—Eloise for placing myself in a potentially risky situation, and Bagwell for my meddling in an investigation. So why not wait and tell them at the same time and avoid getting chastised twice? I sat down for a quick bite of Eloise's field-hand breakfast before he could get there. Better to get yelled at on a full stomach, I always said.

Bagwell showed up thirty minutes later, just as I was sopping the last gravy off my plate with a piece of biscuit. He had a folder stuck under his arm that I took to be Kelly's phone records. Eloise offered Bagwell breakfast, but he said he'd already eaten, so she and Mackenzie cleared the table.

Bagwell turned to me and smiled. "Before we get started, I've got some good news for you. I hope you know that I never considered you a suspect, but as I said, we had to eliminate you. It's the standard procedure in things like this. Well, now it's official, you are cleared as a suspect. One of Ms. Mayfield's neighbors saw two men, one with a ponytail, come through her backyard from the general direction of Ms. Mayfield's place, then, thirty-seven minutes later she saw you pull into the driveway." That's enough for me."

"Thirty-seven minutes? This neighbor timed it that precisely?"

"Seeing those guys in her backyard scared her, so she kept time on the neighborhood comings and goings from that moment on."

"I appreciate you telling me," I said, but the fact that he had even checked me out in the first place, procedure or not, was still absurd. I couldn't be all that grateful for him clearing me. He was still smiling, and I was about to wipe that smile off his face.

I announced to them that I had something to say too, before we got started. I guess I had spoken too gravely. All three of them took their seats and waited.

"I went to the Tiger's Tail Bar and Grill last night and had a little conversation with some of the Dixie Demons biker gang."

I told them all about it, watching Bagwell's jaw muscles roll from the grinding of teeth as I spoke. I'd tried to do his job for him once before, and he didn't like it then, either. I was convinced he would never have learned about Hound-dog hitting on Kelly just twenty-four hours before she was brutally assaulted. I still believed that the Dixie Demons would say things to me they would never say to a uniformed policeman.

I knew I would be in for it when I was finished. And I was.

Bagwell sat with his eyes closed, slowly shaking his head. When he opened them, he looked at Eloise, not me, and I knew that her being there would save me from the worst of his anger. He wouldn't unload on me like he wanted to.

"Dadburn it, Bragg, I ought to lock you up," he said finally. "You had no business interfering with a police investigation."

"I agree with him, John David," Eloise said. "Seriously, did you actually confront a gang of Dixie Demons? What were you thinking? Are you trying to end up in a bed down the hall from Kelly?"

"I thought they would say things to me they would never say to Sheriff Bagwell," I said.

She said, "But at least Arlen wouldn't have been alone. And he and every officer with him would have been carrying guns."

"Okay, okay, enough," Bagwell said. "And you," he said, turning to me. "You stay away from these guys, or I promise you, you will end up being an extended-stay guest of Pickens County. We will look into it. This is our job, so let us do it. If this guy who came on to Ms. Mayfield at the bar doesn't have an iron-clad alibi for Friday night, believe me, he won't be going anywhere. I will hold him over until we find out exactly where he was Friday night."

Then he looked at Eloise and me.

He said, "I hope y'all understand the predicament this creates. If this Dixie Demon is guilty of the heinous attack on Ms. Mayfield, that's one thing. He'll get what's coming to him. But if he isn't our guy, he could still be a problem. If word gets out that a Dixie Demon was even *considered* a person of interest, it could play hell with the upcoming event this summer.

"The fact that we're already having trouble like this, with just a small advance party in town, portends what might happen when we get hundreds of them here. We don't need to stir people up needlessly, which this would, especially those against these Dixie Demons coming here in the first place. That could lead to either a public outcry to cancel the event, which personally wouldn't bother me, or build up animosity with the locals against the bikers and cause trouble, maybe even violence, when the whole bunch gets here. That *would* bother me.

Bagwell took a breath and paused before going on. "Having said all that, don't get me wrong. I will do everything humanly possible to find and arrest the man who attacked Ms. Mayfield, whoever it is. All I'm asking you is to at least keep this quiet until we've had a chance to check out this Hound-dog fellow. This can't get out before we can determine whether he's definitely a suspect or not. I don't want to create a shitstorm—pardon me, ladies—by wrongly casting suspicion on an innocent Dixie Demon."

"Innocent Dixie Demon," I repeated. "That's probably an oxymoron, but I'll agree. But you need to be damn sure this guy is innocent beyond any shadow of a doubt."

I wondered, *who else would have done it?* I would let Sheriff Bagwell and the Clemson Police Department do their jobs, but Bagwell didn't know me well if he thought I'd stop looking into it myself. If it wasn't Hound-dog who attacked Kelly, then there had to be a clue somewhere to reveal who did. And if the cops couldn't find it, I would not rest until *I* did.

With that conversation seemingly over, Bagwell turned his attention back to the reason he came. Kelly's recent phone records.

"These are for both her home and her cell phone," he said, spreading them out on the kitchen table. "I've looked them over, but I didn't find anything meaningful, at least to me. Maybe you two will spot something I missed."

Eloise and I stood examining the print-outs. They revealed the numbers called, as well as date and duration of the call. Not surprisingly, my number frequently appeared. Most of the numbers had names with them, but a few didn't, and none of the ones that didn't were familiar to either Eloise or me. We told Bagwell that, and he already had someone in his office tracking those down. He'd pass them along for us to look at as soon as he could.

The first call that got my attention was to Doctor Michael Stefans last Monday morning, before Kelly's visit to him that afternoon. That would be unheard of in Atlanta, I thought. It usually took me a week to get in to see my Doctor. Maybe living in small towns did have its advantages.

Another name from last Monday caught my eye. Kelly had called an April Cheney, a local number, and I'd never heard of her. Neither had Eloise. The interesting thing was, Kelly had called this person a total of five times over four days. The first call she made was after she returned from the appointment with Doctor Stefans. The second, later that evening, and the third call early Tuesday morning. The last two, the mornings of Wednesday and Thursday. Both Monday calls were brief, probably unsuccessful, or at least only long enough to get a voicemail recording. However, the one made at 9:33 a.m. in the morning on Tuesday lasted for almost thirty minutes, and the two over the next two days lasted even longer. So, when Kelly finally reached this woman, they had long conversations. If this April Cheney was a new friend, Kelly hadn't mentioned her to either me *or* Eloise. I made a note of the name and number.

Outside of those, neither Eloise nor I saw anything else suspicious or curious. I grabbed my phone and dialed the number for April Cheney. I got a voicemail greeting that said, "This is April—not the month, silly—but my name. You know what to do after the beep." She had a very young voice with a definite up-country South Carolina accent.

Beyond my curiosity over April Cheney, and Kelly's visit to Dr. Stefans, I didn't see anything in the phone records to knock Hound-dog off the top spot for Kelly's suspected attacker. I told Bagwell that, and he agreed.

Bagwell gathered up the phone records, telling us that when his men tracked down the identities of the unnamed callers, he'd pass that along too. His first order of business was to get Chief Watson to pay a visit to the Dixie Demons and find out the real name of Hound-dog, so they could run a check on the man's criminal records.

Bagwell said, "If he's our guy, it probably won't be the first time he's done something like this."

After Bagwell left, Eloise and Mackenzie said they would visit Kelly later in the afternoon. I decided to go now, but first, I had another stop to make.

#

I used my copy of Kelly's house key and went inside. The crime-scene people had left a mess with dark smudges of fingerprint dust everywhere, and there was still dried blood on the kitchen floor. There was no police tape, which I took to mean they were finished with their investigation here. I made a mental note to call in a cleaning service before Kelly came home. Some of Doctor Mathis's optimistic nature at the hospital must have rubbed off on me. Believing she would return home at all was a step forward for me.

The house held the familiar aroma of her. I could never remember the name of the perfume she wore—ever the inconsiderate male—but I knew it by smell. Memories of being there with her flooded my mind as I looked through her things, hoping to find something Bagwell and his officers may have missed. I'd come on the off chance that she'd made notes somewhere of whatever she'd been working on, and the sheriff's deputies had overlooked them, not knowing what they were or that they would be important to anyone. I looked through the desk files in the spare bedroom she used as her office, and in the nightstand in the master bedroom, and I didn't find anything. I even went through the pockets of her clothes in the closet, finding nothing there either.

I sat down in a chair in the living room, and my thoughts filled with memories of Kelly and me there: us watching TV on the sofa and fooling around like a couple of love-struck teenagers. The many times that kind of activity led to something far more adult. The sounds she made making love. The tenderness of her touch and the heart-race of my touching her.

These visions should have made me feel good, but they didn't. They made me violently angry. Angry at the latest memory of her, lying unconscious in a hospital bed with her lovely face bloody and bruised. Angry at the scent of her now—the antiseptic odor of a hospital.

I found myself wanting desperately to see the person responsible get what he deserved, if by not meted out by the justice system—then by me.

For the first time in my life, I wanted to kill someone.

CHAPTER TEN

I made the thirty-mile drive from Kelly's house to her hospital room in record time. I sat and watched her, hoping against hope that she would suddenly open her beautiful brown eyes and smile that heartbreaking smile of hers. But she didn't.

I sat there long enough for Doctor Mathis to make his rounds and tell me that Kelly was still stable and there was no change, although she looked a little better. Her bruises were lightening in color, and the swelling in her face and eye was slowly going down.

But even if she was looking better, I found myself having to work harder to stay positive about her condition. Doctor Mathis said the average time of an induced coma was from a couple of days to about a week, and there was no intention to try to bring her out today.

I went out in the hallway and called Eloise, telling her she didn't need to come today. Nothing had changed with Kelly's condition, and I probably wouldn't stay too late myself. I could tell she felt guilty not coming, so I made an argument about something we both knew. Spending so much time with Kelly with her in a coma wasn't helping anything, and might even be hurting. We were in the Doctor and nurses' way, and potentially keeping Kelly from getting the complete rest she needed. Sitting with her was more for our benefit than Kelly's. It made us feel like we were doing something helpful when we weren't. Eloise understood and said she would stay home today.

I couldn't take my own advice. I would continue to visit Kelly every day. Even if I spent most of the time just sitting in the waiting room and out of the medical staff's way. If there were only the remotest possibility that Kelly felt my presence near her and it could comfort her, then I would be there every day until she was well again.

I went back into Kelly's room, squeezed her hand again, then went out and sat in the waiting room. I'd brought in the back issues of the *Clarion* and began looking through them. In the issue dated two weeks ago, an editorial Kelly wrote caught my attention. A local woman had died from an opioid overdose, and Kelly had stepped up on her soapbox to editorialize about the exploding opioid epidemic in America, and how it had made its way into Pickens County. Her point was that no city or community, large or small, was safe.

She talked about May Burgess, the deceased woman, a young divorcee whose life had been cut short because of it. She quoted the woman's mother, a Kate Cheney, who said her daughter innocently started out on prescription pain pills for a back injury and ended up a full-blown addict and buying drugs off the street.

Cheney, I thought, sitting up straighter in my chair. May Burgess's maiden name would be Cheney. April and May Cheney. Too much coincidence not to be sisters. Was Kelly calling April Cheney about her dead sister?

I looked back at what I'd copied from Kelly's phone records. The dates on Kelly's calls to April Cheney were the week after the editorial appeared in the *Clarion*. And so was her visit to Doctor Michael Stefans. Was he the doctor who prescribed the pills that got April Cheney's sister hooked?

Kelly was still working on the subject of her opioid editorial. I was sure of it. Perhaps it was just a follow-up opinion piece, but knowing Kelly's reporter's nose for hard news, my gut told me she was chasing down something of greater significance. Possibly, the illegal source of opioids in the upstate. The implications of that sent my imagination into over-drive. There would be some people who wouldn't want her going there. Dangerous people who had a lot to lose if she dug too deeply into their business, and would be willing to do whatever it took to stop her. Including beating her nearly to death.

Curiosity and suspiciousness were traits that often got me into trouble. They were also the reason for my success as an investigative journalist. Kelly and I both shared these. Had her curiosity caused her to stick her nose someplace that angered some very dangerous people? Like opioid traffickers and dealers?

Perhaps even the Dixie Demons? Was their interest in Pickens County more than just a good place to hold an annual reunion? Were they responsible for the increased influx of opioids in the area? An intuitive alarm bell went off in my head.

If Kelly was digging into that subject, she could easily find herself in harm's way from several possible directions, the Dixie Demons included.

I'd been having a hard time believing that an over-sexed Dixie

Demon would try to kill a woman for just getting snubbed at a bar. That is, unless he was a certifiable psychopath. Add a snoopy reporter to the equation, sniffing around a biker gang's highly profitable livelihood, and it might be another matter. That might cause someone to commit—what did Bagwell call it—a heinous act?

So, I had *two* women to talk to now. April Cheney, Kelly's recent phone mate, with a sister who had OD'd on opioids; and the little red-headed bartender at the Tiger's Tail, who, from the way she acted when I showed her Kelly's picture, knew something she wasn't telling.

I stuck around until late afternoon, combing through the past issues of the *Clarion*, and looking in on Kelly every few minutes. She never moved, and I didn't find anything else in the paper that suggested any different reason for Kelly's beating. I kissed Kelly on her forehead for the last time and headed to Still Hollow.

CHAPTER ELEVEN

The worry alarm on my internal clock woke me up Monday morning. I lay there with Kelly on my mind. I guess I was having a hard time accepting that I had no control over her fate, and the helplessness of it dragged me to the depths of despair when I thought about it too much. The truth was, I just couldn't share Doctor Mathis's blind optimism anymore about her recovery, as hard as I tried. The age-old fear of someone I loved dying on me again was paralyzing. I'd been there and done that and didn't want to do it again. Ever.

I got up, showered, shaved, got dressed, and was on my second cup of coffee in the kitchen when Eloise came down. Still in her nightgown, robe and slippers, she poured herself a cup from the pot of coffee and sat down at the table with me. I could tell that my sister had a lot on her mind too. She looked like she hadn't slept well either.

"What's up, sis? How are you this morning?"

It was a moment before she spoke. "I just don't know what to do."

"About what?"

"The *Clarion*," she said and sighed. "I don't see how we're going to get this week's paper out without Kelly. So, I was thinking maybe I ought to call everybody, give them the week off with pay, of course and just cancel this week's edition. I don't know if I can handle it without her."

"Sure, you can. You've already got your front page—it's Kelly. What's bigger news than that? And I'll help."

"You'd actually come work at the *Clarion*?" she said, surprised.

"Of course, Eloise. At least until we can get this week's edition out. What kind of publisher would I be, if I didn't? By then, we should know more about when Kelly will return, and we can plan accordingly."

If she returns, I thought, but didn't say. We'd cross that bridge if we came to it.

Eloise had raised an eyebrow when I'd referred to myself as the publisher. I'd always been perfectly clear that I'd never take a "hands-on" position with the *Clarion*. The paper was hers and Kelly's to run entirely, and I was publisher in name only. That was our bargain from the beginning. But Eloise was never pleased with it. She'd wanted me there, which was what our grandfather wanted. He'd dreamed of me one day taking over from him. In a way, I would, but not exactly as he'd planned.

"But what about your job with *SportsWord*?" Eloise asked.

"Given the situation, they won't mind me taking a few days off."

This seemed to relieve some of her anxiety, and she reached over and squeezed my hand. "Then I'd better get dressed and go to the office. Why don't you go check on Kelly? She'll be wondering where you are. You can come into the paper when you're ready. I'll gather the troops and find out how much work we need to do."

#

I took my sister's advice and went to the hospital. Kelly's condition hadn't changed. If she was wondering where I was, as Eloise said—or wondering anything—I couldn't tell.

As for the *Clarion*, which occupied my thoughts the entire drive over, even if Kelly recovered tomorrow, I suspected she would miss quite a few more editions of the paper before she was able to work. And that was my optimistic view, which I was trying so hard to adapt. Being realistic, if she recovered at all, it was also possible that due to the severity of her injuries, she might not be able to function well for some time.

I left her room and found a quiet corner to do something I had to do. I called my boss, Joe Dennis, the publisher of *SportsWord* magazine back in Atlanta. Joe used to be the editor there and was responsible for hiring me. The publisher at the time was a spineless bureaucrat who cared more about budgets than news and ended up firing me. He was fired later himself, and Joe became the new publisher, and hired me back.

Joe and I were friends, and we worked well together. He let me choose my own stories, regardless of the sport, and I never let him down. Circulation was healthy, especially since we'd added the digital version, and I was building a name for myself as an investigative journalist that you didn't want on your tail if you were someone with something to hide.

Right now, I was going to let Joe Dennis down. I needed more than just a few days off, I needed a leave of absence until

Kelly was back on her feet and functioning at a hundred percent capacity at the *Clarion*. What I wouldn't tell him was that I was also determined to stay until the animal who did this to Kelly was caught and punished.

Joe knew Kelly. He and his wife, Ann, had invited us for dinner at their house several times, and Kelly had charmed them both, becoming friends.

Joe picked up his phone on the third ring.

"It's J.D.," I said.

"Hey, I was just thinking of you. Wondering where you were."

"I'm in South Carolina, Joe." I told him about Kelly's assault and her condition.

When he got past telling me how sorry he was, how tragic this was, and how I should stay positive, I told him the main reason I called.

"I need to take a leave of absence Joe."

"I understand, J.D., take some days off, but I'll bet you she'll be up and around in no time. She's a strong woman."

"I need more than a few days, Joe."

It was a moment before he spoke. "I'm not sure I can do without you for too long, J.D., I don't mean to be insensitive, I understand your problem, but just being honest, I need to keep this place afloat, too. You're the best I got."

"I'll understand if you need to fire me, but I've got to do this."

"Let's don't go talking about firing or quitting and stuff like that. I'll try to make do with freelancers until you're back, which I'm hoping is soon. But J.D.? I can't continue to pay you while you're gone. Soon as you use up your vacation days, I'll have to cut you off and use your salary for the freelancers."

"I understand, Joe. I do plan to come back eventually, if you'll have me. If there's no job there, then I'll understand that too. You're a good boss and a good friend, and I'm sorry about this. This is just something I have to do."

"Hey, you didn't cause this. Do what you've got to do. Ann and I will keep you and Kelly in our prayers, and you'll see, she'll get over this soon. God wouldn't do this to her."

I didn't remember Joe ever being much of a religious man, but I'd take well wishes and prayers wherever I could get them.

"Thanks, Joe," I said. "I'll keep you posted."

CHAPTER TWELVE

I was sitting in Kelly's room, my stomach telling me it was nearing lunchtime. All I'd had for breakfast was a couple of cups of coffee at Still Hollow before I left. My cell rang and I went out into the hall to take the call.

"Have you eaten yet?" Eloise asked.

"No, I was going to head to the *Clarion* soon, and thought I'd grab a bite on the way."

"Don't leave yet, we're coming there. Mackenzie is with me. I let her play hooky from school today, and she's been at the paper helping me organize some of the regular content that runs each week. We decided to take a lunch break and come see Kelly. We'll need to eat too, so why don't we stop by the Clock Drive-in for some pick-up food—we're going right by there. If I had time, I'd cook us something, but this will still be better than that hospital cafeteria food. I just can't take that. Tell me what you want, and we'll bring you something. We can eat in the waiting room."

I said, "Okay, sounds good." I'd been to the Clock Drive-in so many times in my younger days, I knew the menu by heart.

"Bring me two chili dogs, mustard and onions, with a coke and fries."

#

Forty-five minutes later, Eloise and Mackenzie walked into Kelly's room, Eloise carried a large paper bag and Mackenzie had a cardboard container holding three soft drinks.

"Great, let's take the food into the waiting room, I'm starving," I said.

"Hold your horses, J.D.," Eloise said. "First, we need to say hello to Kelly."

The two of them went to the bed and took turns kissing Kelly on the cheek. Then Eloise and Mackenzie took Kelly's hand, and they bowed their heads. Eloise said a short prayer, her voice too low for me to hear the words. It was a touching scene. I wasn't the only Bragg who cared a great deal for this woman. Eloise placed Kelly's hand gently back by her side and then turned to me.

"*Now* we can eat," she said, wiping a tear from an eye. With Mackenzie and me following she headed out the door. We found the waiting room empty and had our pick of the chairs and sofas. We settled in a corner away from the TV to give us a quiet spot to eat and talk.

When we were all settled and munching away, I looked at Eloise. "I've got something important to tell you. It's about the *Clarion.*"

"You haven't changed your mind about helping me, have you?" she asked, alarmed.

"Oh no, in fact, it's just the opposite. I know that our biggest worry at the moment is about Kelly's condition, and hoping she'll soon be as good as new. But we shouldn't feel guilty if we worry about other things too, like what's going to happen to the *Clarion* if she takes longer than we expect to get back on her feet."

Neither Eloise nor Mackenzie spoke. I could tell from Eloise's expression that I'd hit the nail on the head. Her worries about continuing to publish the *Clarion* made her feel selfish.

I told them, "So, I've decided to take an extended leave of absence from *SportsWord* and help out with the *Clarion* until Kelly can get back on her feet. That is if you'll have me."

"Oh, John David," Eloise said. "You already know I'd love that, but I don't want you changing your whole life and giving up your job at *SportsWord* for it. We'll figure out a way to manage."

Eloise was always a terrible liar, and I could see by the hopeful look she gave me how desperately she wanted me to come. She loved Kelly, but she was worried about supporting herself and a daughter.

Mackenzie was downright grinning from ear-to-ear, the first time I'd seen that beautiful smile since I'd arrived. So she had been worried about this too.

"It's a done deal," I said. "I've already arranged it." I looked at Mackenzie. "But you'll have to teach me the ropes."

Mackenzie said, "Okay, it's a deal. If you'll teach me right back."

Eloise was smiling now. "Are you going to stay with us, or at Kelly's?"

"With you, at least for now. I don't think I want to be in Kelly's house yet."

Her blood is still on the carpet. I saw that they understood.

"By the way," I said to Eloise. "Was Kelly planning to do a follow-up on that editorial she wrote on opioids and the death of that Pickens County woman? I was reading that. Sounded interesting."

She gave me a blank look. "Not that I know of. She didn't mention anything to me about it."

Kelly wouldn't tell her. As Eloise has already explained, that was the way Kelly worked when she was on to something. She would shroud her investigation in secrecy until she had a valid story. I needed to do some follow-up myself.

April Cheney appeared to be the place to start.

We went back and sat with Kelly for a while. I think all three of us felt the same sense of utter helplessness. There was just nothing we could do. I moved over and held Kelly's hand and kissed her cheek numerous times, but if she felt it, or even knew we were there, she never showed it.

Doctor Mathis and a nurse came in, and he was still positive. Everything that could be done for Kelly was being done, and now it was just a waiting game. When he left, I kissed Kelly again, then followed Eloise and Mackenzie back to the *Clarion* to start a new chapter in my career. How long it would last was another uncertainty in my life.

And while I told my sister that I took my leave of absence from *SportsWord* to help keep the *Clarion* running on all cylinders without Kelly, which was the truth, there was another reason I was going to stay. I couldn't carry on my life as usual and just let what happened to Kelly go unpunished.

#

As I drove from Greenville back to the town of Pickens and the *Clarion*, I got a call on my cell phone from Sheriff Bagwell.

"I've got some news about this Dixie Demon Hound-dog character," he said. "He's got an alibi. Hound Dog, or Larry Dean Atkins as the records show his real name to be, was on a road trip with the rest of his gang up to the North Carolina mountains at the time Ms. Mayfield was attacked."

"And he can prove it?" I asked.

"Sort of. He's got seven witnesses. I say *sort of* because they're all his brother Dixie Demons, so I don't know if they're telling the truth or lying to protect him, which wouldn't be

out of character for that bunch. I'd feel better if we had somebody a little more credible to back them up before we close the door on Mr. Atkins.

"They say they were doing a recon for a ride they plan to have when the whole gang gets here in August. Their route was a round trip up to Highlands, over to Cashiers, then back here by way of Whitewater Falls. Last Friday they made a dinner stop at a place in Cashiers called the Ugly Dog Pub for beers and burgers, stayed late, and then they all checked into the Cashiers Village Inn for the night. Didn't get back here until Saturday morning.

"I've got a deputy up in Cashiers right now with Atkins' mug shot to show around to see if anybody there remembers him. So far, nobody has. But I got to tell you, I've seen this Doughboy in person and this picture doesn't look much like him. It's old, he doesn't have a beard or long hair, and was thinner back then.

"The desk clerk at the motel says only one of them came in to register and pay for the rooms, and that's all he saw. They rented four rooms at double rate. The waitress who served them at the Ugly Dog didn't remember seeing him. But she really didn't look at any of them all that closely. They made her nervous. The teenagers from the golf course took a look at the photo, but they couldn't identify him either. They both said they didn't see the guy well enough to do it. So, it looks like a dead-end all around on this road trip unless somebody unexpected comes forward."

"Mug shot," I said. "Does that mean you have Hound-dog's criminal records?"

"Yeah, but it's mostly minor stuff. Drugs, alcohol, traffic charges. And that was quite a while ago. No sexual offenses or assault and battery charges at all. Nothing even close to what somebody did to Ms. Mayfield."

"So, you're letting him go?"

"Never *had* him," Bagwell said. "We didn't have enough to make an arrest, and there's even less now. We can't stop him, or any of them, from leaving. These guys have their own lawyer, so we can't even talk to them. But we won't stop looking at him, Mr. Bragg. Maybe something will turn up. He's got a home address in Rocky Mount, North Carolina, so we know where to find him if we need him."

I thanked Sheriff Bagwell, knowing that he didn't have to tell me all this, and it probably stuck in his craw to do it. His cooperation was because of his fondness for my sister. So, I actually had *her* to thank for it. I drove the rest of the way to the *Clarion*, thinking about where all of this left me. Hound-dog's alibi *was* suspect. I didn't believe a word of anything the Dixie Demons said. I needed absolute proof—or disproof—of Hound-dog's alibi. I couldn't leave him a dangling loose end. I needed to know for sure if he could be *the guy* or not. If not, then I'd forget him and get on with finding the son-of-a-bitch who *was*. If Bagwell and his people couldn't find that out, I would try to do it myself, somehow.

I still had the bartender at the Tiger's Tail who knew something that she wasn't telling, and whatever it was, scared her. Was it about Hound-dog? The Dixie Demons? I could at least try to find that out.

CHAPTER THIRTEEN

Eloise's car was out front of the *Clarion* in her personal parking space. Superstition kept me from taking the spot next to it, designated for Kelly, as if it might jinx her recovery. Anyone who's ever played sports on a high level has superstitions: the baseball player who snaps and unsnaps his batting glove a certain number of times; the basketball player on a scoring streak who won't shave for fear of breaking it. My ritual used to be eating the same meal before every game. I would load up on carbs. A giant baked potato with butter and sour cream.

As I went inside, Mrs. Mozingo came from around her desk and hugged me.

"I can't believe this has happened to Kelly," she said, the tears on her face wetting my shoulder. "God will take care of her, you'll see. Some of us went to see her Saturday, and I took her some flowers. Poor thing didn't know we were there. Will she be alright? I love that girl, and I know your grandfather did too."

I said, "The Doctors have high hopes. The coma is medically induced because she needs time for the swelling in her brain to go down, which they say will happen, soon, and I hope they're right."

"What are we going to do around here until then, John David? I don't know how we can get along without her."

"We're going to have a staff meeting in a little while, and Eloise and I will tell everybody how we plan to do that." I held her at arm's length and looked at her. "Everything will be fine, Mrs. Mozingo, I promise."

I hoped I wasn't lying to her.

Her hair had gone from salt and pepper to completely gray over the past few years, and she wasn't one to dye it, so an attractive aging lady had become an attractive elderly lady. Mrs. Mozingo, long rumored to be Grandfather's paramour, was still the closest thing to a mother I'd had since Eloise and I came to live here. Mrs. Mozingo still treated me like a little boy at times, and I loved it.

Eloise came out and I asked her, "Where do you want me, sis?"

"You're the publisher of this newspaper, John David, you get the big office."

"Grandfather's office?"

"It's Kelly's now, but neithe r one of them will mind. Besides, there's nowhere else to sit without buying some new furniture and adding phone and computer lines."

My superstition pinged again, thinking of taking Kelly's desk. I had no choice. I opened the frosted-glass paneled door near Mrs. Mozingo's desk and went in. Eloise followed me. I sat down in the chair and found a picture of me staring back. I turned it face-down.

"I refuse to sit here looking at *that* guy," I said.

Eloise chuckled and grabbed the picture. "I'll put this

handsome devil on my desk. I like looking at it."

"You're still refusing to wear your glasses, I see."

"I think we should gather the staff and tell them what's going on sooner than later," Eloise said. "They need to know about Kelly's condition and how we're going to run the paper in her absence."

"I agree, they need to know as much as we do. Kelly will be our front-page story this week, and I'll need some help writing it."

"You already know most of the staff, but we have a new employee you should meet, maybe before the staff meeting. Vickie Sayers, our new reporter."

I saw her name when I went through the *Clarion*'s back issues at the hospital. I'd just assumed she was one of the freelancers that the *Clarion* often used, and not a regular employee. I remembered thinking that her basics were good. She had the 6 W's of journalism down, the *who-what-where-when-why and how*, and without a lot of superfluous words. She had presented the heart of the story with a human touch that many with far more experience often failed to achieve. Her writing reminded me of Kelly's.

Eloise was saying, "Vickie graduated last year from Furman University with a journalism degree. Kelly saw some of her school work and was extremely impressed. Her daddy was a newspaperman somewhere, but I've never met him."

"Got it in her blood then. She should fit in around here."

"Well, maybe not. She's good, but maybe too good. She's very ambitious. We've got her handling community news; City Council and Chamber of Commerce stuff, new business openings and the like, but I doubt that we'll keep her doing that for very long. Kelly and I both think she's destined for bigger things. She has a lot more capacity for work, and I think she's already getting bored. She's taken Mackenzie under her wing to teach and already has her performing at a college level."

"Sounds like somebody we need to keep, especially now. What's the budget like? Can we afford to give her a raise? And maybe boost her assignments a bit?"

Eloise smiled. "I'm for it, and I think I can speak for Kelly too."

"Can you get her in here?"

Eloise left for a couple of minutes and came back leading Vickie Sayers into the room.

What struck me first was how young Vickie Sayers looked. If she were a year out of college, I'd be surprised—she looked almost as young as Mackenzie. Then I looked into her eyes and she suddenly became older There was an intelligence and confidence that belied her youthful looks. She was short in stature—and cute, I guess most would say. She wore glasses with heavy black frames that gave her an earnest look.

Eloise introduced us, and Sayers stood examining me like she was placing my image into some permanent file in her head. This was a girl who wouldn't miss much, I suspected.

She said, "You're the mystery publisher on our masthead. So you *do* exist. What's up?"

She spoke frankly and wasn't overwhelmed with meeting me.

"I want to give you a raise."

She looked from me to Eloise, and back to me like we were pranking her.

I told her, "I'm going to take over the *Clarion* until Kelly comes back, and I want you to take on more responsibility. I hear you're up to it. I thought it deserved a pay raise."

"Hard news?" she asked, her voice somewhere between disbelief and excited anticipation.

"You can't give up all of what you've been covering, but you'll certainly have more chances to make the front page now."

"Thank you." She grinned from ear-to-ear, which showed her real age. She wasn't talking about the raise, but the new choice of assignments. Maybe now the *Clarion* would keep her a little longer before she headed for bigger and greener pastures.

"Gather up the staff, Vickie. Eloise and I will come out and fill everybody in on Kelly's condition and how we're going to run this place for a while without her."

As soon as she left, I turned to Eloise. "Let's give our other reporter a raise too, and send an occasional good assignment her way. She won't set the world afire as Vickie Sayers might, but she's been here a long time faithfully doing her job and deserves it. We can give her more city hall, police reports, whatever. We'll keep the freelancers doing the sports, let's not rock that boat. We'll officially make Mackenzie a reporter—no more cub reporter—and have her answer to Vickie, who can continue to serve as Mackenzie's editor and mentor. We'll all probably need to wear several hats if we don't want the paper to slip. We're filling some big shoes here. Kelly will be hard to replace."

Eloise said, "We're already wearing multiple hats, so that won't come as a change. And remember, little brother, just because I handle the business and advertising end, it doesn't mean I don't create content too. After all, I was a journalism major just like you, albeit from a community college. I handle the obits, classifieds, and deal with several outside sources of my own who freely contribute community and church news on a constant basis."

"Good, maybe we can keep the *Clarion* upright after all."

Eloise called in the *Clarion*'s other reporter, Joanne McKinney, and asked her to come in. Joanne, a middle-aged woman married with two grown kids, had been at the *Clarion* since before Grandfather died. I knew her as a hard, dependable worker who seemed to enjoy her work regardless of the mundane subject matter she covered for the paper. She blushed when I gave her the raise, and differed from Vickie Sayers in that she appeared more excited by the increase in salary, the prospect of getting to cover more exciting news.

I caught my sister looking at me, a slight smile on her face.

"What?" I said.

"You haven't mentioned yourself, and what you bring to us. Kelly is very good at what she does, but so are you. You're already proving you make a good managing editor, with what you're suggesting we do, and taking charge like this. And as an investigative journalist and writer, John David, you're famous."

"I'm only famous to you," I said. "You're my sister. To everyone else, I'm just a pain in the ass who's been lucky enough to chase down a few good stories."

I studied her for a moment, then said, "Look Eloise, I'll try to stay on top of any big news that comes along, and maybe even write an editorial or two, but mostly I'll be managing editor for the other reporters, guiding them and helping them carry the major load of what appears in the *Clarion*. I want to tell you this upfront. My main news interest will be tracking down who assaulted Kelly, and why, and nailing their asses to the wall. That's the story I want to write."

"I would expect you to do just that, little brother. I know you well. Now let's go talk to the staff."

CHAPTER FOURTEEN

The staff meeting went well, under the circumstances. We were small in number, but gathered around Mrs. Mozingo's desk in the lobby we still spilled into the hallway.

I read in their faces a mixture of concern for Kelly and varying degrees of anxiety about their jobs. I hoped I could assuage those concerns as they got to know me better and saw that I was there to help, not shake things up. I told them that they were all doing great jobs and to continue doing what they were doing, and that Kelly would be back before they knew it. Whether they all bought that would become evident as time went by.

Afterward, when everyone had gone back to their offices and stations, I asked Mrs. Mozingo, "Who's in charge of business cards? I want to order some for me. I don't want to go around having to explain to people why a sportswriter from Atlanta is interested in their business and is asking them questions."

'You're in luck, honey. When Kelly and Eloise took over, we went ahead and ordered your business cards for you too."

She went to a file cabinet and came back with a small box. Inside were *Clarion* business cards that read 'John David Bragg,

Publisher,' and had both the *Clarion*'s and my cell number on them.

"There's more where those came from," she said.

I was official, I thought, and went back into my new office, closed the door, and sat down at my new desk. All kinds of old memories washed over me. Not so much of Kelly, I'd spent little time there with her. My memories were of times when it was Grandfather's desk. I could almost smell the cherry tobacco he smoked in his pipe and feel the sense of being in forbidden territory every time I came there as a kid. Of course, the office had changed since Kelly took over—there were signs of her everywhere now, and the desktop was neat and uncluttered, which it never was when Grandfather sat there. The only thing of Grandfather's that remained, other than the desk itself, was his Pulitzer, the commemoration still hanging on the wall.

As I sat down, an idea suddenly popped into my head from what Bagwell was saying about the photos of Hound-dog not looking like him. I remembered what I thought the first time I'd seen him at the Tiger's Tail. I thought that he strongly resembled the actor, Jason Momoa. I was no celebrity buff, but even *I* knew who Jason Momoa was. He was hugely popular, having been in the TV series, the *Game of Thrones*, among other popular TV shows and movies.

I got up and went out to see Mrs. Mozingo.

"Who around here would have the software program *Photoshop* on their computer, and know how to use it?" I asked her.

"Photoshop? The computer artwork software program?" she asked.

I was surprised she knew what it was. But then, there were *few* things Mrs. Mozingo *didn't* know. "Yes. I need someone to retouch a photograph for me." *If I couldn't find a good picture of Hound-dog, I'd have one made.*

"If it were anybody, it would be Jason Pilgrim," she said.

"Would you get him for me, please?" I said and returned to my office.

Jason Pilgrim was the *Clarion*'s IT manager. He was the mastermind behind the digital online version of the *Clarion*, and he'd also been working for a year or so converting all the old microfilm records in the morgue into digital files, bringing the paper up to modern times. I'd met him, but I didn't know him all that well. I imagined that converting everything into microfilm was an enormous job. Past copies of the *Clarion* were stored in gray steel cabinets and went back almost a hundred years—since the paper's inception and long before my grandfather bought it.

Jason was a young man, not much older than Vickie Sayers, but of a different type. He looked like he should be playing in a rock band. He had a ring in his eyebrow, one in an ear, his nose, and his lower lip, and a high fade haircut to go with it. Other than that, he wasn't a bad-looking kid.

Kelly had told me about his history. He'd finished top of his class at an upstate Tech College in Computer Sciences and was a whiz kid with computers. But an earlier arrest for hacking some government website left him with a police record that kept him from finding a job after graduation. Kelly met him and took a chance. She thought him a good kid and a genius. For that, he was fiercely loyal to her. I got the feeling that he didn't expect me to regard him as highly as Kelly did. Maybe I didn't, but he was doing an excellent job. Our digital issue was as good or better than many big-city papers, and I agreed with Kelly. We were lucky to have him.

"How are you, Jason?" I asked when he came in and took a seat.

He just shrugged and said, "Kelly."

Jason seemed to be a man of few words, or maybe it was just around me. He was bummed out over what happened to Kelly. Weren't we all?

"Am I to keep digitizing the morgue?" he asked.

"Of course. Business as usual. And I understand you're doing a great job."

"Just wondering, new boss and all." He looked like he was about to say more.

"There's something I'd like you to do for me." I swung my laptop around and showed him the photograph of Jason Momoa that I had downloaded. "See this guy?"

"Yeah, same first name as me. That's the guy played Khal Drogo, Daenerys Targaryen's husband on *Game of Thrones*. He was a *bad* dude."

"Can you take this photograph and retouch it for me?"

"Maybe, I'm no expert, but there are some things I can handle. What do you want done?"

"Trim his beard. Make it shorter and neater. Like a barber did it. Take some arc out of the eyebrows, and remove that scar that runs through one of them."

Jason said, "No problemo, when do you want it?"

"Ten minutes ago, One print, eight by ten."

"You got it, just email me the photo file."

"You don't want to know why?" I asked him.

"Tell me later, I got a rush job to do."

I liked this guy.

He slid out of his chair and left while I was emailing him the photo.

CHAPTER FIFTEEN

After Jason Pilgrim went back to his work station to do the photo retouching for me, I turned to my laptop and opened a Word document to begin writing about Kelly's assault.

I sat for a moment staring at the blank page but couldn't seem to focus on it. Other things were interfering with my thinking. I decided to take care of at least one of those things before I tackled Kelly's story. The *Clarion* didn't go to press until Wednesday night, so I still had some time.

A woman answered on the second ring. I told her who I was, used my *Clarion* title, and asked if she was Kate, Chaney, the mother of April Cheney and May Cheney Burgess. She said she was, proving my assumption right. April and May were sisters.

After offering her my sympathies for the loss of May, I said, "Mrs. Cheney, we're doing a follow-up story to the one we published on your daughter May's unfortunate death, and I'm trying to get in touch with April, but we're having a hard time reaching her by telephone. Is there some other way to contact her?"

She didn't speak for a moment, which I took to mean that she was hesitant to give me that information.

"I promise you, Mrs. Cheney. We won't put your daughter's address or any private or personal information about her in the paper."

"Well . . ." she said finally. "You can probably find her behind the bar at that beer joint in Clemson where she works." The distaste was clear in her voice. "But don't put that in your paper. She might not care, but I do. I ain't proud of it."

"And the name of that beer joint?

"The Tiger's Tail."

That, I *hadn't* guessed. To say I was surprised was an understatement. The bartender who had something to hide was April Cheney.

"I don't like her working in a place like that," Mrs. Cheney was saying. "But she don't listen to me. April is my wild child. May was the good one, but look what happened to her. First, her husband Bobby got killed in that car wreck that tore up May's back, and now May is dead from the pain pills she got hooked on. That wreck killed them both, I guess you could say. April is the one I thought would end up on drugs. Every rough piece of white trash in this part of the county hangs out at the Tiger's Tail. It ain't no place for respectable people."

I thanked her and ended the call. I'd found not only April Cheney, but discovered that I'd met her. And she'd denied knowing Kelly, which was a lie. Going back to the Tiger's Tail for another visit was definitely on my agenda.

#

It took Jason Pilgrim about forty-five minutes to retouch the photograph. It was perfect. It wasn't quite Hound-Dog, but it was a lot closer to him than his mug shot.

I placed the photo in a manila envelope and told Mrs. Mozingo I was leaving for the day. I asked her to pass that along to Eloise, and to tell her not to wait up for me. I'd be quite late.

From there, I fueled up the Jeep and headed to Cashiers. The little mountain town with million-dollar homes and million-dollar views was only about forty miles away but would take an hour to drive because of the snake-back roads once I hit the mountains.

I planned to do what Bagwell's deputy couldn't. Find someone who could positively say that the man in my photo was there with the other bikers—or he wasn't. I had to believe that Hound-dog's striking good looks would have got him noticed—or that his absence was just as noteworthy.

Regardless of what I found, it wouldn't be anything the authorities could use. But hopefully, it would be enough to satisfy me that we had the right guy, or we didn't. If Larry Dean Atkins had attacked and almost beat Kelly to death, then I would find a way to bring justice to him. And I had a lot of ideas on how to do that, none of them for delicate ears.

CHAPTER SIXTEEN

The Ugly Dog Pub was just off going into Cashiers. It was a much nicer place than the name suggested, and more family-friendly than I expected. The Dixie Demons must have made an unlikely mix with the usual patrons. I went straight to the bar, took a spot by the waitress station, and ordered a draft beer. It was still a little early for the dinner crowd and only about a half-dozen people were there.

A waitress came up and plopped her empty tray down on the bar beside me. The bartender, a guy about my age, started to come over to her, but she waved him off. She glanced at me, and I said hello. She gave me a quick, standard customer-smile and went back to looking bored.

"Slow, huh?" I said to her.

"It's a Monday. It'll pick up in an hour or so—I hope," she added.

"When you've got a moment, I'd like to talk to you."

She swept the room with an exaggerated look. "Moments, I've got. Customers, I don't."

"Were you working last Friday evening?"

"If we're open, I'm working," she said.

I placed the photo on her tray. "Do you remember seeing this guy in here?"

She looked at it. "Is this about them motorcycle guys who were in here? You're the second guy showed me a picture today. You a cop? He was a cop."

"I'm a reporter." That didn't seem to impress her.

"*Was* he here?" I asked again.

She looked back at the picture. "This is a different person than the photograph the cop showed me. This guy, I saw. How could I not? He's a hunk. Spent a lot of time at the bar hitting on Susan, a regular in here. Wouldn't surprise me if he went home with her, the way they were carrying on."

I seemed to have hit the first pitch out of the park, I thought. "Where can I find this Susan?"

"I don't know where she lives, but she works at that picture frame store up the street. If you hang around a little while, she may be in here."

I had what I came for, Hound-dog *was* here. It seemed like a good idea to see what else I could find out before I left. Maybe Hound-dog had headed back to Pickens County before the others, in time to assault Kelly. Perhaps this Susan would know.

"So, where is this frame store again?" I asked

"Just around the corner, on the left. Practically walking distance from here."

"I think I'll go try to catch her there," I said, dropping a fiver on the bar for the beer and heading for the door.

I found the frame store easily and went inside, a bell over the door announcing my arrival. There were two women behind the counter, one young, one older. I headed for the younger one. She was blonde and pretty, and looked up and smiled at me as I approached.

"Are you Susan?" I asked.

"Yes I am, how can I help you?"

"I'd like to ask you about this guy." I placed the photograph on the counter.

She gave it a quick look and glanced nervously at the woman down the counter. She wasn't paying any attention to us.

"Not here," she whispered. "Meet me at a bar called the Ugly Dog in thirty minutes."

"Know it well," I said, picked up the photograph and left.

Thirty minutes later to the minute, she joined me at the bar. I was having another beer. The waitress was getting her wish and was busy as more people were coming into the pub, and business was picking up.

"What are you drinking?" I asked as Susan sat down.

"First, you tell me who you are and what you want."

"I'm J.D. Bragg, and I want you to tell me about the guy in the photo."

The bartender came over and said, "Vodka tonic, Susan?"

She nodded yes, and waited until he'd gone.

"What makes you think I know who he is?" she asked me.

"Look, I'm not here to make trouble for you or make moral judgments. It's obvious you recognized the guy in the photo, and you were seen talking to him in here last Friday. So, it's too late to deny it. All I want to do is ask you a few questions and I'll be gone."

"What makes any of this your business? Are you a policeman?"

"Worse, I'm a newspaper reporter." That seemed to alarm her. In truth, it alarmed *me* too. It was the first time I'd used that title since I'd agreed to help out at the *Clarion*.

"I won't be in the newspaper, will I?" she asked, wearing a troubled look.

"Absolutely not, all I'm trying to find out is what time he left town."

She hesitated and said, "I don't know what time he left town, but he left my apartment early Saturday morning."

"Thank you, Susan," I said. *Hound-dog had his alibi.*

I paid my tab, including her vodka tonic, said goodbye, and headed to South Carolina.

On the way, I called Bagwell. He was out somewhere, and I talked the dispatcher into patching me through to him, telling her that he was expecting my call, and would be very upset if he didn't get it. Evidently, he went along with it, and she patched me through.

I told him what I'd learned in Cashiers and that it was enough to satisfy me with Hound-dog's alibi. So, I suggested Bagwell close the books on him and if he wanted official proof, I would take him up there and help him get a signed statement from Susan. I didn't tell him that I didn't even know her last name, but she told me the truth. Bagwell could do whatever he wanted to do. But I was now onto other suspects—and I didn't tell him that either.

CHAPTER SEVENTEEN

The Tiger's Tail wasn't as smoky inside tonight as my first visit. It was Monday, and it wasn't nearly as crowded. There were two things about the place that were just the same. The Dixie Demons still held court around the pool tables in the back, and Pancho Villa and April were behind the bar serving their respective ends of it. The only difference was that I now knew that Hound-dog didn't assault Kelly, and April Cheney had lied to me.

April was talking to a couple of hefty guys, one with long black hair and a bandana tied around his head like a renegade Indian. As I made my way toward them, I had an urge to say "*How*" to him. Not only was it racially insensitive, I'd come here for information, not a butt-whipping. I didn't see any Dixie Demon regalia on him, but he could be one of them if looks counted. He was a tough-looking guy. So was the other man, dressed in jeans and a T-shirt.

April looked up as I approached, and it was clear she didn't like seeing me coming.

"Hi April, I'd like a Bud and a word with you, if you've got a minute," I said.

That got the attention of the two big guys. They turned to look at me.

"Get your beer and fuck off, Jack," Bandana said. "We're talking to the lady here."

"I'm sorry, chief," I said (I couldn't resist). "I'm not trying to break up the pow-wow (again, my urges got the better of me), I just need to speak to the young lady for a minute. Then I'll be out of your way."

"I think you been dissed," the other guy said to Bandana and chuckled.

"Yeah," Bandana said. "And I'm about to show him why he don't want to do that."

"Tone it down, guys," April said and turned to me. "What do you want to talk to me about?"

"Kelly Mayfield, I know you know her."

She shot a nervous glance around see who was listening. "I'm sorry, I don't know anybody by that name."

I looked around too and didn't think anyone had heard me. Bandana and his friend were too busy talking about what to do to me. Pancho Villa down the bar was looking at us. I couldn't see how he could have heard anything with the jukebox blaring and everyone in the place trying to talk over it.

As April pulled a long-neck Budweiser out of the cooler, she turned and asked, "Do you want to start a tab?" She began to write up a ticket with a pen she'd had stuck behind an ear.

I waved a fiver at her and told her not to bother. I wasn't going to be there that long. She didn't seem to hear me and kept writing. I told her again. She turned and placed a napkin on the bar and set my beer on it. She held my eyes for a moment as if she was trying to tell me something. She wanted me to shut up about Kelly.

Bandana turned to me. "Why don't you take that beer down the bar and save yourself an ass-whipping?"

I decided to take his advice. It was apparent April Cheney wasn't going to talk to me here, and just as evident that this guy meant what he was saying. So, I picked up my beer and moved down the bar. When I did, I saw there was something written on the bar napkin.

It said, "I'll call you."

I took the bar napkin with me. April had obviously gotten my calls and listened to the messages I left; she just hadn't returned them—and she definitely didn't want to be seen talking to me.

Pancho Villa watched me take a stool and set my beer on the bar. He gave me the same unfriendly look he gave me the last time. A bit of trivia popped out of the recesses of my mind about the drooping mustache he wore. These days it was called a "biker mustache." He looked right at home here.

He flipped up a folding section of the bar and went through it toward the back of the place. He entered a door with a "private" sign. The bar's office, I guessed. Two minutes later, he came out and went back behind the bar. It might have been my imagination, but he seemed to be deliberately avoiding looking at me now.

I swiveled around with my back to the bar and surveyed the Monday night Tiger's Tail scene. The booths and tables were only about half-occupied. The bandstand still sat empty, the only change, the homemade sign announced a different band performing on Friday and Saturday nights. This week it was the "Ragin

Cajuns." A couple danced on the small dance floor to a slow, sad song from the jukebox. I glanced up the bar at April Cheney and caught her looking at me. I winked, and she quickly turned away.

I spun my stool back around to face the bar and noticed two guys standing against the wall at the back of the bar, staring at me. It was more than just a casual look, they seemed to be studying me. One had stringy blond hair down to his shoulders and was dressed in jeans, cowboy boots, and a western shirt. I could see the shiny pearl buttons from where I sat. The other one was bigger, as tall as me probably, but broader in the chest and shoulders like he'd done some lifting. He had long blond hair too, and a beard to go with it. He was in biker garb, and I didn't remember seeing him from my Dixie Demons encounter. Neither struck me as friendly types.

I met eyes with the cowboy for a moment, then he turned and went through the private door. The other one gave me a last look and followed him in.

I left my beer unfinished on the bar and left. There was something disturbing about the way the two guys were looking at me. If I hadn't been feeling unwelcome in the Tiger's Tail before, I did now.

#

I was about five miles gone when my cell phone rang. It was April Cheney.

"Where's Kelly?" she said. "She was supposed to call me this weekend. She didn't."

"So, you recognized me?"

"Of course I recognized you. You're the boyfriend. Kelly told me about you. Even showed me a picture. And I got the messages you left. I wrote down your number and was going to call you, but not from work. I'm out back on my break now and only have a minute. Now, why am I talking to you and not her? Has something happened?'

"Somebody broke into her house Friday night and badly beat her. She's in Greenville General hospital in a coma."

"Oh my God, I was afraid of something like this. Don't come in here anymore. I'm not saying another word about this, to you or anybody else."

"Saying a word about what, April? What were you and Kelly talking about?"

"You don't know? I'm hanging up. Don't bother me again."

"Kelly didn't tell me everything. Now she can't. You're going to have to do it." It was a lie, Kelly hadn't told me anything. But the last part was true. Kelly couldn't tell me now, only April could.

I said quickly, "If you hang up on me, I'll come back there and camp out until you talk to me. I'm not a guy who gives up, believe me."

She said, "Jesus Christ, you're going to get me hurt too. After you left, Terrell came over and asked me what you'd said to me. He says you're a busy-body reporter out to make trouble for the Tiger's Tail. He told me not to talk to you if you ever came in again."

The one with the mustache?" I said. *How the hell did these guys know me?* I wondered.

"Yes, his name is Terrell Dent, and he's got his nose stuck so far up Sonny Dollar's butt he can smell his chewing gum. He tells him everything that goes on in there."

"Who's Sonny Dollar?"

"He's the manager of the place. Look, I can't talk no more, I've got to get back in before Sonny comes looking for me."

"Then meet me somewhere, tell me everything, and then I'll leave you alone."

It was a while before she spoke. "Call me in the morning. But not too early. I sleep late. I'll meet you somewhere, Then you leave me alone."

#

When I pulled into the drive at Still Hollow, I was surprised to see a single headlight follow me in, accompanied by the growl of a motorcycle. I got out to meet it. The rider stopped ten feet away and sat straddling the chopper, his feet bracing the bike. I could hardly see him, the bike's headlight in my eyes. All I could make out was that he wore what looked like one of those black beanie helmets and had a scarf or something wrapped around his lower face.

"What do you want?" I asked loudly enough for him to hear me over the idling engine.

The rider didn't speak. He pointed a finger at me, thumb cocked like the hammer of a pistol, and mock-shot me with it. Then he slowly raised his arm and made the same motion directed somewhere above me. I looked up to see my sister Eloise standing at her bedroom window, looking down at us.

The guy slowly turned the motorcycle and rode off back down the driveway. I stood and listened as the sound of it faded down Highway 178 to the south.

Eloise was waiting for me downstairs when I went in. I lied

to her, telling her the motorcycle rider was just some lost drunk who had shown up at the wrong address. If she bought that, I didn't know. At least it momentarily dispelled any fear she had that we might be in some kind of danger, and she went back to bed.

I turned in and lay in bed, replaying the night's events. Had this guy followed me home from the Tiger's Tail, or was he at Still Hollow waiting for me? Either way, someone knew me, where I could be found, and that I had a family. What was I up against here?

I'd proven Hound-dog's and the other seven Dixie Demons innocence in assaulting Kelly. Were there other ones in town that I didn't know about? Who was the biker-looking guy at the Tiger's Tail with the cowboy, watching me?

There was a lot I needed to ask April Cheney tomorrow.

CHAPTER EIGHTEEN

Tuesday morning, I broke my promise not to call April Cheney too early and rang her up first thing. She answered with a sleepy growl and agreed to meet me somewhere for breakfast. She picked the place, a Waffle House in the town of Easley. It would be about a thirty-minute drive for me, a twenty-minute drive for her, and a safe bet we wouldn't run into anybody who would know either of us.

I declined the breakfast Eloise was making and told her I was going to check on Kelly and would be into work afterward. I didn't tell her I was having breakfast with April Cheney.

I found April sitting in a booth by the window, and I almost didn't recognize her. She wore none of the heavy makeup she'd worn at the bar, had her long blonde hair pulled into a pony-tail stuck through the back strap of a Harley-Davidson cap, and wore shades. She was drinking a cup of coffee and watching me approach, unsmiling. I took the bench seat across from her.

"I hope you're not going to get me killed for this," she said.

"How about some breakfast?" I asked, spotting a waitress making her way toward us.

"Just don't make it my last meal," April said, and ordered a waffle with bacon.

I ordered bacon, scrambled eggs with cheese, and hashbrowns, scattered, smothered, and covered. The waitress topped off April's coffee, sat a cup down and poured me one too.

"Tell me about you and Kelly, and I'll be out of your life," I said, when the waitress left with our orders.

"She came to me about my sister May's death. Kelly had already written about her, but she wanted to know more—like what kind of drugs May was taking when she overdosed, and where she was getting them. Kelly wanted to know if they were from a doctor, and I told her they weren't. Her doctor stopped prescribing them to her, and she was getting them from somewhere else."

"Was the doctor Michael Stefans?"

"Yes," April said.

So this *was* the reason Kelly had paid him a visit. She was asking him about May Burgess.

April said, "I think Doctor Stefans saw that May was getting addicted and cut her off. She didn't mean to get hooked; she was just constantly in pain from a bad car wreck a year back that injured her spine. It killed her husband, Bobby, so she was messed up both physically and in her head. None of this was normal for her. May was the good sister, church-going and all that. I was always the no-good one. The black sheep of the family."

I didn't tell April that her mother had already told me that.

I said, "So, she began getting her drugs off the street when the doctor cut her off."

"Yeah, and I was shocked. May wouldn't know where to find

a drug dealer if her life depended on it, and I don't think she was friends with anyone who would. All the people she knew were Bible thumpers and goody-two-shoes housewives. I asked her about that. She said a guy came to her. Approached her in the Ingles parking lot. It was like he knew she had run through her prescription meds and was waiting there just for her. His name's Doughboy, and he gave her a number to call when she wanted more. After that, she would meet him in the same Ingles lot to get more pills."

I said, "Doughboy? Did she describe what he looks like or tell you if she ever learned where he could be found?

"Here's the weird part. May didn't have to, I know him. He comes in the Tiger's Tail all the time. I'd only heard he deals drugs, and all I know for sure is he's an asshole."

"Does he know who you are? That you and May Burgess were sisters?"

"He knows me, obviously. I serve him drinks. But I don't think anyone in the Tiger's Tail knows that May and I were sisters. I never talked about her. And May swore to me she didn't tell Doughboy. I believed her."

"Describe him."

"He's kind of fat. A biker type, but no beard. Shaved head. He's one of those white guys who try to talk black. Like that makes him a cool dude or whatever."

I entered Doughboy's name and description on my phone.

I asked April, "What about a guy with long blond hair, dresses like a cowboy? He was with another guy with a beard and long blond hair too. Big guy. Looked like a biker. Do you know these guys?"

"Oh, my God. Did they say something to you?"

"No, I just saw them and wondered who they were. They went through that door beyond the bar. I took it to be the bar's office."

I wasn't about to tell her about the biker who followed me home. April was scared enough already.

"Who are they?" I asked.

"The Dollar brothers, Laverne and Sonny. They run the place. Laverne is the one with the cowboy clothes and is what I call a scary-bad-ass. He's the big boss. Sonny is the younger brother and just your average bad-ass. He's the day-to-day manager I mentioned on the phone. If they know who you are and saw me talking to you, I'm fucked."

"What about the drugs? You said this Doughboy is a regular in there. Are the Dollar brothers involved in that?"

After a moment she said, "The brothers know it's going on. They're tight with Doughboy. So is Terrell. I guess I can't prove they're involved directly, but even if they aren't, they're turning a blind eye to it."

Her thoughtfulness impressed me. She was believable. She made a good confidential informant, and I could see why Kelly was talking to her.

"They have anything to do with the Dixie Demons?" I asked.

"I don't know. They're awfully friendly with them, and I know that one of them had a couple of closed-door meetings in the office with Sonny and Laverne. So maybe there is something there. Sonny is a biker. He rides a Harley. I've never seen him wearing Dixie Demon colors. I don't know about Laverne. Most of the bikers who come into the Tail don't belong to anything.

Some of them are just barely members of the human race. They just want to ride bikes, drink beer, and raise hell. Pretend Hell's Angels, I call them."

"When was the last time you talked to Kelly?" I asked.

"Last Thursday night, when she came into the bar. It was the first time she'd ever done that. We had a deal to always to meet somewhere else, or talk on the phone, and even then, just when I was at home. But she came in that night to talk to Terrell, not me. We only spoke for a minute or two. It was kinda' funny. One of the Dixie Demon bikers hit on her and she put him in his place in a second. She was a tough one."

"Why would she talk to Terrell?"

"She wanted to ask him about who owns the Tiger's Tail. She'd asked me first, but all I could tell her is it's some company called the OMSK Corporation. It's on our paychecks. I used to think that Laverne Dollar owned it, but Terrell told me once that it was one of them parent companies that own bars and restaurants. I couldn't ask Terrell any more about it. He'd want to know why it was any of my business and get suspicious. I didn't want to risk that, and neither did Kelly. So she decided to go in there and ask him herself. She was protecting me."

"Do you know what he said to her?"

"I couldn't hear, but he called her a nosy bitch behind her back when she left, and asked if I knew her. I lied and said no, it was the first time I'd ever seen her. He said for me not to talk to her, if she came in again, if I wanted to keep my job. He said she was a nosy newspaper reporter trying to make trouble for the Tiger's Tail. Then he went into the office to see Sonny. My guess is he told him about her."

"Did you tell Kelly that?"

"I was going to, but I didn't get a chance to call her. Then, since Saturday morning, she ain't been answering my calls. I guess I know why, now."

If Kelly wanted to find out about the OMSK Corporation, I thought, why wouldn't she just get on the internet and Google it? The only reason I could come up with was that it was a shell corporation, heavily layered and protected, and the web gave her nothing.

"Why have you been doing this?" I asked. "Working with Kelly? You had to know it could be dangerous."

She said without hesitation, "My sister May is dead, and she didn't deserve it. I want every son-of-a-bitch that had anything to do with it to get what's coming to them, and I thought I could help a little."

April was wrong about herself, and so was her mother. There was a lot of good in April Cheney. I found myself liking her, and I had to be careful not to get her into more trouble than she might already be in.

I caught her staring at me, deep in some thought. I could almost see wheels turning behind that red hair.

"Kelly was attacked Friday night," she said. It wasn't a question. I nodded.

She gave that some thought, biting on her lower lip. "I want to see whoever's responsible for May's death get what they got coming and burn in hell for it, but I don't know if there's anything else I can do to help. I hope Kelly gets better—I really do. But what happened to her ain't happening to me. Whatever is going on here, I can't be a part of it anymore. Somebody else stronger than me needs to do it from here on out."

She grabbed her purse off the seat and stood up. "I've got a friend who runs a bar in Key West who's been wanting me to come down and work with her. I'm going to think very hard about doing that."

She nodded and left. I watched out the window as she got into a little blue compact car and drove away. I wouldn't blame her if she got out of town, as much as I would like her to stay and to continue feeding information to me. But she was right, she had done about all she could do. And from what I could see, she had helped scrape the top off the iceberg that was probably the opioid problem in Pickens County. I didn't want to see her get hurt over what she and Kelly had started. I didn't think that the violence would end if I continued to follow in Kelly's footsteps. With the biker showing up at Still Hollow last night, it appeared that I had now brought the enemy into my family's house. The problem was, I still didn't know who this enemy was—the Dixie Demons, the Dollar brothers, or the OMSK Corporation. Perhaps they were all the same.

The thing I did know was that I was in over my head. I took out my phone and punched in the Chicago number of Alvin "Big Hurt" Brown.

CHAPTER NINETEEN

Alvin Brown got the nickname "Big Hurt," just like the one that belonged to Frank Thomas, the White Sox homerun-hitting Hall of Famer—not because he hit baseballs, but because he hit *people* with baseball bats. In his younger days growing up on the streets of Southside Chicago, he'd been a gang-banger in one of the most violent street gangs in America, the Gangster Disciples, and was known for his proficiency with a Louisville Slugger.

After Alvin outgrew the gang thing, he'd been a cage fighter for a while, trained for several years in the Orient, and was now a martial arts expert who owned a chain of Chicago dojos. He could probably take out most of the Tiger's Tail Saturday night crowd with one finger.

I'd met Alvin a year ago. He was the cousin of Taylor Johnson, an old college football teammate and friend of mine. Taylor had suffered a terrible injury our senior season which left him a bed-bound paraplegic, and me with the guilt that I was to blame. I'd thrown the wayward pass that caused Taylor to leap for it and expose his blind side to a defensive back who hit him with the crushing blow, breaking his neck.

Taylor resided in a medical institution in Greenville now, and last year, when his teenage brother went missing, Taylor asked me to help find him. The police thought the kid had simply run away. Tayler suspected foul play.

Alvin came down from Chicago to help too and we joined forces in the search. In the process, Alvin helped me through a situation with people who wanted me dead, and he and I became unlikely friends. Alvin watched my back then, and it looked like I needed him again.

"J.D., my man, whassup?" He'd obviously seen my name on the caller I.D.

"I need a big, ugly, black man to add a little muscle to a thing I'm looking into," I said.

"Ugly? Then you ain't talking to me, bro. I'm so pretty I got women jumpin' off the Sears Tower 'cause they can't have me."

"Well, I don't need the good-looking one, I need the bad-acting one."

"What you done got yourself into now, J.D.?"

I told him about Kelly. The two got to know each other last year and quickly became fast friends. "I'm going to find the gentleman who did that to her."

He was silent for so long I thought we'd lost the connection until I heard him breathing. He wasn't taking friendly breaths.

"I'm on the next flight. I'll rent a car at the airport. Where you want to meet?"

"Call me when you land, and I'll meet you at Greenville General Hospital." I gave him Kelly's room number.

"Mother-fuckers who hurt her better be looking for someplace to hide," he said.

I knew that with Alvin, it wasn't an idle threat. "Alvin? Thanks."

"You got it. I'm on my way."

I paid the Waffle House tab and headed out to the Greenville hospital to see Kelly.

CHAPTER TWENTY

After an hour or so of sitting and holding Kelly's hand, I headed back to Pickens County. Just outside of Pickens, I came across an auto accident. Traffic was down to one lane of the highway, moving slowly around a severely damaged, upturned minivan occupying the other lane. Two ambulances were leaving the scene as I neared it, and a wrecker was poised to remove the pancaked vehicle from the road. Debris from the van littered the highway around it, some of it children's things. A forlorn stuffed animal lay near the shoulder. Cars lined the road before and after the wreck, both State Highway Patrol, and Sheriff's Department vehicles. Sheriff Bagwell leaned against one of the county vehicles, surveying the scene.

I pulled over to the side of the road just beyond him and got out.

"You here as a rubbernecker or the press?" he asked as I approached. "Rubberneckers need to move on." He wore a sour look.

"Press, of course. What happened here?"

"Stupidity, or criminal negligence, but you can't quote me on that. A woman, speeding, it looks like. Lost it in that turn back there and barrel-rolled that top-heavy van. Had kids on board. She seems to have gotten out without a scratch, but not the kids. One of them, dead at the scene. The other one pretty bad off."

"Jesus, that's tragic."

Bagwell turned and met my eyes. He still wore the sour look. "I don't think tragic even begins to describe things like this, The carelessness of people never ceases to baffle me."

This had obviously gotten to him. I was glad I didn't get there in time to see the children being taken away.

Bagwell said, "I can't give you any names yet. Got people to notify first. Call the department later and I may have something for you."

I understood and would put Vickie Sayers on it right away.

"There's something else I'd like to talk to you about," I said. "Maybe this isn't the time. I could come to see you later, if that would be better."

"You can tell me now. Maybe it'll get my mind off this for a minute." Bagwell glanced at the stuffed toy animal in the road. "Let's get in the car to talk."

I joined him in the front seat of his cruiser.

"So, talk," he said.

"I believe Kelly was working on a follow-up story to an editorial she wrote a few weeks ago about the opioid epidemic in Pickens County. There's some bad people involved in that business, and if she was asking questions in the wrong places, she might have put herself in danger."

"I saw that editorial. How do you know that's what she was doing?"

"I've found some evidence of it. And it's also what I would do if I were her." I didn't mention April Cheney. I promised her I'd keep her out of it, and maybe it was an outdated and even foolish convention, but I had this funny thing about keeping my word. I probably had my grandfather to thank for that.

"What kind of evidence?" Bagwell asked.

"I think she interviewed the doctor of the deceased woman from her first article, after the article ran. You may remember when we searched Kelly's appointments at the *Clarion*, we found that she had visited a doctor that neither I, nor Eloise knew. That's who he was. I plan to see him myself, when I can. So, now that we know that Hound-dog has an alibi and couldn't have assaulted Kelly, it's the only other thing I've found that could place her in harm's way."

Bagwell considered that for a moment. "We can take a look at a drug-related angle, I guess, and see where that goes. Anything else you learn, let me know, you hear?"

"Yes, sir," I said. "Can you tell me a little about the opioid situation in the county? I'm considering picking up Kelly's story myself."

"Did you just put on your press hat?" he said and chuckled. "Is this an interview?"

"Yes, I guess it is. Do you have the time?"

"I do, if it means we keep a tit for tat working relationship, and you keep me informed of whatever you find out." He looked at me, expecting an answer.

"Deal," I said. *To a degree*, I thought.

"I can't deny that it's a big problem. We do what we can, but it's out of control. We've never seen anything like this. It's an addiction epidemic that's growing out of all proportions. My officers and every other cop in this county are up to their ears in this thing. They've had to become both nurse and social worker, as overdoses sweep the county. They joined the force to solve crimes and make arrests, not spend all their time handling scene after scene of family tragedies and opioid-related deaths."

"What are you doing about it?"

"To tell you the truth, we don't know what to do about it. Nobody does—local, state, or federal. We just try to do the best we can. During the crack epidemic back in the nineties, it was easier to police. You could at least *see* that problem. You could spot a serious crack-head, not only because they were bat-shit crazy, but by the bad teeth and facial sores. And they were a different class of user. The lower class, you might call them. Opioids go across all socio-economic groups. Also, opioids are tougher to stop because many users have actual prescriptions for them."

"I thought that these pill mills with prescription drugs had dried up," I said.

"Well, the ones like we used to see, a single-wide out in the woods somewhere with a line of people out the door, *have* disappeared for the most part. But there's still way too many doctors quick to prescribe pain killers, and big pharma is pushing out pills with incentives to sell them like never before. The government is starting to crack down on that. But what's replacing it on the streets these days is worse than anything we've ever seen. Heroin, often spiked with fentanyl, is coming in, and addictions, overdoses, and deaths are exploding. Fentanyl is fifty times more potent than heroin. It's manufactured in a lab, usually overseas, and smuggled in by the Mexican cartels. But more and more, homespun labs are popping up all over the country. It's too easy to get and too easy to make. Now, anybody can buy the stuff from China off the internet. And there's this latest drug, carfentanil, that's 10,000 times more potent than morphine."

"Can't you catch the guys dealing this poison?" I asked.

"The street dealers, yeah," Bagwell said. "But there's always somebody else in their place the next day. It's harder to get the guys behind them. That's who we want. But you can't get a low-level guy to talk when he's more afraid of his supplier than he is of the police. These are bad people."

"So, don't you have some idea of who the big enchiladas behind this are?"

"Yeah, we have ideas. You might be closer to it than you think with that word *enchiladas*." The Mexican cartels are behind a lot of the drugs that are in the country."

"That's the country," I said. "How about just this county?"

"We're working on it. Along with the DEA."

I took that to mean he couldn't discuss it, or he didn't have a clue.

"A lot of money is changing hands here, Sheriff Bagwell. You ever think that you might have someone in your department who's being paid to turn their heads?" The second I said it, I regretted it. I saw that I'd pissed him off.

"Of course I think about that, Mr. Bragg. "But I can guarantee you that none of my deputies are on the take. I would know."

"How about some of the city cops around the county?" I said.

"I know all the chiefs. They're all great cops who run tight ships, and it would shock me to hear that any of their officers are bent. We can't know everything, Mr. Bragg, but we're doing our best. Budgets keep going down year after year, and we're all short-handed. So far, when we make an inroad into the upper echelon of these drug dealers, we're faced with a wall of silence whenever we talk to anyone. The Feds are doing their best on all this too, but unless all governments—ours, Mexico's, Chinas, or whatever country is making this poison, steps up, it's a losing cause. I tell you, Mr. Bragg, we're overwhelmed here."

I thought of telling him about Doughboy. What Bagwell said was probably right. If he arrested Doughboy, he wouldn't talk and would take the rap if he had to—and someone new would be in his place tomorrow. Bagwell might even know about him already. Besides, as the old saying goes, *better the devil you know.* Turning in Doughboy would slam the door on anything Alvin could find out—I had a plan for Alvin to go under cover and try to get to know him. Selfish of me perhaps, but I wasn't in this to end the opioid business in Pickens County. I was after something on a smaller scale, but much more significant to me—finding out who attacked Kelly. If Alvin and I found that person, then we would drop him into Bagwell's lap.

Or maybe we'd just drop him off a tall building somewhere.

CHAPTER TWENTY-ONE

From there, I went to the *Clarion* for my second day as a hands-on publisher. Eloise said they were rolling along on this week's issue, but nobody wanted to take a shot at writing the story of Kelly's assault, which would pretty much be the whole front page and then some.

"We all think it should be you, John David," Eloise said. "Everyone thinks you'll be so hypercritical about it, that nobody wants to touch it. So you might as well write it yourself."

I said, "You're probably right." Before I got started, I went to find Vickie Sayers. The young reporter was on her computer when I peeked in.

"I know I promised you more exciting projects," I said, "but until I come up with one, will you do something very boring for me?"

"I guess I can't turn you down after giving me a raise on your first day," she said.

"Can you help me with a little research?"

"What do you need?"

"Get me some info on opioids. Facts, figures, and any

interesting stuff you come across. Especially as it relates to this area of South Carolina. I don't want an encyclopedia—just the highlights and talking points. Don't spend more than an hour on it."

I'd already gotten a lot from Bagwell. I wanted a little more detail.

"And why do you want this?" she asked.

"Just boning up on the subject. Every time I turn on the TV, I'm hearing about the opioid crises in this country. I decided I needed to learn more about it."

She held my gaze just long enough to suggest that she wasn't buying that. My guess was that very little got by this girl. However I was the boss and she'd just have to do what I asked and keep her questions to herself.

"You got it," she said, and gave me a two-fingered scout salute. At least it wasn't the *one*-finger salute.

I returned to my office, found the number of Doctor Michael Stefans and dialed it. Based on what April Cheney told me, I thought I already knew why Kelly went to see him. It couldn't hurt to make sure. He might even have more to tell.

A very Southern female voice answered. I gave her my name and asked to speak to Doctor Stefans.

"He's busy with a patient right now. If this is a medical issue, I can make you an appointment to see him."

"I don't need that kind of appointment. I just need to talk to Dr. Stefans for a minute."

"If you're a medical or pharmaceutical salesman, I can make you an appointment for that too, but it will be a few days."

"It's not that either. Can you have him call me?"

"I can pass along your request, sir. Give me your number and the subject you'd like to speak to him about, and spell your name for me."

I did what she wanted. I gave her my cell number, spelled out my name, and identified myself as the publisher of the *Clarion*. The doctor had an excellent watchdog at his gate. I got the feeling that if I just showed up there, I'd never get past her to see him. I would just have to wait and see if he would return my call.

After I hung up, I opened a blank MS Word document on my computer and began to write the story on Kelly's assault..

\#

Fifteen minutes later my phone rang. The caller ID showed it was Doctor Michael Stefans. I was amazed that he got back to me so quickly.

"Am I speaking to Mr. Bragg?" he asked.

"Yes, Doctor Stefans, thank you for returning my call."

"I had the pleasant opportunity of speaking last week with Ms. Mayfield, your associate at the newspaper. She is a lovely lady. How can I help you?"

"That's what I'm calling about. I'd like to go over what you and she discussed."

"I told Ms. Mayfield everything I know about how we doctors are dealing with this tragic opioid epidemic that is sweeping the country. She seemed to get what she came for in the interview and I do not think I have anything else to add. Ms. Is there some reason why Ms. Mayfield cannot tell you that?"

"I'm afraid Ms. Mayfield has been injured and can't speak. I'm taking over her work. If she made notes, we can't find them."

"That is terrible. I was not aware of that. Was she in an automobile accident?"

"No, but she did suffer acute physical trauma." I didn't see any reason to give him more details.

"I am so sorry, what is her condition?"

"She's in an induced coma, and it's wait and see at the moment."

"What hospital is she in, if I may ask?"

"Greenville General."

He said, "At least that is good. They are a Level One trauma center. It is the best place for her. I hope she makes a good recovery."

"Thank you, Doctor."

He was saying, "I will do whatever I can to help. As physicians, we face a major dilemma these days with opioids. We want to do our best to relieve acute pain for our patients, but we must do it responsibly. And that is the trick. Too often in these cases, doing good can go very bad. So, anything I can do to assist in this problem, I am happy to do. But I have patients waiting at the moment, Mr. Bragg. I wonder if you could meet me here after hours today, say about five? I should be free by then. As I said, I want to help any way I can on this issue."

I couldn't think of anything else that I might learn from him with a personal visit, other than maybe getting some idea of the story direction Kelly's questions were taking her, but what other avenues did I have at the moment?

"Thank you, Doctor, I'll be there."

CHAPTER TWENTY-TWO

I went back to writing the story of Kelly's assault, keeping my door closed and trying hard to concentrate. The only interruption was Eloise when she brought me a ham sandwich she'd made along with a coke and a bag of chips from the office vending machine. I wrote in silence, trying to keep from being as nit-picky with myself as I would have been with anyone else. Everyone left me alone, with many of the staff going to see Kelly during the lunch hour.

I did my best on Kelly's story and realized I'd probably never be happy with it. I guess it's always that way when you're too close to something. Every line I wrote was so personal to me, I lost all objectivity. I thought Eloise was wrong. I wasn't the best person at the *Clarion* to write this story. I was probably the worst. I decided to finish up what I had, at least including all the facts, then give it to someone else, like Vickie Sayers. Maybe she could turn it into news instead of an emotional ramble from a guy too worried that the story would eventually have an unhappy ending.

There was a tap on my office door, and Vickie Sayers walked in.

"I've got your research," Vickie said, holding up several sheets of paper. "Want to take a look to see if it's what you wanted? Or are you too busy right now?"

"I need a break anyway. Come in and sit down."

She did and said, "Okay boss, here's what I've got. I'll just hit the high points as I see them." She began to read from her notes. "When we talk opioids these days, we're talking oxys and fentanyl. Fentanyl is a potent synthetic opioid, and all the rage of late. It's a lot more potent than heroin, and far more profitable for dealers. It's also the primary culprit for the growing opioid deaths in this country."

That much I'd heard from Sheriff Bagwell.

"It's been found mixed with everything from marijuana and heroin to animal tranquilizers and formaldehyde."

"Animal tranquilizers?" I couldn't help myself.

"Horse and elephant. I kid you not. And it's easy to get and easy to make. It all starts in China, and here it gets a little technical: labs there manufacture the main ingredient used in the production of fentanyl, as well as analogues—drugs that have chemical structures differing only slightly from the pharmaceutical-grade version. One of the best-known fentanyl analogues is alpha-methylfentanyl, known on the streets as China White. It's available to anyone over the internet, and signing up for an account only takes minutes. You can even buy quarter-ton pill presses from them. The sites guarantee delivery and ask customers only for a shipping address and credit card number. Before it's shipped, the drug is hidden in a decoy package. Like detergent or auto parts boxes, or something like that."

"How hard is it to mix it up and turn it into a street product once you've got the main ingredients?" I asked.

"I'd say it requires about a ninth-grade education, if even that, a protective mask, and a pair of elbow-length rubber gloves. These drugs are not only dangerous for users, but they're also dangerous for those who make it, and the cops and drug dogs who come upon it. If you touch some forms of it you can absorb it through your skin. That can be deadly. If cops conduct a raid on a dealer of fentanyl, they are instructed to wear protective gear—at a minimum, latex gloves, at a maximum, a hazmat suit with a respirator.

"But to make it into a street drug, it's easy. All it takes is an elementary knowledge of chemistry, and a pill press. If you have somebody to teach you, then all you need is a brain a little bigger than a walnut. And it can be produced as a pill, or in powder form where it can be smoked, snorted or injected. Fentanyl is often made to resemble painkillers like oxycodone and hydrocodone, because those drugs fetch a higher price on the street, even though they're less potent. This has resulted in the epidemic of overdoses."

"Wow, no wonder this stuff is suddenly everywhere."

"These home-grown processing mills seem to be gaining on the old methods of getting the product into the country, as best I can tell, which was the Mexican Cartels smuggling them in over the border."

Another thing Bagwell told me.

"The biggest deal about opioids is that they're being consumed by a wider market than your typical drug user. It attracts people dependent on prescription pain-killers, along with the severely addicted illicit-drug users, and recreational users. Overdose victims range from teenagers to seniors, college professors to housewives. Just about anybody, regardless of race, creed or color."

None of this made me an expert on the subject, I thought, but along with what Bagwell had told me, I now had a much better idea of what I was dealing with.

She placed the papers on my desk. "One last thing. I found a report from a recent meeting of Upstate law enforcement officers that said the opioids in Pickens and Oconee Counties are different in make-up from the drugs in Greenville and Spartanburg Counties. They're from two different sources, or so the authorities think."

"So, two different trafficking rings?" I said. Bagwell hadn't mentioned that.

"Looks like it."

"Thanks, Vickie, great job."

She still sat there, making no move to leave. The look on her face suggested she had something else she wanted to say.

"Is there more?" I asked.

"It's about my job."

"Please don't tell me you're quitting."

That seemed to catch her by surprise. "Why on earth would you think that?"

"Because you're good, and sooner or later a small-town newspaper won't be challenging enough for you. I'm just hoping it's later. Right now, the *Clarion* couldn't do without you."

"That's what I want to talk to you about. I want to do more. From what you've had me researching I'd have to be really stupid not to know you're following up on Kelly's opioid editorial that she did a couple of weeks ago. I can help."

I was right. Very little got past this girl. "You're already helping. This research is invaluable."

"That's backroom stuff, and I can still do that. But I want to be on the streets, helping you run down the story."

"What exactly do you think you could do out there on the streets?"

She said, "I know people who are into these kinds of drugs. People my age. I can find out how they get them. Maybe even go in undercover. Whatever."

"You've been watching too much TV," I said, smiling at her. But I appreciated her spunk and tenacity. She was going to make a good investigative reporter.

"I can go places and do things you can't. People know you. Nobody knows me."

I wanted to tell Vickie that what she was suggesting was exactly what Kelly was doing—and look what it got her.

I said, "Okay, you're right. I am going to do a follow-up on Kelly's editorial. But it's still in the incubation stage. I'm looking for a story angle. Maybe you can help later."

"I told you I wasn't stupid," Vickie said. "So don't treat me like I am. I know you think that Kelly's assault had something to do with her interest in the opioid scene. You're trying to find out who did it. *That's* your story angle."

This girl seemed to be a step ahead of me. There was no use lying to her. "You're right again, and I'm not out to solve the world's drug problems. My motive is far less noble—in fact, it's downright selfish. I want to find Kelly's attacker and see that he gets what's coming to him."

"And so do I, so let me help."

This was more than just ambition, I realized. I saw it in Vickie's eyes. And understood it. She felt the same rage inside that I felt about what someone did to Kelly. Vickie had an emotional fire burning in her that transcended newspaper awards and personal recognition. She was a born warrior for justice, the righting of wrongs not just a tactic, but the very thing that drove her. Inside her lived a journalistic idealist. Grandfather would have loved this girl.

"You want to end up like Kelly?" I asked her. "Or worse? College kids didn't do this to her. The people trafficking these drugs are ruthless animals."

"Then find something for me to do. I'll be careful. Just let me be useful."

I sat and thought about it for a minute. "Okay, I'm going to tell you a few things, which I probably shouldn't, and you need to give me your word to keep it our secret. If you do, I'll promise to find a way to involve you more. I don't know how or when, but it will happen at some point. Is it a deal?"

"I guess it will have to be," she said.

"I've got a couple of suspects in my sights, and it wouldn't be a good idea for anyone else to be out there asking questions right now. It could ruin everything, and even get someone hurt, including you. I promise I'll tell you more when I can. Just be patient."

"I'll try," she said.

"There *is* something you can do that would really help me." I turned to my computer and inserted a thumb drive, copied what I'd written of the Kelly story, ejected the drive and held it out to her. "This is the Kelly story I was writing. Make it better.

Rewrite the whole damn thing if you want. I'm too close to it."

She stared at the thumb drive like it was molten metal and it would burn through her fingers.

I said, "This is your chance to own the whole front page. Do you want it or not?"

She practically grabbed it out of my hand.

"I won't let you down," she said, smiling from ear to ear as she left.

CHAPTER TWENTY-THREE

Later, I found Eloise, sat her down and told her about my meeting with April Cheney, who she was, and what kind of story Kelly was working on. I told her the truth about the nighttime motorcycle rider, and about Alvin Brown coming down to watch my back as I followed through with Kelly's investigation—with my interest focused less on exposing opioid distribution in Pickens County than finding her attacker. Although I was sure that one would lead to the other.

I needed to keep her up to date on what I was doing, because the biker's visit showed I'd put her and Mackenzie at risk, and Eloise needed to be on alert. My sister had handled a lot of adversity in her young life and was a tougher woman than her gentle nature suggested. She quickly recognized the danger, and that's what I wanted.

Eloise had met Alvin only a couple of times. She'd heard me talk about him enough to know we had developed a special friendship. She'd once remarked that the way I spoke about him, the two of us were like soldiers who'd been in combat together, with a deeper relationship than just casual buddies. She was right. Alvin and I had bonded well. In a way, we *had* been in a war together, and we'd learned that we could trust each other. She was glad he was coming, and so was I.

I said, "I told him he could stay at Still Hollow with us, if that's okay."

"Of course, it is. Underneath the scary veneer, Alvin has a big heart. I love him."

He did have a big heart. And a good soul. But he could be as violent as anyone I'd ever met if he decided there was the need for it. I'd tried to keep those tendencies subdued last year, but this time I didn't know if I would. My rage was still at level red, and if we found Kelly's attacker, I might turn Alvin loose on him and be right there beside him.

I'd no sooner told her about Alvin when my phone rang. It was him. He should be on the ground at the Greenville Spartanburg Airport about six. He was renting a car and could meet me at the hospital if I wanted. He wanted to see Kelly before we did anything else. So, that was the plan. I was seeing Doctor Stefans at five. I could make it to Kelly's room in plenty of time to be there when Alvin arrived.

I turned back to Eloise. "Dinner with Alvin at Still Hollow, eight o'clock or so? If it's too much trouble, I can stop and bring something."

"John David Bragg, you know I wouldn't have him for dinner at our house with take-out food. Of course, I'll *make* dinner. What's gotten into you? You've lived in Atlanta too long."

"My bad, Eloise, I must have lost my mind for a minute," I said, and laughed.

I left to see Stefans in Clemson.

#

I found Dr. Stefans' office in a stand-alone single-story brick building near the Clemson University campus. The waiting room was empty, as was a glass-enclosed receptionist area. An attractive young dark-haired woman must have heard me come in because she came out from somewhere in the back and asked me if I was Mr. Bragg, and took me back to Doctor Stefans' office. She wasn't dressed in nurse attire, but she obviously worked there.

The doctor wasn't in his office, but the young lady said he would be right in, and she left. I took a moment to study Dr. Stefan's framed medical bona fides on the wall. He had graduated medical school and done his internship up north. So he was an implant, it looked like, which was why I hadn't noticed a southern accent when we talked on the phone.

Doctor Stefans rushed in, "Mr. Bragg, I presume." He gave me a firm handshake, and motioned for me to take a seat across from him at his desk. He was a big man, with a broad face, dark hair, and bushy black eyebrows. "So, you want me to repeat what Ms. Mayfield and I talked about?"

"Yes," I said, pulling out the small notebook and pen I sometimes carried, mostly to try to look professional.

"As I told you, I'm not sure I can remember everything, but I will try. Ms. Mayfield asked about a patient named May Burgess. I think that was the main reason she wanted to talk to me. The police interviewed me when Mrs. Burgess so sadly died, and without breaking patient confidentiality, I told Ms. Mayfield the same thing I told them. I was treating her for a back injury from an automobile accident, but, at the time of her death, she had stopped seeing me. Her last visit here was six months prior. I had my girl look it up."

"Were you aware of her opioid addiction?" I asked.

He frowned. "Not of addiction per se, but perhaps of an inclination toward it. I was treating her for a problem that required pain medication, and she seemed to be taking it more often than prescribed. When I would not refill the prescription for her again, she quit coming to see me. While I was concerned about her, as I am of all my patients, I had no way of knowing what she did after that."

"Do you think that she was getting prescriptions from some other doctor?"

"Not from a reputable one," he said. "The police told me that Mrs. Burgess overdosed on a fentanyl-heroin mixture. No doctor I know gave her that."

"I hear about pill mills, where unethical doctors write huge numbers of prescriptions to addicts or even drug dealers. I have to believe that they exist here too. What can you tell me about that?"

"That may be so, but thank goodness the authorities have been cracking down on those for a long time. I rarely hear about pill mills anymore. Now opioids have taken the same route as other illegal drugs. They are manufactured in foreign countries and smuggled into America by criminals, to be sold on the street corners like all the other addictive poisons."

"So, you had no idea that May Burgess had become addicted, or where she was getting the opioids that killed her?"

"I did not." He paused, sighing deeply. "Unfortunately, I can give patients appropriate expectations regarding the time-frame with which opioids will be prescribed. And I can try to educate them that opioid discontinuation may be necessary, even before the resolution of their pain, and get them on non-opioid meds like ibuprofen or acetaminophen. But ultimately—and sadly—it is their decision and out of my hands. Mrs. Burgess found opioids somewhere else, and it killed her."

"In your relationship with your patients," I said, "or with other physicians, have you heard of any places in this area where these drugs might be illegally obtained? Say, a local bar?"

"No, I have not. A place like that may exist, but I am not aware of it."

"Did Ms. Mayfield ask you that question?" I asked.

"No, I do not think she did. Or at least I cannot remember it."

I thought back to Kelly's phone records and Mrs. Mozingo's sign-out log. Kelly didn't start talking to April Cheney until *after* she visited Doctor Stefans. And April was where Kelly, like me, found out about the drug connection to the Tiger's Tail. So, Kelly wouldn't have reason to ask doctor Stefans about the Tiger's Tail, or any other bars at that point.

I couldn't think of anything else to ask him, and he didn't remember anything else he and Kelly talked about—most of which I already knew or suspected. The visit was a waste of time. It only corroborated that Kelly was indeed working on a story about opioids, and went to Doctor Stefans to learn what she could about May Burgess and her path to addiction. The meeting didn't get me any farther down the investigation trail.

I glanced at my watch. Alvin's plane was probably close to landing about now, and if I wanted to be at the hospital when he arrived, I needed to get going. I thanked the doctor for his taking the time to talk to me and headed to Greenville.

CHAPTER TWENTY-FOUR

I was standing outside Kelly's room watching for Alvin when he came striding down the hospital corridor toward me like he owned the place, nurses and doctors alike casting sidelong glances at him. Alvin got noticed wherever he went. He was built like someone in an exercise equipment ad, only bigger, with fierce eyes that warned you to get the hell out of his way. He wore a sharply trimmed beard which gave him a satanic look. Women who favored the bad-boy type found him very handsome.

We did a man-hug in the hallway, and I took him into Kelly's room. He stood looking at her for the longest time, not speaking. Then he finally turned to me. "She never moves?"

"Not yet. They move her around to avoid bedsores, but that's about it."

"She gonna' be okay, J.D.?"

"Her doctor has high hopes."

"*You* got high hopes, J.D.?" he asked.

"I don't know what I've got, Alvin. It's either hope or absolute terror at the alternative."

We stood and watched her a little longer.

"Motherfuckers who did this need to git got," Alvin said, his eyes fierce.

"We've got to find out who they are, first."

"Where do we start?"

"Let's go find a better place to talk."

He followed me down the hall to the small hospital chapel. It wasn't the most appropriate room to discuss doing harm to our fellow man, but it was the best place I could think of to talk without being overheard.

I filled him in on everything.

"I'm convinced Kelly's snooping was why she was attacked. Somebody wanted her to stop, and one, or all these guys were behind it. Now it seems I'm on their radar."

"What do the Po-Po think?" Alvin asked.

"The Sheriff's Department first thought it was the Dixie Demon biker Hound-dog, who hit on her at the Tiger's Tail bar. But he's got an alibi. I've given my theory, and they say they're looking into it. But I've seen no evidence of that yet. Oh, and I was a suspect too for a while."

"What?" Alvin asked.

I told him about it.

"Been telling you all along, cops ain't always your friends. When you gonna' listen?"

"Sheriff Bagwell is a good guy. I don't think he ever believed it. He was just doing things by the book. I guess the husband or boyfriend is always the first suspect."

"That's 'cause most cops are lazy," Alvin said, "They go the easy way ever time."

Alvin absolutely refused to admit that most cops were smart

and good at their jobs.

"Maybe I should go in undercover at this Tiger's Tail bar for a few days?" Alvin said.

"My thinking exactly." I said.

"You trust this April Cheney?"

"Yes, up to a point. She's genuinely angry about her sister's death and wants to nail those responsible for selling the poison that killed her. But now that Kelly's been hurt, she's afraid for herself. Guess I don't blame her. But if one of these guys threatened her, I think she'd tell them everything she knows. She said something about getting out of town, so she may not be here much longer. It's probably best she doesn't know about you, or that we know each other."

"How well is this gonna' work if you and me are sleeping under the same roof? If they know about you, they'll eventually know about me."

"I've been thinking about that," I said. "We need to find you your own place. Maybe Eloise can help with that. Let's go see her. She's looking forward to seeing you, and she's making dinner for us."

"Lead on," Alvin said.

We retrieved our cars and headed to Pickens County, Alvin right behind me in a bright yellow Mustang convertible rental he got at the airport. Alvin's creed in life could be right out of an old Mel Brooks movie, *The Producers*. "If you've got it, baby, flaunt it."

CHAPTER TWENTY-FIVE

Eloise made us dinner, with Mackenzie helping, while I showed Alvin Still Hollow. Alvin made them feel like he'd known them forever. Mackenzie was enthralled by him, and Eloise whispered to me that she'd forgotten how dangerously handsome she thought he was. Neither of them knew anyone else like Alvin "Big Hurt' Brown.

He and I were out in the yard, looking back at the house.

"This must have been a hell of a place to grow up in," Alvin remarked. "Sort of like the Cleavers gone Green Acres."

He made light of it, but a wistful expression in his eyes suggested there was more to his thinking. I realized how much different growing up here would have been to the South-side Chicago streets of Alvin's youth. Alvin had at least sampled a better life, having spent his youngest few years living with his mother's sister and her family in rural Greenville County, with his cousin Taylor Johnson, long before he'd gone away to college and I'd thrown him that pass that crippled him for life.

Taylor's mother, Alvin's aunt, was a wonderful, kind, woman. It would have been a terrific home to live in. For Alvin, it was like moving from heaven to hell when his worthless father had torn him and his mother away from there, moving them to Chicago where he soon deserted them. Leaving Alvin and his mother to fend for themselves on the streets.

It struck me just how much the events of our early lives determined who we would become. Standing there looking at Still Hollow took Alvin back to a time that might have been the best of his entire life. The time he lived with the Johnsons. The one time he could remember as a child feeling safe and secure enough to calm the never-ending fear inside that, if he didn't keep a constant guard up to defend himself and his world, no one else would.

Alvin had grown up a tough, hard guy, but as Eloise had said, he had a big heart. And I felt that briefly living with the Johnsons kept that heart from withering over the following years.

"There were good times here, I can't deny that," I said. "But there are some regretful memories here too. My grandfather and I didn't always get along, and I spent a lot of years here feeling sorry for myself. But that's another story."

"Dinner's ready," Eloise called from a doorway, and we went in.

Eloise had the table set with a country-cooking feast. She must have thought that Alvin and I hadn't eaten in a week. She'd made sweet tea, fried chicken, biscuits and gravy, turnip greens, black-eyed peas, and sweet corn. A banana pudding sat in the fridge for dessert. Knowing the health-conscious diet Alvin religiously stuck to, there wasn't one dish on the table that he would probably eat. Even the turnip greens were cooked with fatback.

He shocked me by eating everything and even went back for seconds.

I was staring at him as he took another drumstick from the basket of chicken. He looked at me and grinned like a kid at Christmas, then he turned to Eloise.

"Miss Eloise, I haven't eaten food like this since I was a little boy, and me and my mama lived with my aunt Millie over in Greenville County. You sure have brought back some fine memories to me."

I had to smile.

Eloise placed a hand on his arm. "Well, Alvin, since you're going to be staying here, we'll have to do this every night."

I cleared my throat. "Change of plans, Alvin will be doing a little undercover work for a while, and it's best if nobody knows we all know each other. He'll be bumping up against some pretty rough characters, and he won't exactly be making friends with them. If some of them want to follow him home, we don't want them coming here."

Like the one who had already followed me, I thought.

Eloise looked from one of us to the other, a hundred questions behind her eyes. Mackenzie was wearing the same look in the chair next to her.

Both were concerned, and I got the feeling that Mackenzie was also excited to be included in such intrigue. I had some reservations about letting her in on things. However, she needed to know. There was always the possibility that she might run into Alvin at some inappropriate time and give something away. More importantly, my actions had placed her in danger as well as the rest of us, and she deserved to know about it.

"What are you two going to do?" Eloise asked.

I said, "It's better that you don't know all the details. Let's just say we're going to pick up where Kelly left off but this time, it won't be us getting kicked in the head."

"You're going to find the man who assaulted her," Eloise said.

"That be the idea," Alvin said.

"So where *will* Alvin stay?" she asked, looking at him.

"Somewhere nearer the Clemson area, if possible," I said.

Eloise was thinking hard. "I may have a place for you. I've got a friend with a son in the army in Afghanistan. He lives in a small modular home near the town of Liberty, and it's relatively close to that area. It's fully furnished and vacant, sitting on some farm acreage, and very private. My friend owns it and she's been talking about renting it while he's gone. She could use the money. It would be cheaper than any motel."

"I told you she could help," I said to Alvin. "And cheap is good. Because the *Clarion* will be picking up the tab, if you approve, Eloise."

"Of course, I approve, little brother. We can even put him on the payroll if you want to—secretly, that is. Welcome to the *Clarion*, Alvin."

Alvin said, "I don't need to be on any payroll. I got enough problems with the IRS already. Besides, I don't know nothin' bout no newspapering. What would my job title be, anyway, HNIC?"

Mackenzie giggled, and Alvin reached across the table and bumped fists with her.

They seemed to have bonded, and she was looking at Alvin like he was a rock star. The power of Alvin's magnetism.

"What is HNIC?" Eloise asked.

"Forget it, Mom," Mackenzie said. "It's a black thang."

She and Alvin bumped fists again.

Eloise and Mackenzie gathered the dishes up and took them into the kitchen. I grabbed Alvin and we followed them. I opened the dishwasher door, looked at Mackenzie and my sister, and said, "We got this."

"We do?" Alvin said.

"I'll rinse, you load." I handed Alvin a dirty plate.

He took it and gave me one of his looks. "You tell anybody about this and I'll kill you."

I wasn't entirely sure he was kidding.

Later, when we were settled into our chairs in the den, I texted him the names and descriptions of Doughboy, Terrell the bartender, April Cheney, and the Dollar brothers, along with the bar's name and address. Alvin sat and studied the descriptions.

I said, "Become a regular at this place. We'll both be going in there, but separate. As I said, we don't know each other. Make them believe you're one of them. Maybe a dealer yourself, down from Chicago where things were getting a little hot. You're not looking to compete, but to hook up with whoever's running things. You heard that maybe the Tiger's Tail is the place to find that connection."

"But why would I go there?" he asked. "Why not Greenville, or Atlanta?"

"Home folks in the Upstate. Tell them you grew up near there, which is sort of the truth. Just make them think it was in Pickens County, not Greenville County. I would think it's a hell of a market if you're selling party favors. You've got both

Clemson University and Southern Wesleyan University right there. That's a pool of about 30,000 potential customers, all young, away from home, and looking for a good time in an otherwise wasteland of rednecks and country folk, and where they roll up the sidewalks at dusk. Right next door on the lake are thousands of retired baby-boomers with aches and pains who, like May Burgess, are looking for a little help with an addiction that began with a doctor's prescription for Oxy, which they can no longer get."

"While I'm doing this, what'll you be doing?" he asked.

"Working with April Cheney—if she sticks around—and keeping up with the law enforcement's progress. April was helping Kelly, so she's going to have to help me some. I'll work it outside in, you work it inside out. April won't know about you, but maybe if somebody in the Tiger's Tail tips to your game, she'll find out and tell me before they can come at you. Get to know this Doughboy, who was dealing to May Burgess. Try to find out what you can about the Dixie Demon's involvement in the opioid scene, along with the Dollar brothers. Just keep your ears open. If we can find out who hurt Kelly, maybe we hurt them back a little. Or a lot."

Alvin stared at me like he couldn't believe what he was hearing.

"Are you not the J.D. Bragg who about a year ago, when we were into that thing over in Greenville County, was preaching non-violence shit to me?"

"Kelly changed that."

He stared a moment longer. "Then I be your man."

Eloise came in and broke up the conversation with the news

that she'd secured Alvin her friend's small house in Liberty. The friend was happy to oblige and liked the idea of getting a little extra money for a few days rent. Eloise had drawn a rough map to the place and said Alvin would find the key in a blue flowerpot on the porch.

With that, Alvin and I took our leave, driving both cars with me in the lead.

CHAPTER TWENTY-SIX

The drive from Still Hollow south to Liberty took us a little less than a half-hour. With Eloise's map, we quickly found the house, a couple of miles west of town.

The place sat on open farmland and was everything Eloise had said it was. Small and private, and well off the main road. A fenced pasture ran along either side of the long drive, and a half-dozen head of cattle stood by the fence dumbstruck in our headlights as we approached. We parked in front of the house and got out. It was one of those modular homes that had a brick foundation built around the crawl space underneath to disguise it from looking like a doublewide. It almost worked.

"I'll bet you don't have those at your place in Chicago," I said, looking back at the cows.

"I do, but mine come medium rare with steak sauce."

Alvin found the house key where Eloise said it would be, dropped off his bag inside, and was back out in less than a minute.

He said, "All the place needs is a few beers in the fridge and the little woman to come home to, and I'm *all* set. Now where is this Tiger's Butt place you were telling me about?"

"The Tiger's Tail. It's about twenty minutes down the road."
I gave him the directions. "I don't care what time you get out of
there tonight, you call me and let me know how it went."

I got in my Jeep and Alvin in his bright yellow rental. When
we reached the highway, I went left, and he went right.

#

My cell phone rang and woke me from a sound sleep. As I picked
it up, I glanced at the clock on the nightstand. It was 2:22 a.m.

"You awake?" Alvin asked.

"Yeah," I said, not really sure that I was.

"I'm out of there and on the way back to the ranch. Even
stayed for last call."

"You make any new friends?"

"Of course. Nobody can resist my winning personality, you
know that. Me and this Doughboy mother-fucker best friends
now."

"Did you stick to the script?"

"Yes, I did. I told him I was looking for a job and somebody
had mentioned his name. He asked who, and I gave him my
'you-know-fucking-better-than-to-ask-me-that' look, and he let
it slide. I think I got him a little scared of me. Must have been
my Gangster Disciples tatt."

"So, what did he say?"

"He said he'd think about it, but I got the feeling that hiring
and firing be above his paygrade. The guy's a schlepper."

"We speak Yiddish now, do we? I asked.

"I am a man of many languages and cultures, my friend."

"So, is anything going to come of it? Or was that a dead end?"

"After a visit to the head, where Doughboy stayed long enough to have pissed five times, he introduced me to Sonny Dollar, who just happened to walk by our booth at the precise moment Mr. Doughboy returned. Not very subtle. Sonny Dollar, however, was a more interesting character—*and* with a more suspicious nature. He joined us, and they both seemed to go out of their way to avoid the subject of drugs, or the fact that I was looking for an employment hook-up. But it still felt like a job interview. I'm thinking Doughboy works for this Sonny Dollar. And he's scared of him, Doughboy showing the man a lot of respect. But my gut tells me this Sonny ain't the top dog either. He don't strike me as top dog material. He just a thug."

"The older brother Laverne probably runs things," I said. "Or the Dixie Demons."

Alvin said, "By the way, they're gone. The Dixie Demons. Doughboy told me about them being there and said they took off earlier in the day. I think the D-boy was a little star-struck by them."

There went my chance to find out anything else about them. That was completely up to Bagwell and the Clemson Police Department now.

CHAPTER TWENTY-SEVEN

Wednesday was publishing day at the *Clarion*, and I needed to be there, so I did my Kelly visit earlier than usual. Doctor Mathis was an early bird too, I found him in Kelly's room making his morning rounds. He looked around when I walked in.

"Oh, I'm glad you're here. I wanted to tell you that Ms. Mayfield is showing considerable improvement, and if this keeps up, we should be able to bring her out of the medically induced coma soon."

"What is soon?"

"She still has a way to go, but I'd guess the first of next week."

"What will that entail?"

"It's simple, actually. We slowly reduce the anesthetics and the other drugs we're giving her until she wakes up."

"So, she just suddenly pops her eyes open and says, 'What'd I miss?'"

"Maybe not quite that," he said with an uncomfortable smile. He didn't seem to appreciate my sense of humor. "But barring any unforeseen complications, I'm very optimistic that she'll be back to normal very soon."

I sincerely hoped he was right, but I still couldn't get onboard his optimism train. Dissimilar personalities, I guessed.

#

From there, I went straight to the *Clarion* to help put the paper to bed. The staff was busy adding the finishing touches to things, re-proofing others, filling in blanks, and readying the press for printing. Although it was a much, much, smaller operation than the big-city papers, knowing this press run was mine, and my first, I couldn't help being a bit excited.

I read the story of Kelly's attack that Vickie wrote—or re-wrote—and she'd done an excellent job. I told her so.

She beamed. "So, what's next? Are you ready to include me on the opioid thing? I'm ready when you are."

"Not yet, I said. Just sit tight."

"I was talking to a friend last night who goes to Clemson, and he said he knows a guy that was getting oxy from a dealer out of a bar there. I could follow that up, if you'd like."

Jesus, I thought. *Was she talking about the Tiger's Tail?*

"I would not like. I thought we'd settled this. In *time*, girl, in time."

"Jawohl, mien Führer. Your vish ist my command," she said, in a terrible German accent.

Underneath her attempt at humor was a barb I didn't miss. She wasn't the type to take rejection well.

I spent a little more time with Jason Pilgrim as he uploaded the week's digital issue for our web circulation. I'd never seen that process done—Kelly had introduced the digital version of the paper. Jason didn't talk much, but at least he answered my questions when I asked them.

I kept getting the feeling something was bothering him, but if there was, he didn't bring it up. I hoped *he* wasn't about to quit. We'd certainly be lost without him. The number of people who read the digital version was rapidly approaching the hard copy circulation. Kelly had even talked about recording some of the news on camera, and sending it out as a digital video version like a local cable headline news program. The times, they were a-changing.

#

While I was busy at the *Clarion*, Alvin was visiting his paraplegic cousin, and my old college football teammate, Taylor Johnson, in the medical institution in Greenville. I'd told Alvin that I would be tied up all day, and asked him to say hello to Taylor for me and tell him I'd visit soon. I never went too long between visits, and I'd been doing that for years.

I told Alvin to go back into the Tiger's Tail that night and call me if anything big developed. If not, to go home and get some sleep. That's what I intended to do. We agreed to hook up sometime tomorrow, and figure out where we were and what we needed to do now.

As the day progressed, even with my nips and tucks here and there, and a suggestion or two, the staff had this week's publication of the *Clarion* well in hand. I was relegated to an observer, more than a manager. With Kelly's story taking the whole front page, we didn't need another news lead. So, the first-ever John David Bragg supervised issue of the *Clarion* was ready.

Eloise seemed to be in high spirits too. I think that even with my help, she never thought we'd be able to get the paper out without

Kelly. So much for my sister's faith in my abilities. I didn't blame her. I'd never shown any interest in the *Clarion* before, and the truth was, I would never be as good at the job as Kelly anyway.

I couldn't help thinking of my grandfather. This was what he'd always wanted, to see me following in his footsteps as publisher of the *Clarion*. It was too bad he wasn't alive to see it.

CHAPTER TWENTY-EIGHT

The sun had gone down, and Eloise and I were having a last coffee and celebrating a successful press-day when my cell phone rang. It was April Cheney.

"She's gonna' get hurt," April said, in a hushed voice, but I could tell she was excited. "You need to get her out of here before something bad happens."

"Who's going to get hurt?" I heard the distant sound of a car horn beep. She must be calling from the parking lot in back of the Tiger's Tail.

"This reporter from your paper, Vickie something. I figured you sent her."

"Sent her to do what? What's she doing in there, April?"

"She started out by asking Terrell if he knew where she could score some oxy. He stonewalled her, and she wandered away to the back of the bar. She had stashed her purse behind the bar when she came in, like women in here often do—and Terrell went through it—like he sometimes does. He's a nosy bastard with people he don't know. He found a *Clarion* business card in it. I saw it. Her driver's license was in there too, and her looks tonight certainly don't match the picture on it. She's dressed like a slut, her idea of undercover, I guess. But leaving her business card in her purse doesn't make her very smart. But she's been made, and Terrell went back and did some whispering in Sonny's ear, so he knows."

"Shit," I said. It was all I could think of to say. That crazy, naïve girl.

April said, "Somehow, she hooked up with Sonny. I don't know if that was her move or his, but now they're sitting in a booth with Doughboy, and some black dude I don't know, having a gay old time. Sonny is obviously toying with her, and I can tell you, this won't end well. She's gonna' find herself in the backseat of a car in the parking lot with her heels in the air, and three horny dudes taking turns with her, if you don't come and get her."

"I'm on my way," I said and rang off. At least Alvin was with her—assuming he was the black dude. I told Eloise, who was sitting there listening with a puzzled look, that I'd fill her in later, and hit the door.

#

I made the Tiger's Tail in record time, the result of doing ninety miles an hour in the straightaways, barely maintaining a grip on the curves, and the extraordinary luck of not crossing paths with anything wandering across the road or any officers of the law.

Vickie was still sitting with Sonny Dollar but alone at a table for two now. Alvin was in a booth against the wall across the room sitting with Doughboy. I knew I didn't have to worry about Vickie's safety with Alvin there. Whether he knew who she was or not, he'd blow his cover to stop anything from happening to a woman. I hoped that I could get her out before that.

I saw Alvin glance at me as I approached. He didn't move, but a sudden alertness in his eyes said he was anticipating whatever it was that brought me there. I almost didn't recognize Vickie. She'd replaced the horn-rim glasses and bookish look with heavy eye-shadow, black lipstick and nails, and a nose and an eyebrow ring. She looked like she was in the same Seattle garage band as Jason Pilgrim. She was wearing a short, black leather skirt, fishnet stockings and black combat boots laced to the top. *Très* sexy, if you're a goth. Or Sonny Dollar, who was eyeing her like she was a twenty-four-ounce rib-eye and he hadn't eaten in a week. Even I had to admit she was sexy, and I almost smiled until I noticed her expression, which was one of utter fear. She'd recognized what a mistake she'd made. There was a glimmer of relief in her eyes when she saw me. If she'd known what I thought about her being here, she should have been afraid of me too. I felt like killing her.

"Come on, Vickie, it's time to go," I said, as I reached their table.

"You two know each other. Surprise, surprise," Sonny said. "But she ain't going nowhere. We bout' to get a party on, me and her."

"Let's go, Vickie," I said again, and held out my hand for her. "I don't want any trouble," I said to Sonny.

"You found trouble the second you walked in here," Sonny said, and looked at Vickie. "Both of you."

I grabbed Vickie's hand and pulled her toward the rear exit. It was the closest way out. Sonny got up and followed us, with

Doughboy and thankfully, Alvin, right behind him. No one else in the place seemed to notice us leaving. Either that or they didn't want to get caught up in whatever was happening, which would make the Tiger's Tail clientele smarter than I would have expected.

As I passed through the door into the parking lot, I heard Sonny's footsteps quicken and realized he was coming at me. I turned just in time to do a quick juke that barely avoided a haymaker aimed at my chin. His fist went by blowing wind like a passing train. I caught him off balance from the swing and gave him all I had with an uppercut to the soft spot just below the middle of his ribs, then grabbed him with both hands by his leather biker's vest and slammed him down onto the tarmac. If he'd caught me with that blind-side haymaker, it would have been a clear decision for the other side. He didn't want a fair fight, so I wouldn't give him one. I kicked him hard in the ribs while he was down, hoping that if he was the one who hurt Kelly, he would recognize it as the first of a lot of payback that would be coming his way.

As I turned to grab Vickie's hand again and head toward our cars, Sonny managed to scramble up on an elbow, and pull an automatic pistol from under his shirt, racked it, and pointed it at me.

"You lose, Mother-fucker," he said.

Behind him, Alvin took two quick steps and in a move almost too fast to register chopped the edge of an open hand down on Sonny's wrist. I thought I heard a bone snap. Sonny yelled, and the gun went clattering across the tarmac. As Sonny lay moaning and writhing, I led Vickie around the building and she pointed me to her car, a Mini-Cooper, quite likely the only one ever parked at the biker bar. Alvin was close behind us.

CHAPTER TWENTY-NINE

Alvin caught up as we reached Vickie's car. "I guess my undercover job at the Tiger's Tail is over."

"That can happen when you break the arm of the guy you're trying to get in with," I said.

Vickie, who had scrambled behind me as she saw Alvin approach, stepped clear. "Wait! He's working undercover for you?"

"He was, Alvin Brown, meet Vickie Sayers. Vickie is one of my reporters."

"Ex-reporter, probably. Glad to meet you," she said.

I said, "I *should* fire you. You sure as hell don't know how to take orders." I turned to Alvin, "I specifically told her not to do something like this."

"Then you should have told me about *him*," Vickie said, pointing at Alvin. "If I screwed things up, I'm sorry. But I was trying to do what any good reporter would do, whether I had your official okay or not. How can I do my job, if you don't keep me in the loop? And by the way, I was doing pretty well until you came in and blew my cover."

"We'll talk about your cover later. And whether or not I should have told you about Alvin is beside the point. I gave you an order."

"Well, your orders suck. If all you want is an obedient little girl to keep her mouth shut and do research for you, then you've got the wrong girl. So, you might as well fire me."

I turned to Alvin again. He seemed amused.

"Girl's got grit," he said, grinning. "You gotta' like it."

I looked to see if Sonny Dollar and any sidekicks were following us. They weren't, but there was no reason to risk it.

I said, "Let's get out of here. Meet me at that all-night diner up the road, Sammy's. The *Clarion* is buying."

I looked at Vickie. "You, too. If you want to be in the loop, here's your chance."

Alvin and I went to our respective automobiles, Vickie got in her Mini-Cooper and we all caravanned to the diner. We got coffee and ordered food. I sat a moment, quietly looking at her.

"What do you think you accomplished with your little caper tonight?" I asked her.

"I now know the names of three guys who are connected to the drug trade," she said, obviously proud.

"And how can you prove that? Did they offer you drugs?"

"No, but we talked enough for me to know they *could* have. You've got to start somewhere. This was the first step."

"But they made you."

"How do you know that? I mean, yeah, Sonny Dollar was scaring me, but it wasn't because he made me as an undercover reporter, it was because he had plans to *make* me—if you get my drift—and wasn't taking no for an answer. I thought he was about to drag me outside and rip my clothes off."

I said, "Or worse, have you forgotten what they did to Kelly?"

"No, but still, I don't know why you think anyone made me. How would you even know if they had? Did he tell you?" she asked, gesturing at Alvin.

"No, the red-haired bartender did. She's on our side too." I gave Vickie a stern look. "And don't even think of approaching her yourself. It will get her hurt. So, against my better judgment, I'm trusting you to keep this strictly among us."

"I promise. But that still doesn't tell me how I was made."

"The bartender went through your purse, which you foolishly stored behind the bar, and even more foolishly, left one of your *Clarion* business cards in it."

"Oh, I thought I took them all out. Well, chalk that down to a learning experience. Be more thorough, next time."

I had a feeling I wasn't going to get Vickie to admit she'd done anything wrong. Was it stubbornness, or just an overblown sense of self-confidence? Or her tender age? But she did have courage and tenacity—*grit*, as Alvin called it—and I found myself admiring her for that, just a little. Maybe her decision skills weren't all that good. Perhaps those would come with experience and age. I doubted if I would ever win an argument with this feisty young woman.

"It just dawned on me who you remind me of," I said.

"An out-of-work reporter?" Vickie said.

"Kelly," I said.

"I remind you of Kelly? I'll take that as a compliment." Vickie smiled at me for the first time that night. She'd already figured out I wasn't going to fire her.

Our food came, and we dug in.

While we ate, I gave Vickie a brief explanation of who Alvin was and how I knew him. She was impressed.

"So, what do we do now, Kemosabe?" Alvin asked.

"I can tell you what we're not going to do. We aren't going to send anyone else in the Tiger's Tail undercover."

"Fine by me, they were never gonna' trust me anyway. They're a close-knit bunch and suspicious of everyone. And Sonny ain't exactly race-friendly, either."

"Maybe we can get something on this Doughboy that scares him more than Sonny Dollar or his brother Laverne. He looks like a weak link."

"Or maybe we grab him, put him in a locked room, and start breaking his bones until he talks," Alvin offered.

I nodded. "There is that, but for now, I'm getting some sleep. You guys should too."

Vickie had been listening intently, hanging on every word, her eyes wide.

I told her, "You need to go home and wash that gunk off your face. We'll talk in the morning."

She didn't say anything, but she did give me the shadow of a smile. Alvin and I sat and watched her go.

With Alvin "Big Hurt" Brown and a twenty-four-year-old tenacious spitfire like Vickie on my team, I had to have the most inverse weapons that investigative journalism had ever seen.

How could I lose?

CHAPTER THIRTY

As we walked to our cars in Sammy's Diner's parking lot, Alvin clenched a hand on my upper arm and quietly said, "Don't look now, but I think we've got company. To your left, against the concrete wall."

I took a couple more steps and as casually as I could, stole a glance in that direction. A black SUV with the motor running sat at the edge of the lot. The windows were tinted so dark it was impossible to see who was inside. The driver's window was lowered a couple of inches to reveal a pair of eyes watching us. It wasn't enough to recognize who, but they didn't look friendly.

"How do you know they're here for us?" I asked.

"I feel it," Alvin said, and didn't expound on it. "Get in the Mustang."

"The Jeep's closer."

"The Mustang's got more muscle and corners better."

"We about to be into a race?"

"More likely a chase," Alvin said.

"Who are we chasing?

"Nobody. I think we about to be the chasee, not the chasor."

I got into the Mustang with him and we pulled out of the lot. Alvin was right; the SUV came out right behind us.

"Buckle up," Alvin said, and picked up speed, heading east. I looked back to see the SUV close the gap frighteningly fast.

Alvin was looking in the mirror. He stomped the accelerator a little more.

As we left the Clemson town limits, the highway became a divided freeway on its way east to Easley and Greenville. There was little traffic at that time of night, and we had the road to ourselves. I glanced at the speedometer. Alvin already had the Mustang at a seventy-five. The problem was, we weren't losing the SUV. The glare of their headlights was bright on the backs of our heads. The SUV was right on our tail.

Alvin said, "Dammit, why does every white boy down here grow up wanting to be a NASCAR driver?" He stomped the accelerator a little more. "We can't outrun him on a straight-away. I need to get us an advantage."

"So what do we do?" I said. "I left my Uzi at home."

Alvin slowed and slammed on the brakes to make a hard tire-squealing left turn across an open break in the median. We headed back toward Clemson in the opposite lane. The SUV missed the break and shot past it, brake lights flaring, looking for another place to cross over. They must have found one, because it wasn't long before we saw their headlights approaching fast from behind again.

By then we were back in Clemson on the outskirts of the university campus. Alvin made a sudden violent turn into the maze of small streets that make up the college grounds, tires screeching, engine racing and pulling about the same G's as an

F/A Super Hornet jet fighter on a suicide dive. My heart was in my mouth as we zig-zagged through the narrow campus streets. The SUV had made the turn too, but slowly and was no match for the cornering ability of the Mustang. Alvin was right. My Jeep would have been doing sideways cartwheels about now. I was suddenly feeling like we might live to fight another day if Alvin could avoid putting us through the windows of some classroom or dorm.

We made a hard right and flew down the hill, Clemson Memorial football stadium rising up before us, the nosebleed section of the stands visible from this angle. The field beyond the wrought iron entrance gates was lit brightly as if there was some nighttime maintenance work going on.

As the street dead-ended against the stadium, Alvin made a right, then a hard left, and another left to the back of the stadium. The SUV was still behind us, but we lost them from sight momentarily as we made the turns. Behind the stadium was a large opening in the outer wall under the stands leading to a cavernous dark interior. Beyond that, an inner gate leading out onto the lit green field.

Alvin swung the Mustang through the open access, pulled behind a white panel truck that was parked inside, and doused the motor and the headlights. A few seconds later, the SUV came flying by on the street outside and disappeared up and over the hill.

"Maneuverability and cornering," Alvin said, and grinned.

We had lost them—at least for now.

A rap on my window gave me a start. A man in a dark blue shirt and pants stood there frowning at me. I rolled down the window, thinking he was a cop. It turned out that he was a maintenance man.

"You can't be in here," he said, angrily. "This is a no trespassing zone."

Alvin leaned forward and nodded toward the field behind the wrought iron gate. "Sorry, sir. Just wanted to get a better look at the field. I love them Tigers. We'll be leaving now."

Alvin started the Mustang, turned the headlights back on, and drove through the open outer gate. Outside, he took a right, the opposite direction the SUV had gone. We made it back to my Jeep at Sammy's Diner without spotting it again.

Alvin said, "We got the mother-fuckers' attention. So, what's next?"

"We need to know more about these Dollar brothers. If they're involved in the opioid business, then we need to prove it."

"They tailed us, so, let's tail them," Alvin said.

"It may come to that, but there's something I want to try first, and I need a little time to set it up. I'll call you about it tomorrow. It probably won't be until the afternoon."

I could see that Alvin was curious to hear more about it.

I said, "I'll tell you all about it when I call. We don't want to hang around here until these guys come back, so let's get out of here."

"I'll hang loose tomorrow, so just hit me up."

We left, both of us taking the back roads home to avoid running into the SUV again.

CHAPTER THIRTY-ONE

The sound of a car in the driveway woke me up. I glanced at my bedside clock, and it was almost three-thirty in the morning. I'd been asleep in my old familiar bedroom at Still Hollow since my head hit the pillow.

Then all hell broke loose. Automatic gunfire erupted like I was in the middle of a battle in Beirut. I was out of bed and on the floor in a heartbeat. Windows shattered across the front of the house, peppering me with broken glass. The bullets, coming from a low angle, punched holes in the ceiling, well over my head. I heard Eloise scream as the shooting moved to her room.

"Stay down," I yelled, hoping she could hear me over the gunfire. Mackenzie's bedroom was in the back, so she should be avoiding all of this.

As suddenly as it started, the gunfire stopped, and someone revved a car engine. I goose-stepped over to the window, ignoring the glass shards on the floor, in time to see a dark-colored SUV turn the bend in the driveway and roar away. I couldn't see who or how many were in it and didn't catch the license plate number. I had a good guess who it was—I'd been watching an SUV just like it chasing Alvin and me through the streets of Clemson.

My shoes were on the floor by the bedside. I picked my way over to them, avoiding some of the broken glass but not all of it. I slipped my shoes on and went out into the hall where I ran into Mackenzie, making her way to Eloise's room, scared out of her wits and tearful.

"Mom?" she called, anxiously looking over my shoulder as I opened Eloise's door.

Eloise was kneeling on the floor behind her bed, staring at me with her face crumpled in bewilderment and panic.

"What's happening, John David?" she said.

"Are you okay?"

"I'm fine, she said, nodding rapidly, and standing up. "Well, I'm not *fine*, but I'm not hurt." She looked past me at Mackenzie in the hall. "Are both of you okay?"

"Yes," I said, stopping Mackenzie from running past me into her mother's room. "Get your shoes on first. There's broken glass everywhere."

"Why is somebody trying to kill us?" Eloise asked.

"I don't think they meant to kill us. Just scare us."

"Scare us? What for?"

"To get me to stop doing what I'm doing. Same as Kelly. Plus a little payback, I guess. Alvin and me messed up one of their guys. They weren't too happy about that."

Eloise stared at me, a hundred questions roiling behind her wrinkled brow, but she didn't ask them. Mackenzie went flying past me and embraced her mother, tears rolling down both their cheeks.

This was my fault, I thought. I got dressed and went outside. The open lawn of the front yard cleared the way to the star-sprinkled, nighttime sky, the air cooler in the wee hours. It was a serene experience had it not been for the fog and stench of gunpowder that lay atop the smell of fresh-mowed lawn and sweet gardenias.

Back inside, we sat in the den on the sofa, my feet in Eloise's lap. She was working on the glass cuts on the soles, a half-dozen or so, all minor abrasions, but that didn't mean they didn't hurt or need treating. She was smearing on an antibiotic ointment and placing Band-Aids on the more substantial cuts.

Mackenzie sat by watching and wincing every time I winced.

I tried to dissuade their fears as best I could, and convince them that it was just a warning like I said, and not meant to kill us. The most I could tell them was that I thought the shooters were the same thugs who assaulted Kelly and had shot up our house for the same reason—to get me to stop sticking my nose into their drug business. I had ideas on who they were, but not enough evidence yet to prove it. I got Eloise to agree not to discuss any of that with the authorities until I had one more day to check something out. She reluctantly agreed. I wondered if I deserved the trust she placed in me.

She called Bagwell and reported the shooting. At least by calling him, I thought, we'd have a better chance of getting the insurance to pay for the damage, my practical and financial side showing a seldom-seen face. I didn't know if home insurance covered drug dealer drive-bys.

Bagwell came out, and Eloise and I told him our respective stories of what happened, bullet by bullet, and our inability to identify who did it.

He had me follow him outside to view the damage to the front of the house. Several of his deputies were already out there with floodlights, taking pictures of the bullet holes and broken windows.

Once outside, he turned to me. "Okay, who did this?"

"I'm serious, I don't know. I couldn't see them. The car windows were tinted too dark."

He gave me a look that clearly said I was full of shit.

"Okay, I see that you don't want to tell me what you've gotten yourself into, but whatever it is, you've involved your sister and niece, and placed them in danger. I'm not going to let you do that."

"Look, Sheriff. Right now, all I've got are guesses. Theories. But until I can put some merit to them, I can't see any good coming from talking about them. There isn't one factual thing I can give you. I could be way out in left field with my thinking. When I know something, you'll know something."

He'd stood glowering at me, contemplating what I'd said, and obviously not liking it. He took a step toward me, placed the tip of a forefinger in the middle of my chest and said, "I'll give you twenty-four hours to tell me what the dickens is going on here, or I'm putting out an APB on you and hauling you in. I'm serious here, J.D.. You can't go putting Eloise and Mackenzie in the middle of whatever is going on here. Y'all are lucky none of you got hit."

He was back to calling me J.D. again. But he was right. My actions *had* brought danger right to my sister and niece's front door, and it was the last thing I wanted to do. I had to find a way to put an end to all this, and quickly.

"Tomorrow," I said. "You've got my word."

He looked at me a moment longer, then turned and walked to his car, stopping only to say something to one of his deputies. Then he got in his cruiser and drove away.

The deputy he spoke to came over. "When we finish up here, we're going to leave an officer parked at the end of the drive, sir. He'll be there for the rest of the night, and someone will be there tomorrow, too. So, you and your family can go back to bed and get some sleep. Don't worry about these people coming back."

We followed the deputy's advice. After we swept up the broken glass from the bedroom floors and draped sheets over the broken windows, we went back to bed. But, as to the sleep part, I don't think any of us got much of that.

At least I didn't.

CHAPTER THIRTY-TWO

With about two hours of sleep, I left Eloise and Mackenzie in their beds, Eloise having decided that Mackenzie could stay home from school, and since the day after Wednesday's publishing day at the *Clarion* was always slow, Eloise decided to sleep in herself.

I'd promised Bagwell I'd meet him in the afternoon and explain what was going on. For that to happen, I had a lot to do.

I looked up the number of Jim Brandt, a Greenville City Police Detective I knew. I wanted to ask him where I could find Eddie Smoke. Eddie was a Greenville thug, pimp, and drug dealer I'd once met working on another story. Brandt and I met on that same story, and if anyone could tell me anything about Eddie Smoke, it would be him. He'd been trying to arrest Smoke for something for a long time, but Smoke was too slippery and covered his tracks well.

Maybe he'd nabbed Smoke by now, I thought, and he was sitting in a jail cell somewhere. But I guessed that he was likely still doing business as usual. Either way, I wanted to talk to him. Eddie Smoke was the only high-level drug dealer I knew. My idea to see him was based on something Vickie found in her opioid research. That two different drug rings were operating in the Upstate, one in Pickens and Oconee Counties, and the other to the east in Greenville County. Anything going on in Greenville, Eddie Smoke would be a part of it to some degree or another, and if so he might view the Pickens-Oconee operation as competition and be willing to talk about them—if he thought it might help *him*. Or he might not talk to me at all and have one of his goons re-arrange my nose. But I had to try.

I dialed Detective Brandt's number expecting to get a voice mail. The detective answered on the second ring. After swapping "how ya' doins," I asked him about Eddie Smoke. Unfortunately, Smoke was still in the free world, too cagey to ever give them enough to bring him down.

"He'll fuck up eventually," Brandt said. "And we'll get him. But we still can't get anything prosecutable on him. Any witness to anything seems to have a way of changing their story or disappearing before they ever get to court."

"So, if a guy wanted to get in touch with him, how can he be found?'

"Would that guy be you?"

"Yeah. It's related to a story I'm working on."

"What makes you think he'll talk to *you*?"

"I'm working on a hunch that he will."

"And it's something you won't tell me about."

"Probably not. But if Smoke were to implicate himself somehow, I'd think about it."

"All you media types are all assholes," he said, but chuckled. "Maybe he'll shoot you, and I can nail him for that."

"So, you gonna' tell me how to find him?"

I heard him sigh. "It's no secret that Smoke runs a cab company in West Greenville. Jiffy Cab. That's his legit business, and we know he runs his other business out of there too. We just can't prove it."

"Thanks, Detective, good to talk to you again."

"Hey Bragg? You wouldn't want to plant a wire in there for me, would you?"

It was my turn to chuckle. "You *are* trying to get me shot, aren't you?"

"Can't blame a guy for trying," he said and hung up.

#

I found the number for Smoke's cab company and called it.

"Jiffy Cab," a woman's voice answered.

"I need to speak to Eddie," I said.

"Hold," she said and transferred me.

"What can I do for you?" a man with a raspy voice said. It wasn't Eddie Smoke's voice. I wondered if it was the guy I'd hit in the throat a year earlier when Alvin and I had our first run-in with Eddie Smoke's thugs.

"Is Eddie around?"

"Who's asking?" he said.

"J.D. Bragg."

It was a moment before he responded. "What the fuck do you want?"

Now I was sure it was the guy I'd punched in the neck. I'd aimed for his jaw and missed, hitting him in the larynx. He'd gone down making a sound like he had a chicken bone stuck in his craw. It was the one time Alvin accused someone else of being too violent. He said I could have killed the guy, when all we needed to do was discourage them enough to make our getaway. When it came to violence, Alvin had his professional standards. To Alvin, what I did was overkill. He still ragged me about it.

"You got some balls calling here. You and me got some unfinished business, mother-fucker."

"Am I the reason you sound like Marlon Brando in the *Godfather*? If so, I'm sorry. I didn't mean to hit you in the throat. My aim was off. But look on the bright side. I've helped facilitate your bad-guy mobster image. Now, are you going to let me speak to Smoke or not?"

He muttered something under his breath, then spoke to someone else, obviously Eddie Smoke. "Got somebody here wants to talk to you," I heard him say, followed by something indecipherable, muffled as if he'd placed his hand over the receiver.

A moment later, Eddie Smoke came on the line.

"I never thought I'd hear from you again," he said.

"I need to talk to you about something."

"What could you and me possibly have to talk about, Bragg?"

"Not over the phone. We need to meet."

"And why would I do that?"

"I think that the subject might be interesting to you. It's about your competition."

"You want to talk to me about Uber?" he said, deadpan.

"*Another* competitor. I can be there in a couple of hours."

I didn't say I wanted to pick Alvin up first. I didn't think Smoke would allow the thug I hit in the neck to seek revenge, but with these guys, you never knew. I might need backup.

"Okay, I'll see you. But Bragg? We parted on peaceful terms. That could easily change."

"That's the last thing in the world I'd want," I said.

"Then come on. I'll be here all afternoon," Smoke said and hung up.

CHAPTER THIRTY-THREE

I called Alvin and found him still in Taylor Johnsons' room at the medical facility in Greenville.

"We were just talking about your sorry ass," he said.

In the background, I heard a voice scold him. It sounded like Millie Johnson, his aunt and Taylor's mother.

"Sorry, Aunt Millie," I heard Alvin say. "I didn't mean to say ass."

I heard her scold him again, and Alvin chuckle.

"Tell Mrs. Johnson I said hello," I said.

He did, and I heard her say something in the background.

"She said to tell you she brought you something."

"I hope it's some of her peanut butter cookies." Mille Johnson made her living as a wealthy family's cook, and she was a good one.

Alvin told her I'd guessed it, and I heard her laugh. She'd sent them to Taylor back in college before he got hurt, and he would always give some of them to me.

She's fussing at me for trying to eat em' all up," Alvin said. "I'm sposed' to be savin' some for you. But don't count on it."

"How's Taylor?"

"He about the same. You know how he is. He's doing more listening than talking. But he couldn't get a word in even if he tried. Aunt Millie and me been running our tongues nonstop since I got here this morning."

After Taylor's spinal cord was injured, his phrenic nerve stopped stimulating his diaphragm, and it quit functioning. He needed round-the-clock assistance with his breathing and a breathing pacemaker surgically implanted. Otherwise, he couldn't breathe at all. It gave his speech a start-stop effect with sudden short gasps of breath. It was heartbreaking to listen to him try to speak. He knew it, so he didn't talk any more than he had to.

"Say hey to him for me too," I said. "Tell him I'm sorry I'm not there with you."

"He said you came to see him a couple of weeks ago. I told them about Kelly, and he said you're probably doing more than your share of visiting hospitals, and to go find the a-hole who did it to her and don't worry about visiting him."

"How much longer are you going to stay?" I asked.

"Taylor's getting tired and needs to rest, and Millie's got to get home. I'm ready to leave anytime. What's up?"

"You remember me saying last night I had this crazy idea?"

"Yeah?" Alvin said, as if he wasn't sure he wanted to hear it.

"How about Eddie Smoke from last year in Greenville County? Remember him?"

"Greenville's number one thug, pimp, and drug dealer. What about him?"

"I had a girl at work do some research on opioids, and she turned up something interesting. The opioids sold on the streets

169

in Greenville County are different from the opioids sold over here in Pickens County. That suggests two different suppliers. If anybody knows anything about that, it would be Eddie Smoke."

"He's probably the Greenville supplier himself," Alvin said.

"I think that's a good bet, but probably not both."

"That would make the one in Pickens County his competition. So, Smoke might be willing to tell us all kinds of shit, if he thought it would benefit him."

"Great minds think alike," I said.

"But why would he talk to us in the first place? We roughed up a couple of his guys. There's got to be some bad blood over that. You hit one of them in the throat and could have killed him."

"But it didn't kill him. I was talking to him a little earlier. Besides, I didn't mean to hit him there. I was aiming for his chin and missed."

"What you were aiming for probably don't mean a whole lot to him. He might still pop a cap in you."

"You're coming along to make sure that doesn't happen."

"I see," Alvin said. "Okay, I didn't come down here to sit on my ass in the middle of a cow pasture, waiting for something to happen by itself. I'm in."

"You think you can find your way to the corner of Easley Bridge Road and South Washington?"

"Sure. That's why God made GPS."

"There's a Clock Drive-In restaurant in the southwest corner. Meet me in the parking lot in about forty minutes. I've made us an appointment to see Smoke."

CHAPTER THIRTY-FOUR

I spotted Alvin's airport rental the second I pulled into the Clock parking lot. There weren't many bright yellow Mustang convertibles parked there. Alvin was sitting in it and waiting for me.

"So, the Smoke-man knows we coming," Alvin said, when he got into my Jeep.

"He knows *I'm* coming. We'll let you be a surprise."

"I love surprise parties," Alvin said.

"I didn't want to tell you this over the phone with Mrs. Johnson listening, but about three o'clock this morning we had a drive-by shooting at Still Hollow."

That got all of Alvin's attention, and he looked at me in disbelief.

"Nobody got hurt," I said. "Other than me getting a few shards of glass in my feet. I think they were just trying to scare, not kill. They raked the second-floor windows, and aimed high enough for all the shots to go into the ceiling. They had to know that."

Alvin's face filled with fury. "The black SUV?"

I nodded. "But I still couldn't see who was in the car, or get the tag number."

"How are Eloise and Mackenzie handling it?"

"Shook up, but okay. Bagwell came out. All I could tell him was that the windows were tinted and I couldn't see who it was. We don't really have anything; all we've got are guesses. We can't even prove that it was the Dollar brothers chasing us. I'm not going back to the cops until we've got something concrete. That's why I'm hoping Eddie Smoke can confirm that the Dollar brothers are behind the opioid business in Pickens County. If he can, then we might be able to sic the sheriff on them. He's got the law and the legal system behind him, and we don't. It might be the only way to get justice for Kelly."

"There is another way, J.D." Alvin said.

I stopped talking and looked at him.

"We can blow the Dollar brothers' fucking heads off," he said.

"I'd rather we let that be the back-up plan, Alvin."

Alvin just grinned that grin of his at me.

#

We found the Jiffy Cab Company in a seedy industrial area in West Greenville. It was a white-washed cinderblock building that looked like it was once a gas station. A couple of old gas pumps sat out front, for cab use only now. Several white sedans of varying ages sat about, all with a red "Jiffy Cab" and a phone number painted on the front doors.

Alvin and I parked out front and went into the office. A bleached blond with bright red lips and large breasts sat a switchboard. She looked like one of Smoke's call girls, slightly beyond her prime but not bad, now earning her money in a different profession. Behind her was a closed-door that said "Private." Another door to her right stood open and led to the service bays.

I told her who we were and why we were there. She punched a button on her switchboard, said something quick and low into her mouthpiece, and the private door opened. Out came another of Smoke's thugs that I recognized. I heard Alvin grunt beside me. He knew the man too. Alvin had broken the guy's nose in our fight with them a year ago.

He glared at me, then Alvin, and back at me.

"We were expecting only *you*," he said to me, and nodded at Alvin. "Not this mother-fucker. He has to stay out here."

I started to object, but Alvin placed a hand on my arm. "That's okay. I'll keep Betty Boobs here company. You need me, just holla."

I went through the door and found Eddie Smoke sitting behind a cheap metal desk. A couple more of his thugs leaned against a wall. I recognized them as the other two that Alvin and I had tangled with. One of them was Raspy Voice. They both glared at me, but Raspy Voice's look was especially intense. Smoke gestured me to a chair in front of his desk, and I took it. He hadn't changed since I'd last seen him. The same too-black hair that suggested a dye job, low hairline and hooded eyes that gave him a simian look, and a body like an oil barrel.

"You come to interview me for a story?" he said, almost smiling.

"I came to ask you about something."

"Yeah? What?"

"I want you to tell me who's behind the trafficking of opioids over in Pickens and Oconee Counties."

I felt, more than saw, the thugs leaning against the wall stand up a little straighter.

He sat and studied me for a moment. "Even if I knew anything about that, why the fuck would I talk to you about it?"

"Because a hunch tells me you wouldn't mind seeing their demise."

Smoke turned to the three thugs along the wall. He said, "Pat him down."

They came over, pulled me out of the chair, and frisked me like professionals.

"No wire," one of them said when they'd finished.

"Why would you have a hunch like that?" Smoke asked me.

"I know that the product on the street over there is different from the product over here. That says to me there are two different operations going on in the Upstate. I'm only interested in the one over there, I don't care who's doing what over here. But my guess is, whoever it is, they wouldn't like to see anybody encroaching on their territory—if that isn't happening already."

Smoke asked, "So, what's your interest? You're writing a story about this?"

"Someone in the drug business over there badly hurt a woman I care about, and I want to find out who. I don't care if it makes a story or not. I'm not out to write about the evils of opioids, I'm out to find the assholes who beat her up and nail them to the wall. I thought doing that might be in our common interest."

Smoke said slowly, "Let's say, for the sake of argument, your hunch is right and I wouldn't mind the demise of these people in Pickens County. What exactly do you want from me?"

I was right. Smoke and these Pickens County guys were competitors.

"I want names, and anything else you can tell me about them."

"So, you think I'm a rat?"

"No, I think you're a businessman, and this would be good business for you. Nobody will ever hear where I got my information, and I will never speak your name or use it in anything I write. In fact, I wasn't even here."

The wheels were obviously turning in Smoke's head.

"The Dollar brothers," he finally said.

"Laverne and Sonny?"

"Yeah. Laverne runs things. Sonny's a tough-guy, but Laverne's crazier than a shithouse rat. A fucking psycho. They ain't been in business long, but they seem to be expanding rapidly. Let's just say that whoever's got that business on *this* side of the Saluda River is probably starting to feel the Dollar brothers' breath on their behinds. And they can't be too happy about it. Now is that all?"

"That's it," I said.

"Now go away, and don't come back." Smoke looked at one of his thugs and gestured to the door.

The man walked over, opened it, and stood looking at me.

As I got up, Smoke added, "You know why I'll trust you to keep your mouth shut, Bragg?"

I didn't give him an answer. I didn't think he expected one.

"Because if this comes back at me in any way, whatever happened to this woman of yours won't be nearly as bad as what I'll do to you."

With a sense that I'd just made a deal with the devil, I nodded at Eddie Smoke and left.

\#

I took Alvin back to get his yellow convertible, and we went inside and had hamburgers at the Clock. While we ate, I filled Alvin in on what Eddie Smoke had to say.

"That's confirmation enough that the Dollar brothers are who we thought they are. So, what's our next step?" he said.

"As I said, I'm going to see Sheriff Bagwell with it and see what *he's* going to do. For a cop, he's not a bad guy. Maybe he'll go after the Dollar brothers without trying to force me to reveal Eddie Smoke as the source."

"A cop that isn't an asshole. That's a new one," Alvin said.

"By the way, you got Mrs. Johnson's cookies she told you to bring me?"

"You know, I was gonna' bring em', but somebody came in and ate every single one."

"And you don't know who that somebody was," I said.

"No, but they said he was a fine-looking man, and a snappy dresser."

"You owe me, Brown," I said.

Before we headed out, I called Bagwell to see if he was in his office. I told him we were coming to see him.

CHAPTER THIRTY-FIVE

Bagwell was waiting for us. When we walked in, he completely ignored Alvin, whom he'd never met, and focused a pissed-off look on me.

He said, "I'd like to know why you didn't tell me last night that you'd been in that biker bar in Clemson again, just hours before somebody shot up Eloise's house. Was that something else you had to wait until today to tell me? Were you going to tell me about that at all? You're doing it again, Mr. Bragg, interfering with my investigation. It's got to stop."

Mr. Bragg again, I thought. I kept falling in and out of his favor. "Who told you I was there?"

"You saying you weren't?"

"No, I was there. I just want to know who told you."

"Chief Watson has a guy in plain clothes dropping by there about every night now, just to keep an eye on the place. He's been doing it since I told them about our interest in that Dixie Demons Hound-dog fellow. He recognized you, and said you had some kind of altercation in there. A young woman involved."

"The young woman is a reporter at the *Clarion*, who foolishly took it upon herself to go in there undercover to see what she could find out about drugs being sold out of the place. I went to get her out of there before she got herself hurt."

Bagwell didn't say anything about me also being there on Monday. Chief Watson's man must have missed me that night.

"I guess you know the Dixie Demons have cleared out?" I said to him.

"Of course I do, it's my job to know. Now, tell me who you think fired an automatic weapon into your sister's house last night, and why they did it."

"I'm sorry I couldn't tell you then. I was waiting until I had more to back up a theory that I have. Which I did. I'm here now, ready to tell you everything I know, and everything I think."

"I'm all ears," he said.

Bagwell suddenly looked at Alvin as if he'd just discovered him standing there, which was surprising. If Alvin Brown was in the room, you noticed. Bagwell must have really been consumed with chewing me out.

"Who is *this* man?" he said.

"Alvin Brown, a friend."

"What is your part in this, Mr. Brown?"

Alvin said, "Just lending moral support. Here for J.D. in case he needs any help.'

"Moral support," Bagwell repeated, and stared at Alvin. He obviously didn't know what to make of him. Then he turned back to me.

"Talk to me, Mr. Bragg," he said.

"It starts with the reason Kelly was assaulted. The severity of her beating just didn't jive with me. I didn't buy a horny biker wanting to teach her that kind of lesson for just turning down his sexual advances, however humiliating it might have been. So, I concentrated on other possible scenarios. Like I told you, I found out that Kelly has been working on a story about the opioid crisis in Pickens County, a follow-up to that editorial she wrote a couple of weeks ago. This led her to the Tiger's Tail.

"But Kelly didn't go there to write a story about the Dixie Demons being in town. She was there because she knew someone was dealing opioids out of there, and that they had supplied the pills that caused the death of a woman named May Burgess. Kelly was there to see what else she could dig up.

"So, she was sticking her nose into something that could put her into harm's way from many directions. From the dealer who sold May Burgess the opioids that killed her, to whoever is behind the local distribution of those drugs, or anyone who is associated with that business in any way. Including the Dixie Demons outlaw motorcycle gang. I haven't found evidence that they're involved in the opioid distribution here, but I haven't found anything that says they aren't either. The only thing I do know is that they are friendly with the guys who run the Tiger's Tail, two brothers named Laverne and Sonny Dollar, whom I know Kelly did have suspicions about.

"Today, I got substantiation that Laverne and Sonny Dollar are indeed behind the distribution of opioids in Pickens and Oconee Counties. And I think that's who shot up Still Hollow last night. They know I'm sticking my nose in their business. Just like Kelly was doing when they hurt her too."

"How the heck do you know all this?" Bagwell said.

"I've got sources, Sheriff."

"Who are these sources?"

"They're confidential, Sheriff. You know I can't give them up."

Not only would it break the journalist's unwritten law to give up Eddie Smoke or April Cheney, I thought. *Eddie would kill me and the Dollars would kill April.* I couldn't have Bagwell go confronting either of them.

Everything I was saying made Bagwell even angrier. The redness rose up his neck from beneath his shirt collar.

"So, you're saying that the Dollar brothers attacked and beat Ms. Mayfield?"

"Yes, they either did it themselves, or had it done. I know the Dixie Demons that were here have alibis, but I still haven't completely given up on them being involved in this business somehow. They could've brought in someone else to help the Dollars with their problem. Whoever did it wanted to stop Kelly from snooping into their business. Whether they meant to kill her, or just got carried away and went too far, or were interrupted by the pizza guy at the door and fled before they could finish the job, I couldn't say."

"This is who you think did the drive-by shooting last night? The Dollar brothers?"

"Yes, I didn't actually see them, the windows on the SUV were tinted too dark. But I'm sure it was them, and maybe a guy they call Doughboy. He's the dealer that sold the opioids to May Burgess. He hangs out at the Tiger's Tail. There's also a bartender named Terrell Dent there who has to be involved in this too."

"How do they know about you?" Bagwell asked.

"Like I said, I've been snooping in the same place as Kelly, and asking the same questions."

I didn't tell Bagwell about Alvin probably breaking Sonny Dollars wrist, or the high-speed car chase through the center of Clemson. Laws were broken then too, some of them by us.

Bagwell leaned back in his chair, trying to sort through all of this and decide if he believed me or not.

"Do you know the Dollar brothers, Sheriff?" I asked.

"Yes, I know them. They're part of a family with a decades-long history of run-ins with the law. But until now I thought they were just small-time criminals with the habit of going looking for trouble and finding it all too easy. As to drugs, cooking some meth, maybe. Or dealing some weed and a few pills. But I could never even prove that. I've got nothing on the scale of what you're talking about. What actual proof *do* you have?"

"You now have all I've got. I was hoping you could take it from here."

"Everything you've got seems to be hearsay," Bagwell said. "From sources you won't name. There's not enough here to bring them in, or even get a search warrant for their place."

"So, you're not going to do anything?" He didn't like me saying it.

Bagwell suddenly got up and left the room. "Sit tight," he ordered.

I'd obviously gotten under his skin, or was it that I'd gotten out ahead of him with what I'd found? Especially since he didn't seem to have an inkling of what the brothers might be up to, right in his backyard. This wasn't the first time something like this had happened between Sheriff Arlen Bagwell and me. It was my efforts, not his, that led to the man who killed my grandfather a couple of years ago. Bagwell was a proud man; he didn't like me getting ahead of him then, and he wouldn't like it now.

Bagwell returned in about ten minutes. "I've called the DEA, and an agent from their Greenville office is coming over. He'll be here in thirty to forty minutes. We're going to wait for him. I want you to tell him everything you've told me."

Alvin groaned. He didn't enjoy the company of law enforcement, regardless of the reason.

"Do I need to be here?" he asked me.

Bagwell answered. "Why don't you stick around, Mr. Brown? You can lend us your *moral support*."

I got the feeling Bagwell wasn't through trying to find out exactly who Alvin Brown was.

I still hadn't told Bagwell about the motorcyclist who made the threatening gestures to Eloise and me. If he didn't know by now that I'd managed to place her in danger, he never would, and I was tired of hearing him blame me for it. I knew that well enough already.

"So, tell us a bit more about the Dollar brothers while we're waiting," I said to him.

He seemed to roll that around in his mind for a moment. "There used to be five brothers. They had a hell of a reputation growing up. Rough bunch, most of it before my time, but I've had a few run-ins with them. Two brothers are dead now, one died in prison, the other in a motorcycle accident. Three brothers and a sister are left, along with their families, all of them living on the old family property, a rambling old auto junkyard just north of the town of Central. In addition to selling used car parts, they run a wrecker service too.

"I think Wade, the oldest brother and maybe the only one married at present, runs the salvage and wrecker business, along with a couple of grown children. Don't know if the other two brothers or the sister help in the business, but I'd guess they do. Sonny, the youngest, rides motorcycles and belongs to a local motorcycle club that gives us trouble every now and then. Sonny is a tough guy, but the middle brother Laverne is the worst of them. He's probably insane, and pure mean. He beat a guy to death in his younger days and went away for a few years, and did another stint for a while for drugs, I think. He's approaching fifty now. The local police may know, but I wasn't aware that either brother had anything to do with that Clemson biker bar until you just told me. That's all I know." Bagwell finished by saying, "And now, I've got some work I can be doing while we're waiting on the DEA."

He escorted us down the hall to an interrogation room with a one-way window in a wall and a video camera mounted in a corner, up near the ceiling. There was a metal table in the center of the room surrounded by four chairs.

"There's coffee, candy, and cheese crackers in the vending machines down the hall," he said as he left. "Help yourself."

#

An hour had passed when Bagwell returned with a man he introduced as Agent Ben Underwood, the DEA Agent in charge of the Western South Carolina area. He was about my age, dark, shaggy hair, and with that three-day-old unshaved look that still seemed to be in style. He was dressed in jeans, a white T-shirt, gray hoodie, and worn Nike crossovers. I got the feeling he might do more undercover work than deskwork.

Underwood looked at Alvin. "He's the reporter, you're the friend," he decided.

Alvin just nodded.

He kept his eyes on Alvin a moment longer, then turned to me. "So, what's this all about? What have you got to tell me?"

I told him everything I'd said to Bagwell. Evidently, Bagwell had already filled him in on Kelly's assault, my relationship to her, and my intent to follow the opioid story. Again, I didn't mention April Cheney, Eddie Smoke, the midnight motorcycle rider, or Alvin going undercover in the Tiger's Tail.

After I'd finished, he frowned at me. "And you won't give up your sources?"

"That's correct, I won't."

"Then this is all hearsay and of no help to me."

"I would think you'd be at least a little interested," I said.

"What I'm interested in is none of your business. As of now, your involvement in this matter is over. I understand that you run a newspaper, Mr. Bragg, and have a right to cover anything you want, but you are not to interfere with an active investigation in any way, or there will be serious repercussions. You could go to jail for it, and I won't hesitate to arrest you. Leave the police work to the police. Do you understand?"

I just stared at him. He seemed to ignore the fact that if not for Alvin and me, they would have absolutely nothing—either about who assaulted Kelly, or where the dangerous opioids in

Pickens County were coming from.

"I asked you if you understand me," Underwood said.

Then it hit me. His smug attitude gave it away.

"You already know about the Dollar brothers," I said to Underwood.

He gave me a blank look. "I can't discuss that with you."

"If you know, what the hell are you doing about it?" This officious asshole was pissing me off.

"I said I can't discuss that with you," he repeated.

I turned to Bagwell. "I've got a right to know if anything will be done to catch Kelly's assailants."

"We'll be working with the DEA now to do just that," Bagwell said.

I pointed at Underwood. "But it won't be *his* priority, will it? His interest is in busting a drug ring. He doesn't give a shit about what happened to Kelly."

"She should have kept her nose out this," Underwood said. "Just like I'm telling you to do now."

I stood up quickly, fighting the urge to knock the smug look off Underwood's face. I felt Alvin grab my arm.

Underwood said, "All you and your girlfriend have been doing is making these guys more suspicious of *everyone* and putting the whole investigation at risk. I will at least tell you this. This operation is bigger than you think. We believe that the opioids being distributed here are also being manufactured here, and shipped to many other states. There are millions of dollars of illegal and dangerous drugs going out from here."

I asked, "Have you even searched this junkyard where these Dollars live? Sounds like a pretty good place for a drug lab to me."

"Nothing you've told us here today helps us, Mr. Bragg. You have presented no factual information that would establish enough probable cause to get any judge to sign a search warrant. And there are legal complications here that you don't understand, so you're not helping, you're just in the way. You need to stop."

"What legal complications?" I asked him. "From where I stand it doesn't look complicated at all. I've told you who to go after, you know where they live, now go after them."

"Look, Mr. Bragg, I understand how badly you want to see these guys caught for what you think they did to your girlfriend. I get it. But you don't understand the law. That property the junkyard is on is broken into parcels, all owned by the Dollar family, and each parcel has a separate family member owner, making getting warrants even more difficult than usual. So, to search the whole property—which we would want to do—we need warrants for each owner. We're working on that. So, give us time. Leave this to the proper authorities and *butt-the-fuck-out*."

I said, "You don't have power over the press. You can't stop me from investigating anything."

"It is a crime to interfere with the police and their investigations. I can arrest you for that, regardless of who you are. And don't think I won't," Underwood said.

I looked at Bagwell and held out my hands out, palms up, in a gesture of frustration.

Bagwell said, "I'm just hearing most of this myself right now, Mr. Bragg. But I want you to know that *my* priority is still to find and arrest whoever assaulted Ms. Mayfield. If it was the

Dollar brothers, I will now be working closely with the DEA on a coordinated investigation to get them, not only for the opioid distribution, but for the assault and battery of Ms. Mayfield."

The look Bagwell gave me was so earnest I believed him. Bagwell would do his best, not only because of his dedication to his job, but because Eloise was expecting that of him. Was his best going to be good enough? Underwood may have already known everything I told them about the Dollar brothers, but Bagwell didn't. Which meant they weren't keeping him in the loop and probably never would, regardless of how much they promised him he'd be part of their team. I could see in Bagwell's eyes that he knew that too.

I stood up. "Can we go?"

Sheriff Bagwell glanced at Underwood, who nodded.

"Stay out of our investigation," Underwood repeated.

In the car, I said to Alvin, "Maybe they can't search that junkyard, but *we* can."

I got that fierce grin of his again, and took it as an affirmation.

CHAPTER THIRTY-SIX

We left Sheriff Bagwell's office and headed south to Central, about eight miles away. On the way, we dropped Alvin's Mustang at his place and took my Jeep on the hunt for the junkyard.

In Central, I stopped at a gas station, topped off my tank, and asked a guy if he knew of any auto junkyards in the vicinity. He directed me to a couple north of town. We quickly found the Dollar's junkyard well beyond the town limits.

The place was like a redneck gypsy camp surrounded by a sea of automobile carcasses of all vintages and at every stage of decomposition, stacked in places atop one another, along with scattered piles of mufflers, transmissions, engines, bumpers, and every other used car part imaginable. An aging house trailer and several small white-shingled houses were in the middle of the yard, nesting at angles around an old two-story farmhouse that looked a hundred years old—and at least half that since the last painting. The whole place was enclosed by a patchwork fence of weathered wood and rusting sheets of old tin roofing.

A dirty cinder-block building sat outside the front gate, windows and a door on one end, and an open repair bay on the other. A large tow truck sat nearby. Faded blue letters covered the front of the building and announced, "Dollar's Auto Salvage and Wrecker Service," and a phone number. If what I suspected was true, other things were going on here that weren't being advertised.

From what I could see of the junkyard behind the fence, it looked like it covered six or eight acres. The whole place was a blight on the otherwise pleasant woods and open farmland.

We made several passes, then pulled in and parked near the cinder block building. It was getting late in the day, but the place looked open for business. A large dog lay near the door, watching us. It didn't seem to mind our presence.

A long-haired man somewhere in his mid-twenties came out of the bay. He was wearing a tee-shirt and jeans and wiping his hands on a greasy rag. Behind him in the bay an automobile engine hung from an engine hoist, greasy parts strewn on the floor beneath it. I guessed we'd caught him working on it.

"What can I do for you fellers?" he asked.

Alvin leaned down and patted the dog's head. She lolled her tongue out and closed her eyes in enjoyment. He said, "I've heard of em' all my life, but this is the only one I've ever seen."

"What's that?" the boy asked.

"A junkyard dog. But I'm disappointed. This one doesn't live up to the reputation. Don't look like there's a mean bone in this dog's body. Another myth shattered."

The boy looked at the dog, then back at Alvin. "You was to come around here after dark, you'd meet the real thing. We got two more dogs we only let out at night. They'll chew your leg off up to your dick."

There seemed to be a taunt in the kid's voice. I got the feeling that he especially enjoyed telling that to a black man.

"Good to know," Alvin said, and looked at me.

I'd learned never to underestimate Alvin's intelligence and slyness. The kid might have gotten a kick out of saying that to Alvin, but he didn't know he'd helped us. Now we knew we'd have a couple of watchdogs to contend with if we ever decided to go inside the fence at night. If Bagwell or the DEA couldn't get a search warrant, we might just have to do that.

"So, what do you fellers need?" the boy asked again.

"You have a front bumper for a 1953 Studebaker?" I asked.

The boy thought for a moment. "I don't think so, but I'd have to ask my daddy to be sure. But he's up at the house gittin' something to eat."

"What's your daddy's name?" I asked.

"Wade Dollar. I'm Benny, his oldest. And I ain't interruptin' his meal. You'll have to wait, if you want to see him."

"Mind if we take a walk around the lot? I love looking at old cars, and I bet you've got some great ones back there."

The boy gave me a side-eye. "We do, but we can't let you go back there. You get hurt or something and our insurance won't cover it. If you want to talk to Daddy about this bumper, you'll have to wait, or come back later."

"We'll come back later," I said, and Benny Dollar didn't look torn to see us go. I didn't think he took a shine to either of us.

"I noticed something back there," I said to Alvin, as we drove back to Central.

"What? That the whole place would be at home in the movie *Deliverance* if they'd wanted a junkyard in it?"

"Well, that too. There's a line of trees on a hill behind the junkyard, and I saw what looked like a deer-blind in one of them. If we climbed it and staked out the place, we might find probable cause for Bagwell and Underwood to get a warrant to go in."

"I'm game," Alvin said.

"So maybe we'll go up there tomorrow sometime and see what we can see. But first, there's a couple of things we'll need to get."

"What, a sniper rifle to shoot all these redneck mother-fuckers?"

"That's certainly a thought, Alvin, but I was thinking more along the lines of a bag of sandwiches, some bottled waters, and a can of Off."

"Off? The insect repellant?"

"Yeah, for ticks and chiggers. The great outdoors, Alvin. We'll be roughing it for a little while."

"My idea of roughing it is a hotel without room service," Alvin said. "But ticks and chiggers? I might be having some second thoughts here, bro."

"Let's call it a night, Alvin. I need some sleep."

"Tell me something, J.D.. Do the more politically correct white people down here call them *chigroes*?"

I didn't reply to that.

CHAPTER THIRTY-SEVEN

The next morning I was at the hospital early and with a good night's rest behind me. I had undoubtedly needed it and felt like a new man. When I walked into Kelly's room, I found a nurse with a syringe in her hand, apparently about to feed it into Kelly's IV. She must have heard me enter because she quickly turned her head and looked at me over her shoulder as if I'd startled her. Then, she straightened up and without speaking walked by me and out of the room. I stood and watched her disappear down the hall. *Odd*, I thought. If she'd actually emptied the needle into the IV, I didn't see it her do it.

She wasn't one of Kelly's regular nurses. I would have remembered her. She was quite attractive and shapely, with long dark hair and piercing blue eyes. But I usually wasn't here this early, so maybe she was a night nurse still on duty.

I sat and held Kelly's hand for about an hour. She seemed unchanged, which to Dr. Mathis' optimistic view was a good thing. Stabilization indicated normalcy and was why he was planning to bring her out of her medically induced coma soon.

\#

I called Alvin on the way back to Pickens County and the *Clarion*.

"Yo," he answered, breathing hard.

"What did I interrupt?" I was almost afraid to ask.

"Just finished my morning run. It's nice out here in the country. At home, I'd be dodging cars all the way, but here I just have to dodge the occasional roadkill."

"I'm going into the *Clarion* until the afternoon sometime, then I'll come by your place to pick you up and we'll go junkyard spying. Wear something appropriate. Preferably dark, for nighttime."

"There's a dress code for junkyards?"

"Just wear something you don't mind getting dirty. We might take a stroll through the junkyard at some point, if we can get in there."

"No problem, Cosmo says a well-dressed traveler is ready for any occasion. I got a junkyard suit in my bag, right next to the tuxedo."

"You read *Cosmopolitan*?"

"Got several girlfriends who read it in bed, if they can get the time," he said. I felt him grin over the telephone.

#

Eloise still hadn't come in when I arrived at the *Clarion*. She called and said she'd been in touch with a claims adjuster from the insurance company, and yes, there was a clause that covered vandalism and malicious mischief, and there was nothing that said gunshot damage was excluded. She was meeting the man at Still Hollow at noon. She'd arranged a builder to be there too, for replacing the windows and repairing the bullet holes as soon as possible.

Eloise expected Mackenzie and me to pitch-in on the cleanup and everything else, including the repainting. I decided to wait until later to make a case to have it all done through insurance and this contractor. Painting wasn't my thing. Eloise was caught up in the activity of getting things back to normal, and it seemed to be lifting her spirits, so I decided to leave it alone for now.

There were no fires to put out at the paper, and everything seemed to be under control and running smoothly, starting the march toward next week's edition. At a big-city daily, there was never a slow moment like this. I found myself liking the pace of a small-town weekly.

This week's issue had gone out without a hitch, and I'd read it cover to cover several times. Again, I had to admit I was proud of it, the first for me as a hands-on publisher, and I thought of Grandfather again. I'd finally fulfilled his wishes for me to take over the *Clarion*, although it would be short-lived. As soon as Kelly was back to a hundred percent, I'd be back in Atlanta—if there was a job waiting for me.

Vickie had done an excellent job with the story of Kelly, and I was proud of her too, despite her aversion to following orders. The girl had writing chops. Even Mackenzie had a piece in it, and her writing had surprised me. It was a human-interest thing on a local beloved high school teacher who was retiring.

Joanne McKinney had just turned in a story about a City Council meeting where two aldermen got into a dust-up over finances that almost came to blows, and it wasn't bad. I was sitting at my desk making a few small edits to it when Mrs. Mozingo buzzed me.

"I've got a Doctor Michael Stefans on the line for you."

I punched the button.

Stefans said, "I was thinking about you, Mr. Bragg, and wanted to give you an opportunity to learn more about what we doctors are trying to do about the opioid crisis in our area, if you are still interested in the subject. It might give you something else to write about. I'm just down the road at the County Tax Assessor's office dealing with a tax matter, and just minutes away, so if you are free, let me buy you lunch and I will tell you about it."

"Lunch sounds good," I said.

Anything more that I could learn about the area's drug situation could be a subject for a *Clarion* story—whether I wrote it, or handed it over to someone else. I was, after all, running a newspaper at the moment.

He asked, "Is there a good place nearby? I do not know Pickens all that well."

"The Gatehouse Restaurant. Good place for salads and sandwiches, among other things. It's just around the corner."

"How about in thirty minutes?" he said.

I agreed, and he rang off.

#

Doctor Stefans was seated at a booth along a wall and studying a menu when I arrived. We shook hands across the table as I sat down.

"How is Ms. Mayfield?" he asked.

"Still in the induced coma, but the doctors plan to bring her out of it soon."

"That sounds like good news. It means the swelling on her brain is going down. You said she suffered acute physical trauma. What is her doctor's prognosis? I do not mean to scare you, but depending on the severity of her injury, there can be lingering or even permanent brain impairment. Everything from loss of memory to diminished function."

He didn't mean to scare me, but he damn-well did, and I found it insensitive of him. I still hadn't told him how Kelly got hurt and had no urge to do it now. If this was an example of his bedside manner, he sucked at it.

"As far as I know, she's going to be perfectly fine," I said.

He said, "Before we get down to why I wanted to talk to you, let us order first if that is okay. There was a line at the tax office and I am running a little late, but I had to eat. I am famished. I have already moved my morning appointments to the afternoon, and if I make them wait even longer, I will have an office full of disgruntled patients on my hands."

"Fine by me," I said, as I motioned to the waitress.

Once we'd ordered, Stefans said, "The reason I wanted to have lunch with you was to tell you about our monthly meeting of the South Carolina Medical Association in Greenville early next week. I thought you might want to attend. It is a private meeting, but I can get you in. The subject of discussion this month will be about how we doctors can better address this opioid crisis. Given the interest your newspaper has taken in the matter, there might be something newsworthy for you there. There will be up-to-date reports on the current status of it, a discussion of a doctor's responsibilities, and the law as it pertains to both doctors and the drug companies. I guess you know that the government now has lawsuits against them?"

"Yes, I'm aware of that," I said. "Thanks for the information and the offer, Doctor Stefans. If I can't make it myself, would it be all right to send one of my reporters?"

"Why yes, as I told you and Ms. Mayfield, anything I can do to help bring attention to this egregious problem, I will gladly do. I will have someone from my office contact you with the details, and have passes available for you there."

"Thank you again, Doctor," I said, wondering how much of his determination to help was driven by guilt that he, like so many other well-meaning doctors like him, was a birther of this opioid crisis by prescribing them to their patients in the first place.

Doctor Stefans and I finished our lunch with small talk and parted ways.

CHAPTER THIRTY-EIGHT

On the way back to the *Clarion*, I kept feeling a vague sense of familiarity with Doctor Stefans. I was sure we'd never met before my visit to his office, but he reminded me of *someone*. Then it came to me. It wasn't his looks that were familiar. It was the way he spoke. He reminded me of an old fraternity brother from college. They both spoke with the same meticulous speech pattern, pronouncing their words with a kind of overdone precision. And neither used contractions. Both said, "do not" rather than "don't," and "cannot" instead of "can't."

At first, I'd thought that my old frat brother, who came from a very wealthy family, was a stuffed-shirt, and I didn't like him much. After I got to know him, he told me why he spoke that way. As a child, he stuttered, and his parents sent him to a speech therapist who gave him speech fluency exercises. It cured his stutter, but he never got over the fear that it would return. So he continued to speak in that manner, and it became the norm for him. He and I eventually became friends and still were, keeping in touch with Christmas and birthday cards. His stutter never returned.

Was Doctor Stefans a stutterer as a kid, or was he just pretentious? I'd put my money on the latter. He *was* a rather humorless man who took himself very seriously—which could include the way he spoke.

Later that afternoon, I picked Alvin up at his place, and we got what we needed to stake out the Dollar's junkyard at a convenience store in Central. We drove back past the junkyard about a half-mile and found a semi-hidden place to park off the two-lane blacktop. With the binoculars from the Jeep's glove box, a six-pack of bottled waters, several candy bars, insect spray, and a half-dozen pre-packaged pimento cheese sandwiches, we headed toward the wooded area on the rise behind the junkyard.

First, we had to make our way through an open field, out of sight from the Dollar compound. The field was someone's old farmland, now fallow and overgrown with weeds, broom straw, and small bastard pine trees. We would be easy to spot until we made the tree line. If anyone was looking, I didn't see them.

Once we made the top of the ridge, I found the tree, a tall, broad oak with a hunting blind sitting about twenty-five feet up, nestled like a treehouse between three thick limbs that spread into a fork.

What looked like green-painted sheets of aluminum roofing covered the blind, sides and top, with small windows cut in the walls to look down on any prey. From underneath, I could see that the floor was built of two by fours and plywood, and from where I stood looked reasonably sturdy. I hoped I was right.

The wooden ladder that led up to it, nailed to the side of the enormous old oak, wasn't in the same shape. The steps were weathered and rotting, and I wondered if the ladder would support the weight of two big guys like Alvin and me.

We had to try. I couldn't see any other spot that would allow such a bird's eye view right down into the confines of the junkyard. Alvin lost the coin flip and went first. He made it up with only one rung of the old ladder crumbling away underfoot. I broke another one, and the ladder seemed to be about to come away from the tree, but I made it too. I guessed we'd worry about getting down when the time came.

The blind was barely large enough for both of us. The structure creaked and groaned, and leaned a bit. There were two rusted, folding chairs there, and we sat in them, shoulder to shoulder, facing the junkyard below. I hadn't fallen out of a tree since I was a boy, and I wasn't keen on doing it again. Alvin seemed to be enjoying himself probably because there weren't too many trees for a kid to climb on the Southside of Chicago. Or deer blinds.

We set about watching the rambling junkyard, passing the binoculars back and forth. I could make out strings of lights strung on poles weaving through the yard, and if the Dollars turned them on at night, perhaps we'd still be able to see what was going on down there after the sun went down. We'd just have to wait to see.

I took a closer look at the dwellings. We still didn't know for sure if the Dollars were manufacturing drugs here. If they were, it had to be someplace not easily seen. The two-story farmhouse in the middle of the lot was weather-beaten, but looked livable. It had junk on the wide front porch—an old refrigerator with a round top sat and a stack of worn tires. Pots of blooming flowers hanging around the eaves revealed a woman's touch, most likely

Wade Dollar's wife. Since fentanyl was such a dangerous drug, I didn't think they would have it inside a house where a family lived.

There were three small houses and the single-wide trailer scattered throughout the yard, at various distances from each other and the big house. Two of the smaller homes and the trailer looked lived-in, one house looked vacant. Maybe this was the lab.

There was a motorcycle and a pickup truck parked in front of the single-wide, which made me think that it might be Sonny's pad. The big house had another pickup and the two livable small homes had vehicles parked by them, too—one a black SUV with dark tinted windows. Had I seen the plate number, either while we were being chased or at the drive-by at Still Hollow, we would have had these guys nailed.

"Somebody down there is doing well," I said to Alvin and handed him the binoculars. "All the vehicles are late models. That black truck by the mobile home is a Ford F-150 Raptor and goes for over fifty grand."

"Get the fuck out of here," Alvin said. "Who would pay fifty-K for a pickup truck?"

"Somebody with the money. And the SUV is a new Ford Explorer. I looked at those when I'd briefly considered trading in my trusty Jeep. I quickly learned I couldn't afford it."

Alvin studied the vehicles. "The Explorer looks like the one that chased us. And that Harley can run you thirty to forty. You think you can make that kind of scratch running this junkyard?"

"I'd say it'd be doubtful."

"So, somebody's got some supplemental income coming in."

"Could be from the Tiger's Tail, I suppose. If the Dollars are the off-the-books owners."

"Or if they're running a shitload of drugs," Alvin said, completing my thoughts.

A pickup truck pulling into the office out front caught my attention. I took the glasses back from Alvin and watched. A guy in coveralls got out, and a man I assumed to be Wade Dollar came out of the office, followed by his son Benny. The three of them walked over to the bay where Benny had the engine on the hoist. We watched as they rolled the hoist out of the bay and placed it so the engine hovered over the bed of the pickup truck. Wade and the man stood talking and gesturing, haggling over the price of the motor. They must have reached an agreement, because the man pulled out a wallet on a chain from his back pocket, counted out some bills and handed them to Wade. Benny ratcheted the engine down into the bed of the truck, unhooked the chains from the hoist, and the man drove away.

A little later, another customer came and went, leaving with what looked to be a four-barreled carburetor.

As the sun got a little closer to the horizon, Sonny Dollar came out of the single-wide, saddled up, and rode away on his chopper. He was probably on his way to the Tiger's Tail. A cold beer from there would be pretty good right now, I thought. I was drinking lukewarm bottled water. Alvin had grown quiet, every bit as bored as I was, I suspected. This whole idea had all the earmarks of a wasted effort.

A woman carrying several full plastic garbage bags came out of the old farmhouse. I took her for Wade Dollar's wife, but it was just a guess. A kid about five or six walked with her, holding a big yellow cat in his arms, a grandchild perhaps. From what Bagwell and Underwood said, the whole extended Dollar family lived within the compound, each owning their particular plot of land. The woman placed the bags in a big rusty oil drum and set the contents on fire.

I watched as the kid with the cat wandered over to stand by a chain-length pen, which held two full-grown Doberman Pinschers.

I nudged Alvin. He'd seen them too.

"The *real* junkyard dogs," he said.

The dogs began barking wildly at the cat—we could hear them from where we sat. The cat jumped out of the boy's arms, arched its back, hair on end, took a couple of defensive stiff-legged side steps like cats do, and bared its teeth at the dogs. I couldn't hear the cat over the dogs. It was obviously yowling and spitting at them, holding its ground.

I heard Alvin chuckle.

"Junkyard *cat* too," he said.

The cat finally ran off, the boy chasing after it.

A man came out of the small house where the SUV was parked, walked over and stood looking at the dogs, who were still barking. He said or did something that quieted them down. It was Laverne Dollar. He wore a cowboy hat and boots, and even from this distance he radiated a palpable menace.

As he walked away, the boy's cat came out from somewhere and joined him. The dogs started up again. The cat followed Dollar, winding back and forth between his legs as he walked. Dollar stopped and picked it up, holding it in his arms and scratching its ears. As he went by the blazing garbage drum, the flames now roaring three feet into the air, he tossed the cat at the fire with all the casualness of someone chucking in a piece of litter. The cat did a mid-air somersault, kicked off the rim of the drum and raced off. Without missing a step Dollar continued on his way.

"Mother-fucker ," Alvin said, looking at me in amazement. Did he just try to throw that cat in the fire?"

I looked at Alvin, not believing what I'd just seen either. I had the binoculars, and there was no mistaking it.

"I'm afraid so," I said.

"That's cold, man," Alvin said. "Cold."

"And then some," I added, lifting the glasses and watching Laverne Dollar.

CHAPTER THIRTY-NINE

Laverne Dollar walked into the interior of the junkyard along a footpath that lay between the plethora of auto carcasses, a rusting and weed-punched history of Detroit. There were the beetle-back shapes of the forties, the fins and two-tones of the fifties and sixties, and the misshapen, damaged remains from all eras, symbolizing injury, death and wreckage on America's highways. Somehow the presence of Laverne Dollar walking through them struck me as appropriate. He was like some sinister acolyte of death and destruction, visiting his handiwork.

Dollar disappeared from sight. He'd walked behind a six-car stack of wrecks and simply vanished. I watched for a few minutes, and he never came out on the other side.

"What's he doing behind there?" I asked.

"I don't know, but he's got company," Alvin said. "Look to your right."

A young woman was coming down the same path. She was walking briskly like she knew where she was going. She had short bleach-blonde hair and was dressed in tight jeans and a low-cut blouse. She looked pretty from the distance.

"Who the hell is that?" Alvin said, as much to himself.

"The sister, maybe. Bagwell said she was divorced and living there. I didn't see where she came from."

I handed Alvin the glasses. "Did you see her in the Tiger's Tail?"

"No," Alvin said. "I would have remembered. She's hot."

I didn't comment, but she *was* hot, in a trailer-trash way. We watched her go behind the stack of junk cars where we'd lost Laverne Dollar. She didn't come out either.

"They got *something* going on back there," Alvin said, handing me back the glasses.

"I don't think they're removing car parts to sell," I said, and turned the binoculars to my right, examining the trees along the ridge.

"What are you looking at?"

"Another tree to climb. We need a vantage point to give us a look behind that stack of wrecks where they disappeared."

Alvin stared in the direction I was looking.

"Do you see that large tree in the middle of a stand of young pines?" I asked. "About forty yards down? It has spreading branches low enough to reach, and looks sturdy enough to hold the weight of a man."

"Got it," Alvin said.

"I think I can climb that. You stay here and keep an eye out for them if they reappear before I can get up in that tree."

Alvin just nodded.

I made it out of the blind and onto the ground without breaking another rung on the ladder. Using the trees as cover from anyone in the junkyard, I was at the base of the big tree in a couple of minutes. I stood and looked up into its canopy. It was a perfect tree to climb and for some dumb reason, my mind went back to my eleventh grade English class and a Longfellow poem we had to memorize. "Under a spreading chestnut-tree, the village smithy stands," it went. Only, I wasn't a blacksmith, and I was pretty sure this was an oak.

I climbed four levels of branches before I could see what I wanted to see; a clear view of the path behind the wall of junked cars. I'd hoped to see Laverne Dollar and his sister there, but they weren't. There were no forks in the trail, no sheds or buildings they could have gone into. So, where the hell were they? I scanned the lot and didn't see them anywhere else. Even if they had come out while I was making my way to the tree, they should still be walking somewhere. I didn't think they could have come out and made it back to their houses in that short amount of time.

I searched the path again through my binoculars. It ran straight past the solid wall of old automobiles without any gap between them. There was obviously something here that we were missing. I headed back to the blind.

#

We stayed in the blind until well after the sun went down. The few lights mounted on poles came on with most of them situated around the houses. The area where Laverne Dollar and his assumed sister had disappeared remained in darkness, and as far as we could see, they never reappeared.

We'd watched Wade Dollar and his son close-up shop and release the two Dobermans. They now had a free run of the yard. I was surprised that they were trusted not to get out through the dilapidated fence that surrounded the place. Either they were well-trained, or the fence was more secure than it appeared. Was it wired all the way around with an electrical charge at the bottom?

The dogs found what appeared to be their nighttime home near the fence on our side, lying down in a couple of hollowed-out depressions in the ground beneath the bed of an old rusty truck. They remained alert, I could see, periodically raising their heads in unison and turning their gazes at whatever noise or distraction got their attention. Occasionally they would go investigate, but would always return to their spot beneath the truck.

Alvin and I had eaten all our cheese sandwiches and drunk all our water, and I was having a difficult time staying awake. I was wondering whether to call it a day or not, when the dogs went on alert and raced off in the direction where Laverne Dollar and his sister had vanished.

In the dim lights, two people come out from behind the wall of junk cars and head up the path. The dogs were by their side, following along with them.

"What the fuck?" Alvin said.

We watched as they slowly walked side by side toward the smaller houses. They went under the lights as they got nearer, and we could clearly see that it was Laverne Dollar and the woman. She went inside one house, and Laverne in the other. That had to make her the sister, I thought. The dogs hung around for a moment, then returned to their nighttime watch-point.

"They been gone for at least six hours," Alvin said. "So, where they been?"

I couldn't prove it, but I was pretty sure I knew. "Probably mixing up and pressing out a fresh batch of pills," I said, and grinned at Alvin.

"*Underground*," he said. "The lab is fucking underground."

"And the entrance is behind that stack of wrecks somewhere."

He was grinning now too. "Can't nobody outsmart a couple of sharp mother-fuckers like us."

I said, "We've got to get in there. Find the entrance and prove it."

"We'll need to do something about them dogs first," Alvin said.

"A tranquilizer and a half-pound of hamburger should do the trick."

"How you gonna' get that?"

"I usually get my hamburger from the supermarket. You know a better place?"

"The tranquilizers, wiseass."

"I know a guy. I'll go see him tomorrow."

"So, we go in tomorrow night?

"Yeah. We'll watch them for a few hours first, so we know exactly what we're getting into."

We closed up our stake-out shop and went back to my Jeep. I took Alvin home to his rental, and I headed to Still Hollow. I didn't hear Alvin complaining about ticks or chiggers, so he probably went to bed a happy camper.

A day spent up a tree in a cramped deer blind could be very tiring. An hour later I was fast asleep.

CHAPTER FORTY

It was Saturday morning, and I sat by Kelly's bed, trying my damnedest to maintain a positive outlook. Doctor Mathis had dropped by and said he was still pleased with her improving condition and planned to bring her out of the coma either Monday or Tuesday. That was a bright point, along with my belief that I had a handle on who did this to her. I hoped that after Alvin and I went inside the Dollar junkyard tonight, I'd have evidence to tie the Dollars to it. I wouldn't give up until I did.

I'd agreed to pick up Alvin late-afternoon to resume our stakeout position in the deer blind before we went in after dark. Alvin and I had decided that the old farmhouse, the single-wide, or the small houses wouldn't be where they would have their opioid lab.

According to Vickie's research, manufacturing these kinds of drugs was extremely dangerous. They could kill a person just by handling some of the ingredients. People lived in this trailer and these houses. Surely, the Dollars weren't that crazy. Also, it would be too easy for the cops to detect drugs if they could ever get a search warrant. Especially if they brought in drug dogs, which the DEA would. But could you seal off an underground lab tightly enough to remain undetected by the dogs? I didn't know. And if we couldn't find it, maybe the dogs couldn't either—another reason to find the entrance. My gut screamed at me that it was behind that wall of old cars somewhere.

We still needed to take care of the dogs at the junkyard. The first thing I'd done that morning was to call Doctor Earnest Whitmore, a veterinarian I knew. Whitmore was an honest and ethical man, beyond reproach, but I was going to ask him to break the law for me.

I hoped once he heard about what happened to Kelly, and why I needed an animal tranquilizer to find her assailants, his sense of right and wrong would supersede the law.

I planned to spend a while longer sitting by Kelly and holding her hand, then pay Whitmore a visit. I wasn't sure holding Kelly's hand did her any good, it was mostly for me. The warmth of her hand reminded me that even in her condition, she was still with me.

#

An hour later, I pulled in by Dr. Whitmore's office at the back of his home near a stable. A young man was walking a horse around a small circular track to one side. The horse wore a splint on a leg. They didn't shoot all horses that broke their legs, I guessed. I went inside to find the distinguished figure of Dr. Whitmore sitting behind a small, cluttered desk. His full head of silver hair was even more silver, if that was possible.

He came around the desk to greet me.

"Mr. Bragg, it's good to see you. I hope you're here under less-unfortunate circumstances than those that brought you here a year ago. The horse community here still hasn't gotten over those events."

His gaze settled on my eyes as if he were trying to read the reason I'd come to visit him.

I said, "I've come to ask you a favor. I want you to give me something to tranquilize two dogs. Adult Dobermans."

He frowned at my request and took his seat back behind his desk. I took the chair across from him.

"Why do you want to tranquilize them?"

"I need them to sleep for an hour or so," I said.

"I thought you lived in Atlanta. Have you moved up here?"

"No, I'm staying over in Pickens County for a while."

"I can give you the name of a good vet over there who can treat your pets, if you'd like. As you know, my specialty is horses."

"These dogs don't belong to me," I said, and saw his frown deepen. "Do you have a few minutes to listen to a story?"

He said he did.

"You need to tell this to the police," he said, when I'd finished. "Not to me."

"I have. But they need probable cause to search the junkyard, and I think I can get it for them. And I need to get into their junkyard without being seen. Two Dobermans stand in my way."

"It would be illegal to give you what you want," he said.

"I know that, Doctor Whitmore. Believe me when I say I don't want to hurt these dogs. I don't want them hurting me either. I hope you trust me enough by now to know I'd never tell anyone where I got anything."

"I would know," he said.

"I could easily get something off the street, but I don't want to do that. I wouldn't know what I was getting, or how much to give the dogs. I don't want to harm them, I just want them to go night-night for a while. I love animals, but I don't want to get eaten by one. These are real junkyard dogs I'm talking about here. And it's a good thing I'm trying to do, not a bad thing."

Whitmore got up and went to a cabinet. He brought back a glassine envelope containing pills.

"Six tablets, three per dog," he said. "Enough to put them out for an hour or so. Crush them up into something the dogs would eat and give it to them. They should go down in just a minute or two."

"Thank you, Dr. Whitmore," I said, shaking his hand, and left with the tranquilizers before he could change his mind.

#

Back at Still Hollow I spent some time checking out the repairs on the place. Eloise had really cracked the whip on her construction guys. I couldn't tell that the place had looked like a block of swiss cheese just a few days ago with bullet holes everywhere you looked. I almost felt guilty that I hadn't pitched in and helped. Almost. They had done a great job.

Alvin called. He'd gotten bored earlier and staked out Doughboy's pad just to see how he spent his day.

"How'd you know where he lived?" I asked.

"I followed him home from the Tiger's Tail the other night. He lives in an apartment on the outskirts of town. And guess who showed up at his door?"

He didn't wait for me to guess.

"Sonny Dollar. Driving that muscled-up black Ford pickup from the junkyard. He came bearing a package. And left without it."

"Pills," I said.

"Well, it wasn't Doughboy's laundry. Right after Sonny left, Doughboy hit the road. I didn't follow him. I'm sure he was making his rounds, doling out his drugs. So, we still going into the junkyard tonight?"

I told him about getting the tranquilizers.

"Ain't gonna hurt them, is it?" Alvin asked.

"The doc' says they'll just go to sleep like babies."

"Good, don't want to be hurting them. These dogs just doin' what they do."

It amazed me that someone so prone to violence could, at times, be so tender-hearted. I guess like beauty, compassion was also in the eye of the beholder.

I said, "I'll pick you up about six. Sometime after dark, we'll take care of the dogs, and go in. So, dress for stealth."

"I told you I pack for all occasions, bro, which includes a nice little all-black ensemble that's perfect for this occasion."

"You're always a step ahead of me, Alvin. I had to stop by a Walmart and buy mine."

"Be prepared or get fucked, is my motto. Just like the Boy Scouts."

As an ex-Boy Scout, I didn't remember that being the exact wording. But I guess it was close enough.

"I'll see you later," I said.

CHAPTER FORTY-ONE

Alvin and I sat in the blind until the sun went down and the junkyard was cast in darkness. If there was an underground lab behind the wall of junk cars and there was anyone in it, they had gone in before we got there. There had been no activity while we sat there, other than Sonny Dollar leaving again on his Harley, and Wade Dollar closing up the office. Benny didn't seem to be working with his dad this afternoon. We didn't see him, or anyone else while we were there. Wade had released the dogs as he'd gone to the big house and they were in their night-time home near the fence on our side, lying beneath the bed of the old rusty truck.

We finally got down out of our perch and made out way to the fence near where the dogs lay. They growled as I peeked through a small gap in the fence boards. They weren't looking directly at me, but their heads were raised, and they had obviously heard or sensed my presence. Thankfully, they weren't barking.

I opened the grocery bag I'd brought with two balls of doctored hamburger in it and tossed them over the fence in front of the Dobermans, far enough apart so that one dog couldn't rush out and get to both of them before the other one got his share. It came off perfectly. They came out from underneath the truck, each hesitantly examining the hamburger, at first with suspicion, then recognition of something to eat. They gobbled down the meat like they hadn't been fed lately. And from what I'd seen of the Dollar's treatment of animals—Laverne Dollar and the cat—they probably hadn't.

I stayed and watched from my peep-hole and after about five minutes both dogs were asleep, one of them actually snoring. I gave them a couple more minutes, then motioned to Alvin. Before we climbed over the fence, I pointed to the thin wire that ran along the base of it. I was right about the fence being electrified to keep the dogs in.

Once over the fence, we headed toward the wall of wrecks. We found our destination easily and stood in the path between the walls looking for anything that could be an entrance to an underground room. Nothing stood out to either of us. The path didn't fork back there, there were no small buildings, obvious trap doors, or cellar or storm doors visible. Nothing.

Alvin took the right side, and I took the left, looking between the rusting hulks of the cars. Alvin got my attention and pointed to a gap he'd found between two of the cars. I walked over and looked at it. It was just large enough for someone to squeeze through and led out of sight into the shadows behind the car bodies.

Alvin was down on one knee examining the earth leading into it with one of the cheap compact flashlights I'd bought us at Walmart. I bent and looked over his shoulder. The ground through the gap was well-traveled, but I wasn't sure it was from humans, or from the junkyard dogs.

Alvin pointed at himself and then at the opening. He then pointed at me and the other wall, and I got the message. He wanted to check out the gap, while I should keep examining the other side. We didn't have much time before the dogs would be up and around again, so I nodded. He disappeared through the gap, and I went back to the other wall.

I pushed at the cars on the bottom row of wrecks to see if maybe one would swing away to reveal a trap door beneath, but none of them moved. All I did was make a loud squeaking noise when I pushed on the rear end of an old Buick. I stood still and listened for a moment, but if anyone had heard it, they didn't seem to be coming. At least that's what I hoped as I continued my close inspection of the area.

Suddenly, I heard a creaking noise behind me. I turned to see the trunk lid of the Buick raise up, and Laverne Dollar emerge as if ascending the stairs from hell. He was holding a pistol pointed directly at my heart. He stood aside and motioned for me to get in the trunk.

"After you, Mother-fucker," he said.

I'd found the lab. Unless Alvin had returned and was watching Laverne take me, he would have no idea where I'd gone.

CHAPTER FORTY-TWO

With his gun at my back Laverne Dollar pointed me down a short set of narrow wooden stairs, closing the Buick's trunk lid behind us. At the bottom was a small room with a dirt floor, a table and chairs taking up most of the space. An automatic bill counter, one that counts and bands the bills into stacks, sat on the table. Surrounding it was a large pile of loose cash, and a gym bag half full of banded stacks of money, $10,000 stamped on each band. I'd obviously caught Laverne Dollar counting the take.

Beyond the table there was another room with the door standing open. The woman I presumed to be Dollar's sister stood in the doorway, looking at me. A white respirator mask hung beneath her chin, and she wore elbow-length latex gloves. I could see a table along a wall behind her with something on it that could have been a pill press. Shelves above it contained what looked like supplies. I'd never seen one, but this was what I'd expect an opioid drug lab to look like.

"Come help me Delilah," he said to his sister, and motioned with his gun for me to sit in one of the chairs. It was the first time I'd heard the sister's name. *Delilah*. Samson's downfall in the Bible. *Befitting*, I thought. She was about to help with my downfall.

Laverne took a roll of duct tape from one of the shelves, handed the gun to his sister, and began taping me to the chair. No one had spoken a word yet, so I broke the silence.

"You need to think very carefully before you do something you'll regret," I said to Laverne.

"Any regrets will be yours," Laverne said. "All I've done is catch a trespasser on my property. I got the legal right to blow that trespasser's fuckin' head off if I want."

As Laverne taped my ankles and arms to the straight-backed chair, the woman leaned against the door-jam and gazed at me. She was quite pretty, as I'd thought when we saw her from the distance. I suddenly realized that she looked familiar for another reason. She was the nurse I'd found in Kelly's hospital room, who fled when I caught her about to give Kelly a shot. Only then, she was a brunette.

I turned my attention back to Laverne Dollar. He was standing by my chair, frowning at me as if contemplating what to do with me. There was a deadness to his light-blue, hooded eyes that suggested whatever he would do, I wouldn't like it. He had tattoos, like Sonny, but Laverne's weren't as artfully done. Jailhouse tats, I guessed.

"Nice place you got here," I said. "You dig it yourself?"

"My grandpa built it a long time ago. Storm shelter. He was a-feared of tornadoes."

"So, what now?"

"First, you gonna' answer my questions."

"And if I don't?"

"You will," he said and grinned. He put on a pair of thick leather work gloves. It made him even more menacing if that were possible.

"Then ask your questions, and we'll see," I said, trying to sound tough. Inside, I was anything but. I was in a bad predicament.

"First question, why the fuck are you here?"

I looked about the room. "Looking for this place. Thanks for showing it to me."

"How'd you know it was even here?"

"I didn't, until you stepped out of that Buick."

"So, why were you standing right there when I came out?"

"Blind luck," I said.

He punched me in the face, filling my vision with shooting stars.

"Why were you standing right there?" he asked again.

I didn't see any reason not to tell him. I probably couldn't get into any worse trouble.

"I've been watching you from the hill behind the yard. I saw you go behind this particular stack of old cars, and you didn't come out. I figured there was something back here. So, I came to see what."

"Who knows you're here?"

"Nobody."

He hit me again.

"That's the truth," I said, when I was able, the bells ringing in my head.

"How's that girlfriend of yours?" he asked. "We should have finished that job. But we're gonna' remedy that."

I realized that Laverne had just confessed to Kelly's assault, but I might never get the chance to tell anyone about it. And they would go after Kelly again. The thought of that, I couldn't handle. Somehow I needed to find a way to warn somebody.

"You been talking to the cops about this?" he asked.

"I don't talk to cops," I managed to say, still a bit punch-drunk. It wasn't the answer he was looking for. He hit me again.

"Do the cops know about this place?"

I said, "Obviously they don't. Or they would have been standing outside the old Buick and not me." He seemed to buy that. He didn't hit me again.

I heard the trunk door over our heads open and footsteps clamber down the stairs. I turned to see Sonny Dollar, one wrist in a thick white cast and held up in front of him to keep from banging it against the walls of the tight stairwell. He was holding a paper bag in his other hand. He stopped in his tracks and stared at me tied to the chair.

"Whoa," he said. "What's *he* doin' here?"

Laverne said, "I caught him poking around the Buick. I don't know why the dogs weren't raisin' hell. He must have silenced them somehow. He was by hisself as far as I could see. You didn't see nobody out there when you came in?"

"Not a soul. It's all quiet."

"He says the cops don't know about this place," Laverne said.

They were talking about me as if I wasn't in the room. A bad sign.

"You don't believe him, do you?" Sonny said.

"I think I do," Laverne said. "I think he's just like his girlfriend. He stumbles around like a blind squirrel looking for acorns, but ends up sticking his nose in a yellow jacket's nest. I ain't taking any chances though, so we gonna' move the lab until we find out if anybody else does know about it. If they don't, we can come back."

"Let *me* ask him," Sonny said.

"Later," Laverne said eyeing the bag in Sonny's hand. "Is that dinner?"

"Cheeseburgers from the *T-Tail*," Sonny said.

"Then let's eat, we got a lot to do."

Sonny passed out the burgers, they took seats around me and I watched as they ate.

"Sorry we ain't got one for you, asshole," Sonny said to me. "But you'll be having a knuckle sandwich later. I owe you for this," he added, holding up his bandaged wrist.

Delilah giggled, and leered at me. "Don't mess his face up too much, Sonny, he's pretty."

"She was as sick as her brothers, I thought.

Laverne said, "He ain't gonna' be around long enough to do what you're thinking, so get it out of your head, you dirty little bitch."

Delilah stuck out her lower lip, pretending to pout. "Y'all don't *never* let me have any fun," she said.

They finished eating and Laverne turned to Delilah. "You go on back there and start packing things up. Sonny, go help her."

"I got something I want to do in here first," Sonny said.

He got up and stood in front of me.

"Okay hotshot, I'm giving you one chance to tell me if the cops know about this place. You don't give me a straight answer, and you gonna' get some payback from that sucker punch you gave me the other night."

"Sucker punch?" I said. "You came at me with my back turned."

I saw Laverne glance up at his brother and grin.

"Is that right, Sonny boy?" Laverne said. "You try to sucker punch this boy and he still got the best of you? And you let that black feller break your arm. Thank God your brothers ain't alive to see this. Mama must have stepped out on Daddy to have you. You can't be a Dollar."

"Don't go callin' me a bastard, Laverne."

"If the shoe fits, little brother, wear it."

"You gonna' be the one wearin' a shoe. Mine. Up-side your head."

It dawned on me that I was listening to a six-foot-three redneck biker thug and a fifty year-old homicidal manic exchanging brotherly banter like a couple of schoolyard adolescents. How the hell did these two guys successfully run an opioid manufacturing and distribution operation the size and scope of this one? What was I missing here?

"Fuck you, Laverne," Sonny was saying, and turned his attention back to me. "And fuck you too," he said, and punched me in the jaw. The bells rang again, playing the same tune as when Laverne hit me, but not nearly as loudly. I remembered that Sonny had held his gun in his right hand, which was now with a broken wrist. He hit me with his left, and the punch was weak, but I pretended that he knocked me out, dropping my chin to my chest. It seemed like the best way to defend myself from another punch.

"Damn, Sonny," Laverne said. "You don't understand the principle here. You hurt him to *get* him to talk. You don't hurt him so he *can't* talk."

"He wasn't going to tell us anything anyway," Sonny said.

I let a minute go by pretending I was out cold, and thankfully Sonny seemed to lose interest in me. They had worse things planned for me, and getting beaten to the point where I couldn't at least put up some resistance wasn't what I needed.

"Where we moving to, Laverne?" I heard Sonny ask.

"I was thinking we'd go up to Ray-Ray's old cabin for a while."

"That place still standing? Last time I saw it, it was in pretty bad shape. All grown up around it, big gullies in the road leading up to it."

"That's what makes it a good place. Don't nobody ever go up there. It's been deserted since Ray-Ray stopped keeping it up. We may have to do a little work on it, but I like it looking deserted like that. So, go help Delilah pack things up. I'll take care of what's out here."

Sonny just stood looking at him for a second.

"*Now*, Sonny," Laverne snapped.

Sonny jumped into action like he'd been stuck with a cattle prod.

Laverne said, "Bag it all up. Everything's going with us. And get that Dahlgren Decon decontamination stuff we got and be ready to spray down everything with it. Put on a hazmat suit, and bring me one. Delilah, get yours on too."

CHAPTER FORTY-THREE

I'd been sitting silently for a time, not talking to anyone and no one talking to me. But no more punches to the face, thankfully. The room had almost stopped spinning.

Laverne had finished counting the money and I watched as he began to fill the three gym bags with it. He turned and looked at me, his light blue eyes as cold and clear as a couple of round-cut sapphires. They say you can see a man's soul through his eyes. What I saw through Laverne Dollar's was the emptiness of no soul at all. This man made chills run up my spine.

"Delilah?" he said calling back to his sister. "Fix up an industrial strength cold-shot to go," Laverne called out to his sister. "Mr. Bragg is going with us and I want him walking. He's too damn big to carry. We'll take care of him when we're off somewhere."

He'd said that in a voice totally void of emotion. I knew from Vickie Sayer's research that a cold-shot was a mix of drugs and tap-water, dispensed with a hypodermic syringe. The fact that Laverne had asked for *industrial-strength* sounded lethal, and was probably the same mix Delilah gave Kelly at the hospital. This time it was intended for me.

I was watching through half-lidded eyes as Delilah came out a few minutes later and handed Laverne the hypodermic needle filled with my death sentence. Laverne took it from her and put it into one of the bags with the money.

"You know that decontamination stuff won't clean up all traces of the fentanyl," she said to Laverne. "Should we even bother with it?"

"It might do just enough to keep drug dogs from sniffing out traces of fentanyl if somebody does come looking and gets right up close to the Buick," Laverne said. "They can't prove what they can't find, and we'll let that high-priced Jew lawyer we got handle the rest."

"What about him?" Delilah asked, nodding at me.

We'll let him set there until were ready to go. You and Sonny can begin taking some of that stuff out the back way and putting it in the SUV."

"The back way?" Delilah said raising her voice. "There's spiders and God knows what else in that old tunnel. I don't like going in there. Why can't we take it out this way. Sonny said they ain't nobody out there."

"That tunnel's a lot easier than hauling that stuff up these stairs. Now do what I say."

"We can get Wade and his boy to help us," she said.

"We ain't gettin' Wade to do shit. He don't want anything to do with this, and I don't want him to. So, get on back there. I'll be out to help, directly."

Delilah went back into the other room. Laverne added the last of the cash into a gym bag, and began trying to fit the money counter in on top of it.

For two hours I watched the Dollars, decked out in hazmat suits, continue to box up and remove almost everything in the lab that wasn't nailed down. They'd left the door between the two rooms open, and I could see them as they made multiple trips through a door in the back into a dark tunnel.

I thought of Alvin. He was probably turning the junkyard upside down looking for me. I could see him hanging Wade Dollar by the heels out an upstairs window of the old farmhouse trying to find me. I didn't know where the tunnel came out, but I hoped Alvin would see the Dollars coming and going. He would need to find me soon because the lab was about cleaned out. The only things left were the bags with the money and needle on the table in front of me. Delilah was spraying down the walls and floors with a pump sprayer, harsh chemical fumes from it making my eyes water. It had to be that decontamination solution they talked about. They were close to wrapping up here and taking me out. In more ways than one.

I'd heard Laverne Dollar say that he wanted me walking out with them when they left, because it would be easier than having to haul my lifeless body out with them. Perhaps that would present the best moment to attempt an escape. But with my eminent death in a hypodermic needle in a bag a few feet from me, could I just sit there and risk Laverne changing his mind? They were hauling boxes and equipment out some hidden escape tunnel, why not a body? I thought about the chair I was in. It was sturdy—but it was wood, and wood breaks. If I could ram myself back into the wall behind me, maybe I could break it and somehow get my hands on Laverne's pistol, which he kept tucked in his belt. A long shot, but I had no other ideas or options, and sitting around just waiting for things to happen was not something I did well.

I was gathering up my strength to propel my chair back into the wall when I heard a scrunching metallic sound from above, as if someone was opening the trunk lid. Was the older brother Wade or his son Benny coming to join the party?

It was now or never with the chair, I thought. I thrust backward with all my strength, but my taped ankles wouldn't give me the drive I needed to smash the chair against the wall. I only managed to hit it hard enough to bang the back of my head and leave me dazed and dizzy again.

Then someone yelled, amplified, as if through a bullhorn.

"Sheriff's Department! Come out with your weapons down and your hands up!"

Laverne and Sonny stood frozen. Then in unison they sprang into action. Laverne came out and gathered up two of the gym bags of money from the table.

"Get the other one," he shouted to Sonny, ignoring me. They spun and headed into the back room, shutting the door behind them.

The voice from above came again, announcing that this was the last chance to throw down weapons and come out. I recognized it as Sheriff Arlen Bagwell. The offer didn't last long. Seconds later, a couple of black canisters s came tumbling down the steps, my foggy brain registering the words "flash-bangs" before they exploded and took most of what was left of my coherence.

There was another explosion, this time from the back room of the lab, blowing the separating door off its hinges. Raging flames shot out, blasting me with heat. The lab was an inferno.

Had the Dollars self-immolated themselves? Somehow, I didn't think so. They had gone out the tunnel.

I had no time to think about it as Bagwell and several uniformed deputies in bullet-proof vests and guns came rushing down the steps. The force of the raging fire pushed them back, but they grabbed me, still taped to the chair and with my clothes beginning to smolder, and dragged me up the stairs and out into the cool night, chair and all.

CHAPTER FORTY-FOUR

Outside they took the tape off and had me sit on the ground, away from the black smoke and flames pouring out of the old Buick's open trunk. Bagwell and Alvin hovered around me with deputies and what appeared to be Central town-cops moving busily all around us. Alvin must have seen Laverne take me after all, and called for help. A crazy thought swam through my muddled brain. This had to be the first time in his life that Alvin actually called for the police.

"Who's down there?" Bagwell shouted to me.

"Laverne and Sonny Dollar, and their sister Delilah" I managed to say.

"They didn't get out somehow?"

"Maybe," I said. "There's a tunnel."

Bagwell turned and yelled at one of his deputies. "Escape tunnel! Go find out where it comes out." A half-dozen officers took off in different directions, Bagwell going with them.

"You need medical attention?" Alvin asked. "Looks like you took a couple of licks to the face, and your eyebrows are singed, but I don't see any other burns."

"I'm okay. The fresh air is reviving me."

Alvin was looking at me with a sorrowful face.

"I'm sorry, bro. I let you down. When I came back, you were gone. I went looking for you and was about to go breaking down doors at those houses and getting medieval on somebody when Sonny came riding in on that hog of his. I followed him here."

"You've got nothing to apologize for, Alvin. You're the only reason I'm not shot full of enough fentanyl right now to overdose a rhinoceros. You brought in the cavalry just in time and saved the day. Thanks, bud."

"Yeah, but I should have gotten to you earlier. I watched Sonny unlock the trunk and go down inside it. I tried to follow him, but it locked back when he closed it. I couldn't get in. I was looking around for somethin' to pry it open when I heard them dogs. They were growling like they were coming for my black ass. I went a row over and climbed in an old wrecked school bus I'd seen—still had its doors and windows. I needed a dog-free zone to figure out what to do."

"Damn it, Alvin. You shouldn't have even been thinking about coming after me by yourself. We would probably both be dead right now. That was a heavily armed and crazy bunch down there. Even the sister is scary."

"That's what I finally decided," Alvin said. "I was pissed off, but I ain't no fool. This ain't no movie and I ain't no super-hero. So I called your buddy Sheriff Bagwell. But I couldn't just sit there doing nothing until they showed up. I tore loose the hand-rail at the front of the bus to fend off them dogs and was going to come back out here. My thinking was that if the cops didn't show up real soon, I'd start banging on the Buick to get the

Dollars' attention, hoping to distract them from whatever they might be doing to you. If they came up to see who was banging on the door, I'd use the hand-rail to play a little Whack-a-Mole with them."

I almost laughed at the mental image of that.

"The cops got here quicker than I'd expected. At least one of them did. I saw flashing blue lights coming through the front gate and went to meet it."

"What about the dogs?"

"I found them surrounding a squad car, a lone cop behind the wheel looking out at the dogs like he might shoot them. I was afraid he was the only one coming until I heard a siren off in the distance and realized more were on the way. One of the dogs lunged at me, and I had to bump him on the nose with the hand-rail, and that backed him off a little. I was ready for him to come back at me when he did the damnedest thing. The cop had left the front gate standing wide open, and the dog took off right through it, and the other dog followed. Looks like the Dollars are such detestable shits they don't even merit the loyalty of man's best friend. Them dogs hauled ass at the first chance to get away from them."

It became impossible to talk as a firetruck, lights blinking and siren blaring came up the path and rolled to a stop as near to the fire as they could get. Alvin and I moved out of their way and went to lean against a wreck that didn't look too dirty.

Alvin continued telling me his story. "When the rest of the cops got here, I showed them the way to the Buick, with Bagwell firing questions at me every step of the way. I have to hand it to him though, he and his guys crow-barred the trunk lid and stormed right in. Gutsy fuckers, even if they are peckerwoods."

We watched as the firemen began dragging a hose to the back of the Buick which was still belching smoke and fire. I didn't think there was enough stuff down there to burn like that. What had I missed?

An unmarked, official-looking sedan pulled in behind the firetruck. DEA Agent Underwood got out, glanced in our direction but walked the other way.

I suddenly remembered what Laverne said about Kelly and grabbed Alvin by the arm. "We've got to put someone on Kelly's door at the hospital. Right now. They want to finish the job they started on her. They've already tried once. Yesterday, I caught a nurse in her room about to give her a shot. She took off when I walked in, and I didn't think anything about it. But when I met the Dollar sister tonight, I recognized her as the nurse. She was going to give Kelly the same thing they were about to give me. And Laverne Dollar implied they'll keep going after Kelly until they get the job done."

Alvin thought it over. "Seems to me that they'll forget about Kelly now since you've escaped. What else could she know that you don't after tonight? This bunch's been totally busted. All that's left is rounding the mother-fuckers up."

Alvin had a good point, and it made me think. When Laverne Dollar said what he did, he was convinced I'd never walk out of there alive. But I was still concerned about it.

Alvin saw the worry in my face. "I'll take care of it. We'll get somebody on her room twenty-four-seven until all these mother-fuckers are caught. I can be there part of the time myself."

We saw Bagwell coming toward us. Trailing him was Agent Underwood.

Bagwell said, "They're in the wind. We found the exit to the escape tunnel in a shed up by the big house. It looks like they went out a back gate. According to the brother, Wade, they were driving a black Ford Explorer SUV. We got an APB out on them, and anybody wearing a badge within two hundred miles of here is looking for them."

Underwood was glaring at me.

"You guys are fucking something," he said, "pulling a stunt like this. What you've done here tonight will get any chance of a case we've got thrown out of court. There may be more prosecutable crimes here against *you* than them—breaking and entering, trespassing, cruelty to animals. I ought to lock you up myself."

"You wouldn't *have* a fucking case if J.D. hadn't found this lab," Alvin said. "The Dollars would still be down there making pills while you'd be standing around somewhere, scratching your ass and eatin' Krispy Kremes."

Underwood stood glaring at Alvin, his eyes filled with rage. I fully expected him to arrest him—or at least try. He'd managed to tip Alvin's tipping point, and I wasn't sure Alvin would let him. Whatever was on the Agent's mind to do, he seemed to get over it. He turned and stormed away, cursing.

I asked Bagwell, "Does he have a point? Will the Dollars get off?"

"Anything's possible I guess," Bagwell said, "the way the courts are these days. Agent Underwood has been trying to nail these boys for a long time, and he's just sensitive about anything screwing it up for him. I would need to discuss this with the District Attorney, but you being a reporter and discovering this lab by your journalistic investigation, they can't accuse you of working on behalf of the police, which would be one reason a smart lawyer could get everything found here thrown out in court. We were notified of a possible kidnapping in progress by a man with a legitimate reason to suspect it," he looked at Alvin, "and from there, everything we've done is by the book. Even though the caller was trespassing by being here, and this is private property, we were officially required to investigate. I don't see a problem with it."

I hoped he was right.

"I'm sure Agent Underwood will cool down," Bagwell added. "Especially if, when you write this story, you make sure he and the DEA get some credit. Underwood has his pride."

"I can do that," I said. Bagwell would get his share too. I wouldn't be here if he and his men hadn't responded to Alvin's call so quickly.

Very little smoke was coming out of the Buick now, and what there was had gone from black to white. White smoke meant that the water the fireman was pumping in was doing its job. Two other firemen had brought over a steel ladder from the truck and were placing it down the entrance to the lab. The stairs must have burned away, I thought.

Bagwell, Alvin, and I stood and watched them descend into the lab. I noticed they put on respirator masks before they went in.

I turned back to Bagwell. "You said that Wade Dollar told you what make the get-away car was. Does that mean he's cooperating?"

"He seems to be," Bagwell said. "We got both him and his son Benny in custody, and Wade is claiming he didn't have anything to do with the drugs. He said it was all Laverne, Sonny, and their sister. Says it's been years since he's even been down in that storm shelter, and to beat all, the plot of land the lab is on belongs to Laverne, not him. When their daddy died, he carved up the property and left them each a piece of it. It's what Agent Underwood was saying, remember? So, all Wade may be guilty of is turning a blind eye. And I don't know if there's a law against that. We'll see."

"Sheriff, I overheard Laverne Dollar talking about moving the operation to somewhere called Ray-Ray's cabin. Maybe that's where they went."

"Who is Ray-Ray?"

"I don't know. Somebody they knew at one time, I think. It sounded like he's not even around now. Maybe dead. An old friend or a relative perhaps."

Bagwell said, "By saying that in front of you, I'm assuming they weren't planning on letting you leave there to tell anybody about it."

"You're right about that. Laverne had a lethal dose of fentanyl ready to give me when your men broke in."

"We'll charge them with that, too," Bagwell said. "Attempted murder. But if they now think you got out of there alive, they'd probably forget about going to this cabin, wouldn't they?"

"I don't think so. At the time they talked about it, I was pretending to be knocked out. I don't think they knew I heard them."

Bagwell looked at my face. "I can see where they roughed you up a bit. If you need a paramedic to look at it, they're here now."

"I'm okay, Sheriff. Compared to a blitzing linebacker's elbow through a face-guard, this ain't nothing."

I almost got Bagwell to smile.

"Ray-Ray, huh?" he said. "We'll see what Wade Dollar knows about him and his cabin."

There was no smoke at all coming from the lab now, and the firemen began to emerge, bringing their equipment with them.

One of them came over to speak to Bagwell.

He said, "They had the place set up to incinerate deliberately. Beats anything I've ever seen. They triggered it by a wall switch a few yards up the tunnel. Guess they done it as they left. It had to be something extremely flammable and long burning. Maybe with a small explosive of some kind to set it off. The Fire Marshal can probably tell us. They made damn sure nothing would be left. It's just a blackened hole in the ground now."

"Is it safe to go in? I want to see," Bagwell said.

"To tell you the truth, Sheriff, I just don't know. We went in, but you might have noticed we didn't stay long, and we were wearing our protective clothing and boots, including face masks, but they aren't much more than surgical masks, so, we might have already made a big mistake. This fentanyl stuff—which is what I understand we're dealing with here—is all new to me. We're just a small-town fire department. I don't know what was aerosolized by the fire, or if it's dangerous, or what precautions to take. Hell, it might even be dangerous breathing the air out here. We need to get some experts in. My advice to you, and everybody else is don't go in there until we do. I'd shut this whole junkyard down and get whoever lives here out until further notice."

Alvin and I were listening. He turned to me, raised an eyebrow and said, "I'm ready to get the fuck outta' here. Whaddya say, homeboy?"

Bagwell looked like he might want to join us. He was wearing an expression like he was already smelling something noxious.

"DEA Agent Underwood is still here," he said. "I need to get him. This sounds like a job for the Federal Government."

The fireman went to his truck and Bagwell stood casting an eye around the junkyard, probably looking for Agent Underwood. If the possibility of breathing dangerous air wasn't enough to make me want to leave, the prospect of seeing Agent Underwood again, was.

"Can we go now?" I asked Bagwell.

He gave it some thought. "Sure," he finally said. "But I need to see you tomorrow. There's a lot more to talk about here."

I Said, "What about the dealer called Doughboy that hangs out in the Tiger's Tail, and the bartender there, Terrell Dent? Are you going to round them up? They're involved with the Dollars and this business somehow."

"Looking for them now. Doughboy's real name is Homer Addis, by the way."

"And the rest of the Dollars who live here?" I asked, thinking about the boy with the cat. "I saw a little boy here earlier. You're not leaving them here with all these unanswered safety questions, are you?"

"The kid belongs to Wade Dollar's son, Benny, and his young wife. We're getting Social Services out here tomorrow to look into their situation. But now I think we ought to get them all out of here tonight," Bagwell said.

"Let's hit the road, Alvin," I said.

How? He asked.

I suddenly realized what Alvin meant. The Jeep was a half-mile away, where we'd left it to get to the deer blind.

"Think we could get deputy dog over there to give us a ride?" Alvin said, looking at a police car parked by the fence, a uniformed cop standing by it.

"Let's walk," I said. "We could probably use the fresh air."

"Right behind you," Alvin said.

CHAPTER FORTY-FIVE

Eloise woke up when I got in Saturday night—or early Sunday morning—which was more accurate. I guess she was sleeping with one eye open, waiting for me. We sat together for a while, and I'd told her everything about the events at the junkyard. She listened raptly, saying very little other than uttering an occasional "Oh" or "My God, J.D."

When I finished, Eloise sat there looking at me with misty eyes.

She said, "I don't know whether to laugh with joy that you came out of this alive or scream at you for being such an idiot for going there in the first place. You can't keep doing things like this, John David. I don't know what I'd do if anything . . ."

She leaned over and hugged me without finishing.

"Thank God for Alvin," she said, "At least you had the good sense to take him with you. But I'm mad at him too for going along with it."

She went back to bed after that, and I headed to my bedroom. Sleep came quicker than I'd expected, exhaustion overpowering my lingering adrenalin rush.

I slept until almost noon, and Eloise was sitting at the breakfast table when I came down. She gave me a look that said she had something on her mind.

"What?" I said to her, expecting her jump on me again. But she surprised me.

She said, "I think we should put out a special edition of the *Clarion*. This drug bust is a major story, and who knows more about what happened than we do? Or, *you* do, to be precise. We could certainly put out a far more comprehensive presentation of the story than anyone else."

"The TV news will have run it before then, Eloise. In fact, they're probably already running it."

"Okay, so it won't be a scoop. But that doesn't matter. Neither TV nor any other news outlet will have the details that we do. They weren't there. You were. If we could get it out Monday—even late afternoon—it would still be news."

I sat and gave it some thought. "The story from a reporter's eye-witness viewpoint," I said. "Up close and personal, with a bit of human interest. Not about me, but by me, and we tie in Kelly's assault. That could be interesting."

"Maybe Pulitzer territory, John David."

"Let's not get ahead of ourselves, Eloise. But it would be a unique angle, I'll grant you that. You've become quite the newspaperwoman, big sister. Grandfather would love it."

"Don't make me cry, John David."

Mackenzie came into the room. "Why are you making Mom cry, J.D.?"

I told her about her mom's idea.

She said, "I love it. I want to help."

"Okay," I said to Eloise, "call in what staff we'll need, and I'll go visit Kelly for a little while. I feel like I ignored her yesterday with all that was going on. The drive will also give me some quiet time to organize my thoughts and start framing a story. I'll see you at the *Clarion*."

#

Kelly lay unchanged, of course, and I did my daily ritual of kissing her forehead and holding her hand. Doctor Mathis stopped by and told me he was still planning to bring her out of the coma on Tuesday and had scheduled it for eleven in the morning. I got butterflies in my stomach just thinking about it. I tried hard to follow Dr. Mathis' lead and stay positive. Sometimes it worked for me, sometimes it didn't. Tuesday loomed large for me, both with anticipation and fear.

I stayed for about thirty minutes and was off to the *Clarion* forming a basic outline in my head of the story that I would write for the special edition.

#

Eloise was waiting for me when I got to the *Clarion*, and we sat down together for a planning session. She said she'd called the sheriff's department and there would be a press conference at two o'clock today at the front gate of the junkyard. However, no one would be allowed inside, which means we can't get any photographs of the actual lab. I told Vickie Sayers that—she's also the paper's photographer now—and she said that wouldn't stop her. She's got one of those camera drones, and she'll sneak and get some aerial shots."

"Is there anything she doesn't do?" I asked.

"Not much. That girl is a piece of work."

We discussed the basic layout of the issue: number of articles, content, who would write what, last-minute ads from regular advertisers that she could drum up, the aerial photographs, and so on.

That done I said, "Have Vickie cover the press conference, too. And get her notes of all the opioid research she did for me and give them to Joanne McKinney. Have Joanne do an 'all-you-ever-wanted -to-know-about-opioids' background piece. And maybe we'll even rerun Kelly's original editorial too. Then everybody has a part."

Eloise said, "Oh, I almost forgot. Sheriff Bagwell wants you to call him. He says he has a couple of questions for you."

"When are you going to start calling him Arlen, Eloise? Give the poor guy a break, will you?"

"Shut up, John David, and mind your own business." She was wearing a smile when she said it.

Eloise left to attend to matters and I picked up the phone and called Bagwell.

"Sheriff Bagwell." He answered.

"This is J.D., Sheriff. You wanted me to call you?"

"I was wondering if you can remember anything else the Dollars said about this Ray-Ray or his cabin. Anything, no matter how small or insignificant you may think it was."

"They said it was deserted, rundown and all grown up around it. By calling it a cabin, I assumed it was in the mountains somewhere. And like I said, I don't believe this Ray-Ray is around any longer. Perhaps he's dead. But as to who Ray-Ray was to the Dollars, they didn't say. I don't know if he was a friend or a relative."

"I've questioned Wade Dollar and his wife at length about this guy and his cabin," Bagwell said. "They claim they don't know anything about a cabin, or anyone named Ray-Ray. I tend to believe them. Wade's trying to get as far away from this thing as he can. If this Ray-Ray was a relative or something, I can't find him. I've had people combing the land records for Pickens and Oconee Counties, and the adjacent counties over in North Carolina, but can't find any other property belonging to any Dollar."

"What about Doughboy, did you get him yet?"

"Can't find him. Maybe he's with the Dollars, or helping them hide somewhere."

"How about Terrell Dent?"

"He's still in the wind too. We've talked to all the other employees there, a bartender name April and two daytime bartenders, George and Kenny. None of them seem to know anything."

If Bagwell only knew, I thought. April was still keeping her mouth shut and probably would until the whole gang was rounded up.

I got off the phone and went to work. This was a complicated story to write. How did I make it an eyewitness report without making it a story about me? Reporters should stay out of their stories. The Dollars and the drug bust was the news, but in this case I guess I was too. It was a delicate tightrope I would have to walk.

Later, Alvin called. He was sitting in a chair outside Kelly's door. "All quiet here, he said, "They got any leads on the Dollars yet?"

"As a couple of minutes ago, no. I was just talking to Bagwell. He's still trying to find Ray-Ray's cabin. If the Dollars had any sense—which I know they don't—they'd be on the way to someplace that doesn't extradite. But who knows? I'll come over and spell you later."

"Don't bother, I've slipped a friendly hospital security guard a few bucks to watch over her tonight."

"Good, I'll get the *Clarion* to reimburse you."

"I'm not worried about that. I've also told the nurses they need to be on the lookout for anyone who doesn't belong. I particularly trust one of the night nurses. She'll keep an eye on Kelly for me too. She's a fine-looking, young black woman who seems to have taken a certain interest in me."

"Why is that not surprising?" I said and rang off.

I had the story almost finished at about nine-thirty p.m. My mind was mush, I was beat and needed a break. I decided to face the story with fresh eyes in the morning. The others had already left, and I would check their work then too.

Hopefully, we would have it all set up, stories and ads in their proper places, the digital edition prepared, and everything done by late afternoon tomorrow. If Eloise could have the pressmen standing by and ready for the run, the paper should be on the streets and on the way to our subscribers by six in the evening.

I turned out the lights and locked up the *Clarion*.

#

Everyone was already in bed when I got to Still hollow. I made myself a sandwich from some leftover ham in the fridge, poured a glass of cold milk, and went out to the den to eat it. I turned on the TV low to not wake anyone and found a sports program on a cable station. For the past week, I'd been ignoring my chosen profession. I saw that back in Atlanta, the rebuilding Braves, with a couple of seasoned veterans and a team full of incredibly talented newcomers were tearing up their division, and were the talk of baseball. The personal drama that had surrounded me for the past few days had displaced the excitement of sports in my life. I felt completely out of touch with it. Kids games played by grown men didn't seem all that important to me at the moment.

I finished my sandwich and went to bed.

CHAPTER FORTY-SIX

Monday morning early, I was back in Kelly's hospital room. A young security guard sat in the chair outside Kelly's door. I got him a cup of coffee to keep him awake, handed him an extra twenty dollars for his help, and thanked him for being there. A pretty young nurse came in twice while I was there. I didn't ask, but I was sure she was the one who had a crush on Alvin. That seemed to happen to many women when they met him.

Kelly was her usual. I sat and told her about the special edition *Clarion* we were putting out today. I even told her we were re-running her editorial. Common sense told me she couldn't hear me, but some small superstitious niggle in the back of my mind said she could. Either way, it didn't hurt to talk to her. It might not help her, but it helped me. I'd found myself talking to her more and more as the days went by.

I thought about tomorrow, the big day. Could Dr. Mathis bring her back to me? Would she ever be the same after this? I left those unanswerable questions alone. I would know that a little more than twenty-four hours from now.

Alvin showed up and spelled the security guy outside her

room. We talked about the authorities' progress in catching the Dollars—or the lack thereof—and the unsuccessful hunt for Ray-Ray's cabin.

"Somebody has to know where it's located, and who Ray-Ray is," I said.

"Maybe the guy was just a friend," Alvin said. "Or an old running buddy. Laverne's an asshole, but he's bound to have friends who know him and his history. We need to find one of them."

I thanked Alvin again for playing hall-monitor outside Kelly's room and said I'd come and spell him as soon as we could put the special edition to bed.

By noon I was in my office checking my story for spelling and typos. I'd finished it in an hour, read it over and decided it was good to go as soon as I could do that.

I looked over Vickie and Joanne's shoulders and saw that their pieces were progressing nicely. They should be able to finish them in a couple of hours, I thought. Vickie's story of Bagwell's news conference was excellent as usual, and Joanne was doing a remarkably good job with hers. I realized I'd let Joanne's low-key personality and willingness to cover the most mundane community news make me believe she might be a little sub-par on the writing end. She surprised me with what so far was a concise report of the ugly details of the opioid crisis, written like a crack reporter. We only had two full-time reporters, and I now believed they were both good at it. I was pleased and proud of them.

Eloise said the pressmen and delivery people would be there mid-afternoon, as would Jason, ready to do his part in turning it all into the digital edition. Everything was on track, and she seemed to have it all well under control. She said she would get me for a last-minute approval if I wanted; otherwise, my job was done. And here I thought I was running things. My big sister had just let me know she was still my big sister.

She showed me the photography, which she'd given a whole page. Other than a shot of Bagwell and DEA agent Underwood standing at a podium, it was all shot from overhead with Vickie's drone, and still interesting to see. Vickie had gotten closer to the burnt-out back-end of the Buick than I'd expected, and with some further enlarging, it was as if you were right there. Unless one of the TV stations had sent in their helicopter—and I didn't think they had—no other news source would have that shot. Add that to the first-hand aspect of the story, and nobody could match the *Clarion's* extensive coverage of this story.

I hugged Eloise. "You hit this one out of the park, sis."

"*We* hit it out of the park," she said and hugged me back.

I felt her tears on my neck. Eloise's cry box had always had a hair trigger—she would cry regardless of the emotion—joy, sadness, anger, it didn't matter. The result of an exceptionally tender heart. It was just one of the reasons I loved her so.

#

With my job on the special edition done, and in the capable hands of Eloise, I thought of something Alvin said at the hospital that morning. Somebody has to know who Ray-Ray is, and the location of his cabin. That had been on my mind too. I felt like Ray-Ray was either a relative or an old running buddy. With Laverne Dollar and his brother's long record of arrests, even though they were a tight gang, they had to have their friends in crime. If the *Clarion* had covered any of those arrests, perhaps accomplices were named.

In the paper's morgue in the basement I did a search of past *Clarion* issues with stories that included the name Dollar. There were three. All of them still on microfilm and not yet digitized by Jason Pilgrim. Unless he could spend every waking minute of his time on it, it was a project that would take quite a while.

I found the appropriate microfilm reels in the steel filing cabinets along the wall and strung the first one up on the viewer that sat in the room like a relic from another age.

I hit the jackpot with the third reel. There was a twenty-year-old article about the conviction of a Laverne Stanley Dollar for manufacturing or distributing methamphetamine. He received a three-year sentence to the Tyger River Correctional Institution, a Level Two state prison in Enoree, just on the other side of Greenville in Spartanburg County. I didn't know if he'd done the whole time or not. The news that was most interesting was that a "William Raymond Rayford" went down with him, but for ten years. *This had to be Ray-Ray.* The story went on to say that Ray-Ray's father, Edward Rayford, testified for his boy before the court, claiming that Ray-Ray was a good boy who just fell in with the wrong crowd. The judge pointed out it was William's third offense for the same crime and threw the book at him. They sent Ray-Ray to the same state prison as Laverne.

I did a quick computer search and found an Edward Rayford listed. I gave him a call.

"Who's this?" an elderly voice asked.

"My name is J.D. Bragg, I'm with the Pickens County Clarion and I'm trying to get some information about a Ray-Ray

Rayford, whom I believe to be your son."

There was a long silence. "Ray-Ray's been dead several years, sir."

He didn't say how, and I didn't ask. I was sorry the guy was dead. At least the man had confirmed that his late son was indeed nicknamed Ray-Ray.

"You're not gonna' drag up old stories about him, are you? Let my boy rest in peace. He's paid for his mistakes."

"No sir, this is about a man named Laverne Dollar. I think your son knew him."

Another long silence. "He did, the two of them were cell-mates over at Tyger River. I've been seeing pictures of him on TV. Is that what this is all about?"

"Yes, sir, it is. Did Ray-Ray have a cabin in the mountains somewhere?"

"It belongs to me, but Ray-Ray had access to it. It's probably fallen in on itself by now. I ain't been up there in years, and the way my old hip is I'll probably never be going up there again. Ray-Ray used to spend time there before . . ."

Before he died, I thought.

"It was run-down, even then," he added. "For a while, Ray-Ray was trying to fix it up, I guess to take girls up there, or have a place to play cards—he did that a lot. Or maybe he just wanted somewhere else to live. He was a grown man and still living at home. I should've sold it years ago when it was worth something."

Can you tell me where that cabin is located?"

"It's off Highway 28—some people call it the Highlands Highway—about fifteen miles north of Walhalla. The turnoff to it is right before you get to a sign for the Sumpter National

Forest. You can't miss that. It's a brown wooden sign with yellow letters settin' on a stack-stone base. But the cabin is quite a-ways off the highway, and the little road that leads up to it might be hard to find these days. It's probably all grown over by now. Aint' nobody been up there in years, as far as I know. But what's this got to do with Laverne Dollar?"

"Maybe nothing, but it bears checking out."

"So, Dollar ain't been caught yet, huh? You thinking he may be hiding out in my cabin?"

"Probably just a long shot, Mr. Rayford. But I would advise you not to go to that cabin, or tell anyone about our talk until it can be checked out. The Dollars are dangerous. Anybody that goes up there could get killed. My next call is going to be to the authorities, telling them what you've told me. Let the police handle it."

I had to laugh at myself for what I just told him; it was precisely what Bagwell had been preaching to me—*let them handle it*. But it wouldn't be Sheriff Arlen Bagwell who would handle it anyway, I thought. The cabin was in Oconee County and wasn't in his jurisdiction.

"I got no plans to go up there," Mr. Rayford said. "And I ain't telling nobody about you calling me. I don't want no part of it."

Mr. Rayford hung up abruptly. I looked up the number of the Oconee County Sheriff's Department, then hesitated. Bagwell would still want to be involved as much as he could. I owed him the call. I'd let him bring in the appropriate authorities.

I rang him up, then had second thoughts and hung up before anyone answered. What if the Dollars weren't at the cabin? Did I want to call out every cop in two counties, which would most likely include a battle-ready SWAT team, for something I hadn't first checked out? What self-respecting investigative journalist would do that? Besides, selfishly, I didn't want to be left out. I'd found the cabin for them.

I went to Eloise and told her she was in charge of getting the special edition out, and that I was leaving it in her capable hands. I was out the door, heading for my Jeep before she had a chance to argue. I thought about calling Alvin to come to help me, but there was no time for that and I didn't want to pull him off Kelly's door. Rightly or wrongly, I figured that one person could approach the cabin with more stealth than two. After all, all I wanted to do was see if the cabin looked occupied. I wasn't stupid enough to try to apprehend the Dollars if they were there. I'd call Bagwell from some safe and well-hidden spot, and wait for them to show up.

I gave Alvin another thought, but decided not to try to take him with me. He was too valuable where he was, watching over Kelly. All I was going to do is take a look, anyway. It didn't take two sets of eyes to do that.

CHAPTER FORTY-SEVEN

The drive to Ray-Ray's cabin was about forty-five miles from Pickens with the last fifteen being on some very curvy mountain roads, so it took me most of an hour to get there. I made it to the Sumpter National forest marker, but missed the turn-off. I turned around and went back, driving slowly and finally spotting it— a small path barely wide enough for a car, overgrown with weeds and small saplings, and easy to miss. When I pulled in and took a closer look, I saw recent tire tracks cutting through the weeds. Someone drove in here in the past couple of days, and more than once. Was it the Dollars?

I parked the Jeep and set out on foot. All I wanted to do was get close enough without being spotted to see if the cabin looked inhabited. It wasn't easy going. The road was steep in places and nearer the top of the mountain than I had expected. I had to wade through knee-high weeds and young saplings, Mother Nature taking back her land. My pants legs became covered in beggar's lice, tiny pods that stick to your clothes like Velcro.

Finally, through the trees, I glimpsed a weathered old house with a rusted tin roof. I found a large poplar tree by the path and got behind it. A black SUV sat in front of the cabin. It was like the one Laverne Dollar drove. I took out my cell phone to call Sheriff Bagwell, but there was no signal.

I kicked myself for not thinking of that. Before I went back to get the Jeep to drive back close enough to Walhalla to get a signal, I decided it was worth taking a closer look at the cabin to make sure the Dollars *were* here and hadn't dumped their SUV. A part of me still believed they were smart enough to put as many zip codes between them and this part of the country as they could.

Using a thick cover of trees I circled the cabin to come at it from behind. The cabin was small, two rooms and a kitchen probably, with a fallen-down outhouse in the back. If anyone was in house, they were using the great outdoors as their bathroom. It was a weird thing to be thinking about when someone might be pointing a gun at you.

I made my way to one of the windows in the back. It was dark with no light coming from within. The place may not have the electricity hooked up, so sitting in the dark didn't seem any more unreasonable than anything else about hiding out here.

The window panes were broken out. I approached, crouching low. I chanced a peek over the sill and what I saw scared me enough to duck back down.

Someone was sitting in a chair by a table, looking straight at me.

I was about to flee back into the woods but realized there were no sounds of anyone making a clamor to come after me. It was eerily quiet inside the house. Maybe the person in the chair didn't see me after all. I chanced another look.

The seated figure was Delilah, the light streaming through one of the windows behind casting her in silhouette, creating a bright yellow-white halo around her head. She wasn't moving. Laverne lay slumped over one end of the table, his head in a pool of dried blood. Between the table and the door, Sonny Dollar lay face down on the floor. The back of his shirt, a mess of dried blood. It looked like he had been shot in the back several times, trying to flee. The front of Delilah's blouse, the same one she was wearing when I'd last seen her, was also bloody.

Sonny's gun was still stuck in the back of his belt. I didn't think they'd been expecting this. This was done by someone they knew well enough to let into the cabin.

I went back to the Jeep and drove toward Walhalla until I got a cell phone signal and called Bagwell. He was in his office and didn't ask how I'd found the cabin or why I didn't call him earlier. He just told me not to return to the cabin, park out by the entrance and wait for the Oconee County Sheriff's department to get there. It wasn't his jurisdiction, but it was his case and he was coming too and bringing DEA Agent Underwood.

I figured I was probably in for another ass-chewing from Underwood, even though I'd just solved another problem for them. I went back to the entrance to the overgrown driveway and sat in my Jeep, waiting. After a while I heard sirens coming up the highway. From the sound of it, the Oconee County Sheriff was bringing every deputy he had. When they came into view, he'd also brought a CSI unit, and several EMT vehicles, all followed by a short train of lookie-loos, and what appeared to be the local press.

The Oconee Sheriff had apparently made a big show of leaving town. If he knew this was Bagwell's case, he certainly wasn't going to be left out of its publicity. He probably had an election coming up.

The Oconee Sheriff was leading the pack and came straight to me when he arrived. I told him, as briefly as possible, where the cabin was and what he would find there. With a suspicious look, he told me not to go anywhere and had a deputy lock me in the back of his patrol car to make sure. If I'd expected a hero's welcome, I wasn't going to get it.

I spent the time watching various police cars, official vans and trucks go up to the cabin, each one squashing down the weeds further. Most of the lookie-loos left when they realized they couldn't get to see what all the commotion was about.

The local press was joined by reporters from farther afield and were all hanging around like vultures on a fence waiting for road-kill. Every time one of them would peek through the car window at me, or rap their knuckles on it, or try to photograph me, I would turn away. Once again I was making the news, not reporting it. Sometimes, I was ashamed to be one of them.

Since my mobile phone was again out of range, I couldn't make a call. I wanted to call Eloise and tell her where I was and why. If she hadn't yet gone to press with the *Clarion* special edition, the news about what I'd discovered should be in it. Otherwise, we were going to get scooped by all these yahoos gathered alongside the road, and our special edition would be yesterday's news when it came out.

I saw something that gave me an idea. An Oconee County deputy was walking by and I rapped my knuckles on the car window hard enough to get his attention. He walked over and looked in on me.

I said, "Excuse me, can I ask you to do something for me?"

"What would that be, sir?"

He had the fresh-faced look and demeanor of a rookie and was probably just out of military service.

"You know who I am, right?"

"You're the guy who found the bodies?"

"And you know I'm not under arrest?"

"Yes, I am aware of that, sir."

"My sister doesn't know where I am, and she's got to be worried sick. I can't call her to tell her. Was that a satellite phone I just saw you on?"

"Yes, sir. There's no cell phone reception up here."

"Yeah, I know it. That's why I'd like to ask if I can use your phone, just for a minute. My sister is easily upset. She suffers from a nervous disorder." I almost laughed. Eloise was one of the calmest people I knew.

The deputy seemed to buy it, and I got the feeling he wanted to help me but was having a hard time deciding without somebody up the chain of command okaying it.

"Look," I said. "I'll give you the number. You can dial it."

He looked at me, then behind him, and back at me. He took the phone off his belt.

I gave him Eloise's number.

He dialed it and held the phone up to my face.

"Don't say one word about what's going on up here or I'll take the phone back," he said.

He wasn't as green as I thought.

Eloise answered, and I said, "It's me. Can't really talk right now, but I'm okay, so don't worry about me. Has *Clarion* gone out yet?"

I looked at the deputy and mouthed, "*Clarion* is my sister's daughter."

He gave me a blank look, but wasn't taking his phone back.

"Oh, good," I told Eloise, over-riding her confused questions. "Don't let her go until I get back. I mean it. Wait for me. I have something to tell *Clarion* that she shouldn't miss. Okay?

Eloise asked, "Is this a weird way to ask me to hold the presses?"

"Yes, it is, my darling sister, and I will see you and *Clarion* soon.

I yielded the deputy back his phone and thanked him. He closed the door on me and walked away.

I'd caught Eloise in time, I hoped, and thought she'd understood my message. We couldn't go to press without this new episode. With it, we could cover this whole story from start to finish. All it would take to put a happy ending on it would be for Kelly to come out of her coma tomorrow as good as new.

I could at least use my phone to begin writing the story of today's events. The trickiest part would be to make this a news story, and not a narrative of my actions. The Dollars were the news, not the reporter who found them.

I got to work.

CHAPTER FORTY-EIGHT

Two hours later they'd turned me loose from the back of the patrol car—the last hour spent with Sheriff Bagwell and his Oconee counterpart firing questions nonstop. I told them everything I'd done and how I did it. DEA Agent Underwood was there too, but he had little to say to me. I guess he was getting accustomed to finding me in the middle of police investigations. He and I were just not destined to be best buddies.

The only question I couldn't answer is why I didn't call them in earlier. No explanation I could offer up would keep them from being pissed off at me, so I didn't even try. Had Alvin been there, I'm sure he would have told them how we'd done their job for them again, but I chose not to do that. I only wanted to get back to the *Clarion*.

They let me go after I promised to meet with them again the next day if needed to tie up any loose ends. I guessed that they didn't want to spend any more time with me than necessary. Bagwell had to be downright sick of me. They took the Dollars to the morgue, and the CSI unit was working hard to find any clue on who killed them.

On the way to Pickens, when I finally drove back into cell phone coverage, I called Eloise and briefly filled her in on the Dollar murders. She had understood my cryptic message and had put everything on hold for me.

Then I called Alvin and told him about everything that had happened. I got an earful from him almost as bad as I'd received from the two sheriffs for going it alone. I told him he'd helped me more by watching Kelly. It was a great relief knowing she was safe, and by the way, at no time was my life at risk from three dead people.

I added that I was on my way in to help Eloise put the finishing touches on the *Clarion* special edition, and he should go home and get some rest, I'd see him tomorrow.

The sun was sitting on the western horizon when I arrived at the Clarion. We'd missed getting the edition out by this afternoon, but working into the night, we could have it on the streets by day-break—the digital version even earlier. I sat down at my desk and with what I'd already written on my phone, finished the story of the Dollar's murder, with a segue from the other stories so that all of the content worked together seamlessly. I rushed it into Eloise to put into the layout of the edition and prepare it for the press run.

To those of us with printers ink in our blood and a reporter's passion in our guts, hitting the streets with the breaking news of a big story is a thrilling experience. It's an exciting moment that defies description, flooding you with pride, accomplishment, and a tinge of nostalgia for an earlier time when newspapers ruled the world of news. That was before cable news and the internet, when people waited by newsstands in the wee hours for a delivery truck to drop off the nation's news in banded bundles on the sidewalk, or sat at their kitchen tables over their first cup of coffee, waiting for that thud on the doorstep.

Granted, the *Clarion* was a small-town affair, unlike the big-city papers with their giant rolling presses and fleet of delivery trucks standing by, but we were still getting an informative work of substance out to the people, and there was a nobility in that which made your chest swell. I kept feeling like Grandfather was standing somewhere watching with the same sense of pride in what we were doing.

But even when we put the special edition to bed, we had more work to do. We still had this week's regular edition to put out, only now with less time to do it. At least we had a handle on the front page news. There had been a convenience store robbery in Easley with a clerk pistol-whipped. The Easley police had a couple of suspects in custody, and Vickie was already on that. And there had been a city council zoning change in Powdersville that had a lot of homeowners upset. Joanne was all over that. Between those stories and the area sports coverage by our freelancer and Mackenzie, Eloise's community news, the ads, including classifieds, and we had the major bones of the issue in the works.

I gave kudos to the staff and told them all to go home. Then I went home myself. It had been another long day.

CHAPTER FORTY-NINE

Tuesday morning early, the big day for Kelly. Eloise and I sat in her hospital room, listening to Doctor Mathis. He was saying that tests and monitors continued to show her condition stabilized, and the brain swelling reduced to the point of normalcy. He explained the procedure by which he would bring Kelly out of her medically induced coma today. It was the same as he'd told me before, but Eloise hadn't heard it, and she sat riveted to his every word. The process was simply to begin reducing the anesthetic drugs they were giving her until she regained consciousness.

While we were there, April Cheney came in bearing flowers. She stared at Kelly for a moment and sobbed, "Oh my God, I can't believe those bastards did this to her." She gave me an expectant look. "Tell me she'll be okay."

"We've got our fingers crossed, I said. "They're bringing her out of the coma today, so we'll see."

"I got a copy of the special edition of the *Clarion* this morning and read all about what's happened. It's incredible."

She looked at Eloise and Mackenzie, and I introduced them.

"I'm so sorry about this," she said, nodding at Kelly. "I feel like it's my fault, telling Kelly all I did about the Tiger's Tail and everything."

I told her, "You have nothing to be sorry about. If it weren't for you, the Dollar brothers would still be making and selling the poison that killed your sister May. The things that you told Kelly—and me—are what led to the end of the Dollar brothers' opioid organization. You helped bring justice to your sister May, and you should be very proud of that."

"Thank you," April said, fighting back the tears. "I appreciate you keeping me a secret and not putting my name in the paper. And I could tell by the questions the police asked me when they came and talked to everybody at the bar, that they didn't know I was a snitch for you and Kelly. I'm still frightened of all these people and would just as soon not have what I did made public."

"I gave you my word I wouldn't tell anyone," I said. "All I was doing was just keeping it. But there is one person who needs to know what a hero you've been. And I'd like your permission to tell them about it."

"Who is that?" she asked.

"Your mother. She would be very proud of you."

April stopped trying to hold back her tears and they flowed like a broken water pipe. She put her hands over her face. Eloise, Mackenzie, and I gave her a group hug.

She smiled through her tears and wiped her nose with a tissue Mackenzie gave her from a box on a bedside table.

"How are things at the Tiger's Tail now?" I asked her.

"I'm out of a job, for one thing." The Tiger's Tail is closed and the doors padlocked."

"So, what are your plans?"

"I'm going to Florida to take that bartending job I told you about. I'm all packed. I just came by here to see Kelly before I left."

I hugged her again. "You're a brave woman, April Cheney. When Kelly wakes up, I'll tell her you came to see her. Or, you can stay and be here with us when that happens."

She said, "No, that should be a family thing. But I'll be thinking about her. I'm not normally the praying type, and this would shock my mother to death, but I'll be praying that Kelly comes out of this healthy and happy. Call me and let me know how things go."

I promised I would.

She hugged me back, another tear rolling down her cheek, and left.

I hoped her prayers would be answered.

#

Eloise and Mackenzie went to get us coffees, and I went out in the hallway to call Kate Cheney while it was still on my mind. I told her all about April's heroic actions and how they helped smash the opioid ring that furnished the pills that killed her daughter May. I left her in tears, just like April. She seemed as proud now of April as she was of May. Mission accomplished, I thought.

I called Sheriff Bagwell to see if they'd made any progress in the Dollar killings. "Anything new happened?" I asked.

"You know, Mr. Bragg, I don't remember a part of my job description saying I had to keep you informed with every single thing I'm doing."

I was wondering when the special treatment I was getting by being Eloise's brother would run out. I guess it had.

"Have you found Doughboy or Terrell Dent?"

I heard him sigh.

"We picked up Homer Addis, AKA Doughboy, last night. He's in County lockup. It seems he has a pretty good alibi for the time of the Dollar's death. So we don't think he had anything to do with that. As to his drug dealing, or any connection to the Dollar brothers' opioid ring, or supplying May Burgess with the drugs that killed her, we don't have enough hard evidence to hold him on any of that. We can try, but he'll probably be out by this afternoon."

"What about Terrell Dent?"

"He's still out there somewhere. Mr. Addis says Dent has relatives over in Mississippi someplace and we're checking that out. But according to Addis, Dent was just a wannabe thug and little more than a gofer for Sonny Dollar. The man had little to do with the drug side of things and couldn't see any reason why Terrell Dent would want to kill the Dollars.

"Addis did say, however, that while he didn't know the details, the Dixie Demons motorcycle gang *was* involved with the Dollars. To what degree, or what their position was, he says he doesn't know. But he wouldn't be surprised if the Dixie Demons were the ones that killed the Dollars. Last week when the Demons were in town, Sonny and Laverne were in the bar's office with a couple of them, and Addis heard raised voices coming from behind the door. He couldn't make out what they were saying, but it sounded like they were about to come to blows. And afterward, every time the Dixie Demons came in the bar, there was visible tension between them and the brothers.

They weren't as friendly with each other as they were before. So he thinks they had a falling out over something."

"Think there's anything to that?" I asked.

"I got in touch with the authorities up in North Carolina where the gang calls headquarters. They do suspect that the Dixie Demons are into the distribution of opioids and other drugs up there and in several other Southern states. I sent them a sample of the pills collected on the streets here to see if they match the ones up there. If they do, we're all going to join forces: North Carolina, the DEA, SLED, my department, and Oconee County, and go after this bunch. With what Mr. Addis is telling us, we might be adding a triple homicide to the charges."

I said, "Wow, the Dixie Demons. That would be an interesting turn of events, but not all that uncommon, I guess. Fallout amongst drug dealers probably happens a lot."

"And Mr. Bragg? I'll keep you posted on things, but not because I have to. I've just grown fond of you for some reason."

I was glad he liked me. If it were because he hoped to one day become my brother-in-law, that was well out of my area of influence and entirely up to Eloise. I held no sway with my sister in matters like that.

I heard footsteps coming down the hall and looked around to see Alvin approaching. "Yo," I said to him.

"This thing still on?" he asked.

"Waiting for the Doctor."

"Elizabeth and Mackenzie here?"

"Gone to get coffee."

Alvin must have seen something in my face that made him put his hand on my shoulder.

"She gonna' be fine, J.D.." he said.

"I hope you're right," I said.

"You ever know me *not* to be?" Alvin said and gave me the *Alvin* grin.

Alvin's confidence was contagious, and it made me feel better. "Are you here to lend me more moral support?" I asked, grinning back at him.

"If you'll let me. But this is a family thing, so I'll stay out here and out of everybody's way. I'll be here if you need me."

"Bullshit, Alvin. You're as much a part of this family as anybody. You aren't going to be anywhere but by my side."

Alvin dipped his chin at me and squeezed my shoulder. There was no more to be said about it.

CHAPTER FIFTY

Forty-five minutes later, Eloise, Mackenzie, Alvin, and I were at Kelly's bedside, waiting for Dr. Mathis to show up and bring her out of the coma. I sat and studied Kelly's lovely face, as I had every day since she'd been here. Her bruises were almost faded away, still a faint reminder of what brought her here. Even if the assholes who did this were no longer walking the Earth, I didn't think I could ever get over hating them for it.

I noticed my hand shaking as I placed it on hers. I was trying as hard as I could to stay calm and have positive thoughts, but that wasn't working too well. No matter how much I tried to visualize Kelly opening her eyes and smiling at me as if nothing had happened, that little voice of insecurity in me that never seemed to leave me alone kept whispering that I wasn't worthy of having someone this beautiful and wonderful in my life. And that fate was about to teach me a cruel lesson for even thinking I deserved it.

Doctor Mathis came striding in and broke me away from my dark thoughts. A nurse and another doctor were right behind him.

He said, as bright and cheery as ever, "Okay, it's time to bring this young lady back to the waking world. I'll explain what we're going to do again, if you'd like."

"We would," I said, Eloise and Mackenzie nodding.

"First, let me introduce you to Doctor Amos, the anesthesiologist. I think you've met Nurse Jackson. Doctor Amos will gradually begin the process of taking the patient off her cocktail of medications that are keeping her unconscious. Nurse Jackson and I will be assisting and monitoring the patient's condition as this happens. This part won't take long, but it may be a little longer for the drug's effects to wear off and she actually wakes up. I'd like you all to step outside as we wean her off the anesthetics, and then I'll come out and speak to you. After that, barring any complications—which I don't expect— you can come back in and sit with her until the moment she awakes. But I suggest you don't stay too long after that and tire her out. Just because she's been asleep for days, she still needs more rest to get over this completely."

We went out to the waiting room and took seats. Regardless of Doctor Mathis and his positive attitude that all would be well, Eloise, Mackenzie, and I sat there anxiously, barely speaking, worried and nervous. Alvin sat quietly beside us.

After what seemed like forever, but wasn't all that long, Doctor Mathis came out and announced that everything went well. Kelly was off all the coma-inducing drugs. However, as he'd said earlier, she wasn't awake yet. They would continue to monitor her recovery closely, and we could now go wait in her room if we wanted to. We unanimously wanted to.

After an hour or so of sitting by Kelly's side, I saw her arm move slightly. Once, twice, then three times. Then her fingertips fluttered. My heart raced, and Mackenzie and Eloise had seen her move too. They were sitting on the edge of their seats, watching her closely. Alvin, leaning against a wall, stood a little straighter. He'd noticed it too.

Then she opened her eyes. I grabbed her hand and squeezed, and her eyes met mine. She smiled that beautiful smile at me, and it was like a ray of sunlight had suddenly broken through the clouds, found me in her hospital room, and warmed me to the core.

"John David," she said weakly, but still smiling.

I laughed out loud before I could stop myself. "Kelly."

She looked around at Eloise and Mackenzie standing at the other side of her bed. Somehow they were managing to grin ear to ear and cry at the same time. They clasped her other hand and we held on to her from both sides.

Kelly's eyes went past them and found Alvin, grinning at her too. "Alvin" she said. "*You're* here."

"Welcome back, sweet lady," he said, grinning.

"How long was I . . ." Kelly said.

"Ten days," I said, and she turned back to me.

"You've been here . . . all along. Somehow, I knew it."

"Yes I have," I said, unable to remember ever being happier.

#

We'd spent half an hour with her, with me squeezing her hand the whole time and grinning like an idiot before Doctor Mathis came in to shoo us away. Kelly remembered her attack only vaguely, enough to say there were two of them. I discouraged speaking too much about it now, telling her we could talk about that later.

She was groggy, her eyelids beginning to droop as she was struggling to stay awake. I stood up to go and let her get some rest. Kelly reached out and touched my arm as if she wanted to say something to me. Her voice was weak, and I leaned down to better hear her.

"He spoke *Russian*, J.D.," she said.

"*Who* spoke Russian?"

"The man . . . who beat me. I fought back. I think I hurt him and he called me a *bitch* in Russian. Right before he began to kick me."

"Are you *sure?*" I asked, wondering if this was just a product of a wounded memory.

"Yes, this man said, *Ty chertovski suka*. You fucking bitch."

"How do you even *know* Russian?" I asked.

"A College friend. Exchange student from Moscow. She taught me to curse in Russian so we could swear without people knowing. It was our little joke."

Kelly seemed so sure of it, but did she just imagine it? Was it something from a coma-induced dream about college days? Who knows what went on in her mind over the days she lay drugged up and comatose?

I started to ask another question, but she'd closed her eyes and began to snore gently.

I would have to wait.

CHAPTER FIFTY-ONE

We'd come in separate cars, so Eloise and Mackenzie headed for the parking lot. I'd told them I'd be right behind them but motioned to Alvin to hang back. I didn't think that anyone but me heard Kelly's puzzling news that her assailant spoke Russian. I wanted to tell Alvin about it.

There was no one in the waiting room, so Alvin and I went there, taking seats in the far corner. I told him what Kelly had said.

"And you don't think it was like a *hallucination* or something?" Alvin asked. "A kick in the head can scramble your brains pretty good."

"I don't think so. She was pretty sure about it. Are we wrong about the Dollar brothers assaulting her?"

Alvin said, "Can't see dumb peckerwoods like them speaking *Russian*. They can barely handle English."

"I agree, but they're part of it somehow. Laverne said as much when he had me tied to that chair. We've missed something."

"Yeah. We got us a *Russian* in the woodpile somewhere. So what do we do now?"

"We keep looking," I said. "And looking *out* for Kelly. If the Dollars didn't do it, then the creep who did is still out there somewhere. He might take another run at her."

Alvin read my mind. "We need somebody on her door again. I'll take care of it."

"You can stay a few more days?"

"Ain't no way I'm leaving until we catch this mother-fucker."

"I appreciate it, Alvin," I said.

"You said we keep looking. Where?"

"I don't know yet. I need to do some thinking on it."

Alvin said, "Well when you do think of something, this time don't go trying to do anything without me. I'll add another man on Kelly's door if I need to."

#

I left Alvin at the hospital and headed to the *Clarion*. On the way I called April Cheney. There was a dull roar in the background when she answered, like she was in her car and on the road somewhere.

"You already on your way to Florida?" I asked.

"I hope you're calling to tell me Kelly's okay," she said.

"She's fantastic, she's going to be fine."

"Thank goodness. And no, I'm on my way to my mother's house. She called and asked me to come over. Would you believe it, she doesn't want me to leave? All of a sudden, she's a different person. We're actually getting along. Is this your doing?"

"I might have said something to her," I said.

"Well, whatever you said seemed to make things better between us than they've been in years. Thank you."

"You did it, not me. I just reminded her of who you really are. I want to ask you something else about the Tiger's Tail."

"That place is *so* in my rearview mirror now, but what is it?"

"Did you ever see the Dollars talking to, or associating with, anyone who was Russian, or who spoke Russian?"

"That's a weird question. I heard a lot of stuff in that place, but never anybody talking Russian. Why are you asking me that?"

"It's just something Kelly said when she first woke up. She probably wasn't over the meds yet, so don't worry about it. And April, I'm happy about you and your mom."

There was someone else I wanted to talk to about Russians. I called the Sheriff's Department again, but Bagwell was out. They gave me a deputy, and I asked if I could get into the lockup to see Doughboy. The deputy said no. I started to argue then he Homer Addis was released an hour ago. He's made bail.

Alvin had told me where he lived, so I made a detour from my route to the Clarion and headed to his apartment in Clemson. Hopefully, he would be home by now.

Thirty-five minutes later, I knocked on his door. I could tell he recognized me, and he wouldn't take the chain off the door. Through the gap, I asked him if he knew anybody who spoke Russian. I guess the question so surprised him that he didn't slam the door on me. He just stood staring at me through the opening.

He said, "If this is a joke or something, then I don't get it. Now, go the fuck away."

"I'm not going anywhere until you answer my question. Do you know anyone who speaks Russian?"

He was looking at me like I was a madman.

"*No*, I don't know any fucking Russians, and I don't know

why you're asking me such a stupid fucking question.

"Who told you May Burgess was in the market for opioids?"

He stared at me a moment. "I ain't admitting to nothing. But it sure wasn't no Russian. Now leave, or I'm calling the cops. This is harassment or something."

A drug dealer calling the cops, I thought. That would be different. But his genuine bafflement at the question made me believe him. I headed to the *Clarion*.

As I drove, I went at the Russian problem from a different direction—not from what I knew, but from what I *didn't* know. Laverne Dollar had revealed that he was *part* of Kelly's beating. He didn't actually say that he or his brother Sonny did it. Did they bring in someone else to do the dirty work on Kelly? Someone who spoke Russian? Maybe there was a Dixie Demon with a Russian background. Anything was possible, I supposed.

The other big question that I had no answer for was who was behind the OMSK Corporation? All I knew was that according to April, OMSK owned the Tiger's Tail Bar and Grill. I had assumed that the Dollar brothers were behind it, using it as a shell company to launder their drug money.

Something had been nagging at me about the Dollar brothers since I'd gotten to know them better in our underground soiree. The Dollars were nasty individuals, but neither was the brightest bulb on the tree. I still had a hard time seeing them as the masterminds of an opioid manufacturing and distribution operation. They struck me as labor, not management.

Perhaps there was an unknown faction involved here. Someone or something above the Dollar brothers in the hierarchy. Like the OMSK Corporation, maybe. April said that when Kelly grilled Terrell Dent about OMSK, she was sure Dent told Sonny Dollar about it, and Sonny would have told Laverne. If OMSK was controlling the Dollars, then the news that Kelly was sticking her nose into their business would have soon reached them. And shortly after that, Kelly was assaulted and beaten.

So her attack was either a big coincidence, something I rarely if ever believed in, or the Dollar brothers, the Dixie Demons, or someone in the OMSK Corporation was willing to use violent means to discourage her. And it was someone who spoke Russian, who I was pretty sure wasn't one of the Dollars. Finding out who was behind the OMSK Corporation became my first order of business.

#

The chatter around the Clarion was about the special edition. It was a huge success. The sidewalk stands and outlets had sold out everywhere. Even the extra copies we kept at the *Clarion,* with the exception of the couple we kept for posterity, were gone. By noon there wasn't a copy to be found anywhere . . . and there was a huge boost in sign-ups for our digital version. The *Clarion* was seeing the largest circulation bump in years.

I got on my computer and searched OMSK. The first thing that showed up was an interesting surprise. OMSK was the name of a city in south-central Russia, on the Irtysh River. *Russia.* Another coincidence? I didn't think so. I had expected OMSK to be an acronym for something, not the name of a town in Russia. Now, I *definitely* had to find out who was behind it.

I was out of my league here. To find the hidden owner of a

shell company, I needed help. I needed someone with the skills to find things on the internet that people didn't want found. I needed a hacker.

CHAPTER FIFTY-TWO

Jason Pilgrim was in his cubicle, working on this week's digital issue. He looked up from his computer screen as I approached, an apprehensive look on his face like he thought I was bringing bad news.

I said, "I need your help. I want you to find out who's behind something called the OMSK Corporation."

He ignored my question and asked, "Is Ms. Mayfield okay? I heard she's awake."

"She's going to be fine. It will just take her a little time to get back to a hundred percent."

"Great," he said, visibly relieved. "She's an awesome lady and I owe her big-time. She hired me when no one else would." He paused. "You know about that?"

"The hacking? Yeah, I know about that."

"And that don't matter to you? My record?"

"Christ kid, for someone in the news business hacking should be a prerequisite. Now, what about this OMSK Corporation? Will you look into it for me?"

"Kelly already had me doing that. She said they owned that

bar—what is it? The Tiger's Tail? Kelly thought it was a shell company."

I shouldn't have been surprised. "Did you find out who owns it?"

"No, I didn't get that far. I only found the name of the Resident Agent of the corporation, and that in addition to the bar they own carwashes and coin laundries. That much was easy. But the Resident Agent isn't the Beneficial Owner, whose identity is hidden. That's the point of a shell company. When Kelly got hurt, I stopped looking. I was waiting for her to get better and tell me what she wanted me to do, because the next step would be to look into some things that might require breaking the law. Sometimes, that's the only way to connect the dots to get what you're looking for."

"Why didn't you tell me all this earlier?"

Jason shrugged and gave me a sheepish look. "I was afraid you'd fire me. Digging into this was heading in the same direction that got me arrested before. At the time, I didn't know you knew about that, or how you'd take having a jailbird hacker working for you."

"It wouldn't have been a problem and it still isn't. So, who is the Resident Agent?"

He punched a key on his keyboard and opened a file. Looking at it, he said, "Gregor Popov, a New York Attorney."

"Popov," I said. "A Russian."

Jason looked at me like, *Duh, so what?*

"I think we just connected a dot," I said, and told him about Kelly's attacker speaking Russian. I could see wheels turning behind his eyes as I spoke.

Jason said, "That special edition we just ran about opioids and those Dollar brothers. Kelly was working on that story before you were, wasn't she?"

"I just picked up where she left off." Until she told me that her attacker spoke Russian, I had the Dollar brothers down as the kingpins behind everything, including assaulting Kelly and owning the OMSK Corporation. Now, I'm not so sure. This Russian thing has thrown a monkey wrench into my thinking. I'm starting to wonder if the brothers had bosses and that's who runs the OMSK Corporation. This Russian lawyer is no coincidence, and if he's a Russian, and the person who assaulted Kelly was Russian, then perhaps the Beneficial Owners are Russians too."

"Holy shit," Jason said. "I just had a wild thought. The attorney is from New York. And what New York Russians—from the Brighton Beach area of Brooklyn called Little Odessa to be exact— are known for dealing in criminal stuff, like illegal drugs? The Russian mafia."

As crazy as it sounded, he might actually be on to something, I thought. Had he just connected all the dots? "An interesting and creative thought, Mr. Pilgrim."

"I watch a lot of TV," he said.

"If the Dollars didn't personally do the beat-down on Kelly, maybe they were just an assist to OMSK, and some Russian thug did the hands-on work."

"So then, who killed the Dollars?" Jason asked.

"The authorities seem to think it was the Dixie Demons. What if it were the Russians?"

"The Russians? But why?"

I said, "Maybe the Dollars had outlived their usefulness. The operation here was certainly finished, and they had become a risk, I would think. It was time to cut all ties. The Russian mob isn't known for working well with others anyway."

"Damn," Jason said. "We sat right here and solved the whole thing."

"We haven't solved anything. All we have is a theory. We don't have a shred of real proof for any of this. And the first dot on the string—Kelly's attacker calling her a bitch in Russian—could just be some goon who simply took a Berlitz course."

"You don't believe that," Jason said.

"No, I don't. But it doesn't matter what either of us believes. It's no different than the newspaper business. We can't publish a story without substantiation and verifiable sources, and the authorities can't do anything with what we've got either. We need some proof. Hard evidence that ties the Russians into everything, and I don't see a way to get it."

Jason sat quietly for a moment.

"It doesn't mean we don't keep trying, though," he said.

"And how do you propose we do that?".

"What I do best—prowling the hidden corners of the internet."

What he was talking about would probably be breaking some hacking law. I gave it less than two seconds thought. "Okay, do it. I'm going to check up on Kelly. Let me know if you find anything."

I could hear the keys on Jason's computer already clattering behind me as I walked away.

#

Kelly was asleep when I walked into her room. I didn't try to wake her. A nurse I recognized was removing a dinner tray from an over-bed table on wheels. It looked like they had Kelly on a liquid diet. There was a small half-empty bowl of clear broth and a half-glass of apple juice, both with straws in them. There was also some lime gelatin dessert with a bite or two taken out of it. She hadn't eaten much, but at least it was something.

"She's still pretty groggy," the nurse said. "It's going to take her a while to get back to normal, but she will. Doctor Mathis was just in here. He's pleased with how she's doing and wants her to sleep as much as she can for now."

"Is that a way of telling me that I shouldn't wake her up?" I asked.

The nurse gave me an apologetic look and smiled. "That would probably be best. I'll bet you anything, she'll be far more alert in the morning. More like herself if she gets another good night of sleep."

I hung around a few more minutes and watched Kelly sleep. There was a peace on her face that wasn't there when she was in the coma. This was a different kind of sleep.

More than anything yet, it made me feel like everything was going to be okay. I left her to her rest.

CHAPTER FIFTY-THREE

The next morning I was back at the hospital to find Kelly awake this time, having breakfast, but still on the liquid diet. She looked better, but I wasn't sure she felt better. She kept going in and out of sleep and would close her eyes for long moments as we talked. I wasn't sure she was hearing a lot of what I said.

The nurse came in, and I asked her about it. It was normal, Kelly was improving, but it took time. It was a gradual process and Kelly would remain groggy and needing a lot of sleep and rest for at least a couple more days. I'd heard all that before, but I had to keep asking.

I told Kelly about us doing a *Clarion* edition on everything, and Kelly mumbled that she wanted to read it. But with her drowsiness, and apparent difficulty concentrating, I didn't think she was ready to do much reading yet—or was prepared for the many questions I wanted to ask her.

We talked about inconsequential things for a little longer until finally I leaned over and kissed her on the mouth. I'd had enough of kissing her on the forehead and cheek. She surprised me by returning the kiss and for the first time in a while, it felt like old times. Maybe she was getting better after all.

#

Jason was standing in my office doorway two minutes after I got back to the *Clarion*. Beneath the rings in his nose, lip, and eyebrows, I thought I detected an excited face.

"I've connected a few more dots," he said. "Attorney Gregor Popov, the Resident Agent of the OMSK Corporation, is a partner in the New York law firm of Vasily, Barnes & Popov. Ten years ago, one of the partners, William Barnes, defended a man accused of being part of a huge pill mill in New York City. Drum roll please—the defendant was a known associate of the Russian mafia.

Jason grinned at me. He had now found a connection between Gregor Popov—and therefore the OMSK Corporation—with a law firm that handled cases for members of the Russian mafia dealing illegal opioids. One dot away from tying the Russian mob to OMSK.

"Well done, Jason," I said.

"Thanks, but I'm not finished. There's got to be more to learn here. I want to spend a little more time looking, but right now, if you want a digital edition for this week's paper I've got to get to work on that."

"Okay, I said, "I've got some work to do on that too. Come see me if you find anything else."

After Jason left, I got back to doing my part in finishing this week's *Clarion*. Vickie and Joanne had handed in their stories, and I went over them, making minor changes. The robbers who robbed and pistol-whipped the convenience store clerk turned out to be two seventeen-year-old males, who as minors, we couldn't use their names. Times were truly terrible when more and more, children were committing serious crimes.

I wrote a small follow-up to the special edition, but it was mostly about Kelly's improving condition and how we expected her back at the Clarion soon.

I didn't put anything in it about the Dixie Demons being suspects of interest in the murders of the Dollars. First, because I didn't think Sheriff Bagwell was ready to do that yet, and I didn't want him on my ass again, and second, deep down, I didn't believe it. They probably were in the drug thing somehow, maybe pushing the Dollar brother's opioids, but I couldn't see them involved in any more significant way. Besides, my gut was telling me that I was on the right track with this Russian angle. I just had to prove it.

By late afternoon I had sent everything over to Eloise with my stamp of approval for a morning run. Two editions in one week—a first for the Kelly-Eloise-John David *Clarion* era. Then I went to see if Jason had dug up anything else on the Russians.

I found him taking a sheet of paper from a copier. He held it up and grinned at me.

"I found the original *New York Post* story about the pill mill bust," he said. "This shows that the pill mill headed up by the Russians in New York City also distributed opioids to a network of dealers as far away as—get this—South Carolina. So, I've got the Russians pushing opioids right here in the Palmetto state."

He handed me the copy of the newspaper article to read.

As I read it, something lit up a darkened corner of my brain just for a millisecond as if the beam from a lighthouse had swept across it and revealed something. I ignored the sensation and kept reading, but it nagged at me. I stopped, went back and reread it. This time it was like a bolt of lightning struck me.

I quickly folded the article and stuck it in a shirt pocket. "I need to go," I said to Jason.

He stood with his mouth open in surprise at my abrupt exit. I headed for the parking lot. I would fill him in later if what I'd seen in the article turned out to be what I thought.

As I got into my Jeep, I was torn between doing what I was about to do or calling Bagwell and Agent Underwood and bringing them in on it. I was still working on a theory with no hard facts, *this* theory, based on what could be a coincidence in the New York pill mill article. I was tired of getting jumped on for bringing Bagwell and Underwood things they couldn't prosecute. I would check this one out first before I went to them with anything less than solid proof.

CHAPTER FIFTY-FOUR

The sun was low in the west as I approached the address I'd found on my cell, which turned out to be a two-story townhome in a lakeside community on the east side of Lake Hartwell, not far from Clemson. The house was out on a point with a dock and ski-boat in the back. I'd say the place was in the three-quarter to one-million-dollar range—and although it wasn't at the conspicuous consumption level, the place was pretty impressive.

I rang the doorbell and listened as footsteps approached behind the door.

"Mr. Bragg," Doctor Michael Stefans said as he opened it. "This is a surprise. What brings you to my humble abode?"

"Zdrahst-vooy," I said. *Hello.* The only Russian word I knew. I couldn't remember where I'd learned it. Probably from a Boris and Natasha cartoon as a kid.

"Hello to *you*," he said, then paused and gave me a surprised look. "Do you speak Russian?"

No, but you just showed me that you do, I thought. That was easy. Question number one answered.

"Oh, I just picked that up somewhere," I said. "Don't

288

remember where. I say things like that sometimes to keep people from thinking I'm some dumb southern redneck. Which I am, of course."

He tried to smile at that. It didn't quite work. He knew he'd revealed something that he shouldn't have and was wishing he could take it back.

"Well, come *in*," he said, moving aside to let me pass and closing the door behind us. "I was making dinner and had I known you were coming, I would have made enough for two. I am what you would call a confirmed bachelor, and eat too often alone. Dinner guests are always a welcome change.

The house smelled of garlic, and spices I didn't recognize. Whatever he was cooking, it wasn't southern fried chicken.

I saw no reason to beat about the bush. "I wanted to ask you about the OMSK Corporation, through which you own carwashes, coin laundries, and a bar called the Tiger's Tail. Did you name your company after the town in Russia?"

I had obviously caught him flat-footed. He stood looking at me like he was trying to decide how to answer—or *if* he was going to answer.

I added, "I first thought the name was an acronym, but I guess not, huh?"

The doctor must have decided that I already knew too much for him to deny. Wearing the forced smile again, he said, "OMSK is the name of the town where my parents were born. But why would you be interested in that, or my investments?"

Question number two answered. Stefans had just admitted that he was the Beneficial Owner of the OMSK Corporation.

He said, "I am not one for gambling on the stock market. I

289

would just as soon take my money to Las Vegas."

"But your investments sound a lot like a money-laundering scheme," I said.

He suddenly lost the fake smile.

"That is the kind of talk that can get you sued for slander, Mr. Bragg. And libel, if I ever see a false accusation like that in that insignificant little newspaper you run. What money am I supposed to have that needs laundering?"

Insignificant? I thought. I'd finally touched a nerve. "How about drug money? The manufacture and distribution of opioids, to be exact. The very thing you pretend to be so against. Your association with the Dollar brothers hasn't just been as their anonymous landlord, has it?"

I wanted to ask him a question about May Burgess but didn't think he would answer it. Besides, I thought I knew the answer, anyway. Stefans wouldn't tip off Doughboy directly, he wouldn't deal on that level, but I was sure he passed May's vulnerable condition on to the Dollars, and they sent Doughboy to sell her what Stefans would no longer provide her. What kind of man would do that? Certainly not one who had taken the Socratic oath. That made him even more vile and greedy than I'd thought. Instead of curing her, he killed her. For what gain? Several bucks profit for OMSK? He disgusted me.

Stefans was giving me a hard look. He said, "My only connection with the Dollar brothers was keeping one of them on as manager of that establishment when I bought it—which, based on what I have seen in the news about their nefarious activities, was a regrettable mistake. But I certainly was not involved in any part of that. Now, I will ask you to leave, Mr. Bragg."

I pulled out the *New York Post* article. "What do you have to say about these *nefarious* activities—running a pill mill operation with the Russian mafia. It says you escaped and are hiding out in Russia. Guess we both know that isn't true, don't we? Should I call you *Mikhail Stefanovic* as it says here? I guess you've anglicized yourself a little since this, huh? But the similarity of Mikhail Stefanovic to Michael Stefans is a little hard to miss."

I pushed the clipping at him. He took it, looked at it quickly, and handed it back. I got the feeling it wasn't the first time he'd seen it.

"This is all absurd. I don't know this Mikhail Stefanovic or anything about him. And he is *certainly* not me. You were looking at my medical degrees on the wall in my office when you came there. I saw you. You must have noticed my name and the date on them."

Before I could reply, he jabbed a forefinger on the article in my hand, almost hard enough to tear it. "This article is dated years later. My degrees and medical documents precede it by a decade. Any similarity between the name in this story and mine is purely coincidental. I am outraged that you would come to my house and make these accusations. I will ask you again to leave, sir."

"So, you'd anglicized Mikhail Stefanovic to Michael Stefans before you reached college age," I said. "What I noticed about those documents on your wall was that they were all from schools or hospitals in the New York area. You have a degree, for instance, from *Brooklyn College*. Did you grow up there? Perhaps in Brighton Beach, in an area known as Little Odessa? Russian neighborhood? Russian friends? Russian *mafia*? Like the guys working with you at this pill mill?"

I waved the article at him again, and he ignored it.

I said, "Ever since I met you, I've been curious about the way you speak. So deliberate. So precise. It's because English is your second language, isn't it? What I don't understand is why you *de-anglicized* your name for the pill mill operation when the two names are so obviously similar. Anyone would make the connection. That seems like a dumb mistake for someone smart enough to be a doctor. If you thought you could get away with living two different lives, it didn't work. The Mikhail Stefanovic in this article *is* you and I can prove it."

"How can you prove it?" he asked. "You are delusional, and these allegations are ridiculous. Do not tell me that you are basing them entirely on such a sheer coincidence of names. I see nothing factual here that ties me to this man, not a photograph, not *anything*. Go away, Mr. Bragg, and take your psychosis with you."

"In the parlance of a friend of mine called the *Big Hurt*, go fuck yourself, Ivan," I said. "You're responsible for trying to kill the woman I love, and I will make sure you pay for that, regardless of what else you're guilty of. I'll let the police and the DEA take care of that part."

"My God, now you are accusing me of *another* crime. You are certifiably mad, Mr. Bragg, and I would recommend serious psychiatric help." He pushed past me and walked away. "I've had enough of this," he said, "I'm calling the police."

"You called her 'a *fucking bitch*' in Russian," I said. I can't think of any other suspects around here who speak that language. And I believe the cops will agree with me. So, *call* them."

He had stopped walking and turned to glared at me.

"Who told you that?"

"Kelly, she's awake. She understands Russian, and thinks she might even be able to recognize your voice in a lineup. *That part was a lie, but he didn't know it.* Who knows what else she can tell us? You're done, Stefans—or Stefanovic—whatever name you choose to go by."

Suddenly he was pointing a large pistol at me. He'd taken it from a drawer in a table in the foyer before I even knew what he was doing or could react. But he had answered question number three, the most important one. He was the asshole who assaulted and beat Kelly.

Dropping all pretenses of who he was or wasn't, he said, "You called *me* dumb? But it is you who are dumb for coming here today. If I am who you *say* I am, with the friends you say I have, what makes you think you will live long enough to make me pay for *anything*?"

He had a point. Maybe I should have thought this visit through a little more before I came. "So what do we do now? You're the one with the gun."

"I admit going by my birth name in the New York business *was* a mistake, but I didn't make it. The person responsible for me being identified by that name was someone who had known me since childhood. It's what he had always called me. So everyone else involved in our little operation did the same. Had I the choice, I would have chosen a dissimilar name, but we had begun using it already. All I could hope was that when I became a doctor here with my official certifications in the name under which I earned them that no one would ever come looking and see the similarities. Amazingly, you did. But as they say around here, that is now water over the bridge."

"*Dam*," I said. "Water over the *dam*. Or under the bridge, whichever you prefer. This English is hard to learn, isn't it? All these years and you still don't have it quite right."

I heard the front door open and shut behind me. The doctor glanced over my shoulder, and smiled broadly. "I guess I won't have to shoot you after all, Mr. Bragg. *He* will."

I turned to see a man wearing a flat newsboy hat, a windbreaker, dark shades, and a droopy mustache so obviously phony it would have been laughable if it weren't for the sizeable automatic silenced pistol he was holding.

"I was not expecting you back so soon," Stefans said to him. "But I am glad you are here. You can help me with this new problem that has arisen. This gentleman and his girlfriend have sped up my departure date."

"Good. Nachal'nik tell me to come and help you leave," the man said in a heavy Russian accent.

Great, I thought. The Russian mob had arrived.

"You can assure the Nachal'nik that everything is going to plan," Stefans was saying to the man. "The Dollars are no longer here to implicate us, as you well know, and the authorities do not have a clue as to who disposed of them. And you can tell him I do not need him to bank-roll me on this next operation. I will use the money we took from the cabin, along with some of my own, and as soon as I find the place and the people to help me run it, I will be setting up in new territory. We will be back up to speed in no time. But he needs to know that my piece of this operation will have to be more. I have shown him how successful it can be."

"Which one of you tried to kill Kelly?" I interrupted. "If you're going to shoot me, you owe me that much."

Stefans said, "With all the trouble you and Ms. Mayfield have caused us, asking your questions and sticking your nose in business that does not concern you, we *do* owe you something. A comfortable spot at the bottom of Lake Hartwell would be my suggestion. Like they say in that movie *The Godfather*. You can sleep with the fishes. Literally." He chuckled at his wit.

I didn't laugh, and neither did the Russian behind me. At least I knew what they had in store for me. I turned to the other Russian. "Did *you* do it? Assault and beat the woman I love?"

He stared at me with a curious look, either contemplating the question or deciding where to shoot me.

"*Nyet*," he said and nodded at Stefans. "This man," he said. "With man name *Sonny*. Stupid mistake. Unnecessary."

I saw that his words surprised Stefans.

"She *hit* me," Stefans said. "I lost my temper. So? We went there to scare her, and I *did* scare her."

Stefans had answered question number three, the most important one to me. He was the asshole who assaulted and beat Kelly.

"Stupid mistake. Unnecessary," the Russian repeated. "Cause too much attention, and Nachal'nik not like it."

He raised his pistol and shot Stefans between the eyes. The doctor collapsed to the floor. The Russian moved closer and put another bullet in Stefans' head.

My knees went weak, and I almost fell on top of Stefans. I stared at the Russian, waiting for his next shot, this one to *my* head.

Instead, in his heavy accent and entirely without emotion, he said, "The Nachal'nik tell me to come. Help doctor leave. So I *help*. He *leave*." He smiled, an unnerving sight. "You must forget about me. This is not your business. Or I will come back for you, and maybe girlfriend. I am ordered to kill him. Not you. Do not make that become so."

He looked at me until I gave him a nervous nod. But I'd never learned not to look a gift-horse in the mouth. I said, "I don't suppose you'd tell me who or what Nachal'nik is, would you?"

He looked at me a moment longer. "Nachal'nik mean 'boss man' in Russian."

I watched as he put the gun inside his jacket. Then he said something else to me that sounded like, *Coro shego dinya*. I gave him a puzzled look.

"That mean, 'Have nice day,'" he said, and then he was gone.

Once I'd come to grips with the enormous sense of relief that I wasn't lying there next to the doctor, my thoughts went to the man who shot him. His disguise was almost ridiculous, but I still wouldn't be able to describe him to anyone.

I took out my phone and with shaking hands dialed 911.

EPILOGUE

I was back in Kelly's hospital room, sitting there holding her hand again and talking to her. She was still groggy and kept dozing off. Her recovery was coming along, and the doctor was giving her good marks for it.

The room was practically floor to ceiling flowers from friends and co-workers—and I had contributed two dozen roses myself. The fragrance was cloyingly overpowering from them, but I would have put up with anything to be able to sit there, look upon her beautiful face, old bruises aside, and have a conversation with her. I'd told her everything that had gone on. I wasn't sure Kelly heard it all. She kept going to sleep on me.

The authorities hadn't been able to find the Russian who shot Stefans. That didn't surprise me. They guessed that while he may have been Russian mafia, he didn't live in this country and he was already long gone. I had not seen hide nor hair of DEA Agent Underwood. Apparently, he had moved on to other investigations and was probably happy that I hadn't popped up in of any them. "Yet," I thought, and chuckled at that prospect.

Alvin came walking in and went straight to the bed. He

leaned down and kissed Kelly on the forehead. "I'm heading home," he said.

Kelly pulled her hand from mine and took his. "You're leaving, and *I've* just arrived," she said. "Can't you stay a little longer?"

"Wish I could, but I got business to attend to back home."

"They said you sat outside my door . . . watching over me," Kelly said. "Thank you, Alvin. I love you," she added, her eyes tearing up.

He leaned over and kissed her again. "I'll watch over you anytime, sweet thing," he said. "All you got to do is call, and I'll be right here. I love you too."

He stood up and turned around to face me.

"You, on the other hand, ain't got no love coming," he said. "You don't deserve it."

"You're still mad I went to see Stefans-Stefanovic without you," I said.

"You remind me of that clichéd scene in bad horror movies, where the innocent young girl, knowing there's a crazed killer in a hockey mask on the loose, goes into the dark cellar in a run-down old mansion, when everybody in the theatre knows that only an idiot would do that."

"I suppose I did have a hiccup in my decision-making process there," I said, and laughed.

We bumped fists and exchanged a bro-hug, same as we did when he arrived.

"I put the key to the rental house back in the flowerpot," he said. Are Eloise and Mackenzie here?" he asked. I need to say goodbye to them.

"They're around somewhere," I said. "Maybe in the waiting room."

He gave me a nod, turned, and went looking for them.

I watched him leave, the nurses at their station all raising their heads as he walked by.

I sat down by the bed and picked up Kelly's hand again. We would be able to take her home soon, but Doctor Mathis said she would still require bed rest and attention until she was one-hundred percent—which he said would happen before we knew it.

I'd promised to stay on and help with the *Clarion* as long as needed. In the last few days, my thoughts on that took a surprising turn. The last thing I'd ever wanted was to take over the *Clarion* and run it, as my grandfather had always wanted. After having done it for a while, I discovered that I actually liked it. I'd talked to Joe Dennis at *SportsWord*, and he was amenable to allowing me to freelance for the magazine from Pickens on specific *SportsWord* assignments, rather than losing me altogether. I was considering it.

I could handle that job no matter where I lived. I only needed an airport nearby, and I had that with the Greenville Spartanburg Airport. Not as handy as living in Atlanta, but without the ATL traffic, it would almost be as convenient.

As to the *Clarion*, I still had no desire to run it day to day, nor to usurp Kelly's position or authority. When she got back to a hundred percent and able to return, she would be the boss, and she and Eloise would run the place as before. I would help when and where I could, keeping a toe in that water, but *SportsWord* would be my main job. If there was ever a "have your cake and eat it too" situation, this had to be it.

I hadn't told Kelly this yet. I had something far more important to ask her. I looked over and saw her smiling at me, and somehow found a burst of courage to do it—something I had wondered if I'd ever do. It felt right, and it was what I wanted more than anything in the world.

I looked down at her hand, which I was holding a little too tightly.

"Kelly, will you marry me?"

When I looked up, she was asleep again.

Thank you for reading *The Junkyard*. I hope you enjoyed it. As an independently published author, without the big bucks of the giant New York publishers, I rely on you, the reader, to spread the word. So, if you enjoyed this book, please tell your friends, and if it isn't too much trouble, I would appreciate a brief review on Amazon. Thanks again. All the best to you and happy reading.

–Ron

To submit a review:

1. Go to the product detail page for THE JUNKYARD on Amazon.com

2. Click **Write a customer review** in the Customer Reviews section.

3. Click **Submit**.

ABOUT THE AUTHOR

Ron Fisher has been a creative director and writer for several of the top advertising agencies in the country, including his own, and has won numerous awards including a Gold Lion at Cannes. Originally from South Carolina, he's lived in San Francisco, Dallas, and now Atlanta, where he can be found happily writing more J.D. Bragg mysteries

BOOKS BY RON FISHER

CADILLAC TRACKS (J.D. Bragg Mystery #1)
DARK CORNER (J.D. Bragg Mystery #2)
THE JUNKYARD (J.D. Bragg Mystery #3)

COMING SOON
WILD THING (J.D. Bragg Mystery #4)
STILL WATERS (J.D. Bragg Mystery #5)

Sign up here to find out when the next exciting new J.D. Bragg mystery will be out, and get a chance to win free books and autographed copies in our monthly giveaways.
www.ronfisherwriter.com

Made in the USA
San Bernardino, CA
30 November 2019